DIVISION BY ZERO ③

HALEY BROWN : SUE ANN CULP : MATTHEW ROHR
TIM ROHR : BRION SCHEIDEL : STEVEN VALLARSA

Then Again

MifiWriters

MIFIWRITERS.ORG

x/0 : 3

© 2014 MiFiWriters, All Rights Reserved
Published by MiFiWriters
Holland, Michigan

mifiwriters.org

ISBN: 978-1-312-07337-1

Cover by Digital Dreaming

The illimitable, silent, never-resting thing called Time, rolling, rushing on, swift, silent, like an all-embracing ocean-tide, on which we and all the universe swim like exhalations, like apparitions which are, and then are not...

— Thomas Carlyle

Contents

Preface vii
    Sue Ann Culp

Purify 1
    Sue Ann Culp

Time Enough 29
    Matthew Rohr

Look Forward to Tomorrow 77
    Haley Brown

Saving JFK 97
    Brion Scheidel

Screaming Mimi 129
    Steven Vallarsa

Silent Night 159
    Tim Rohr

Preface

Sue Ann Culp

Man has been fascinated by time since... well, since time began. Scientists have performed countless experiments trying to understand the concept, just as writers have penned thousands of words. The idea of time is just concrete enough to warrant study, yet illusive enough to excite the imagination. Therefore, Division by Zero offers its third anthology, *Then Again*, an exploration of very different viewpoints, woven together by the notion that time travel actually exists.

This year's theme isn't new. Samuel Madden wrote one of the first novels about time travel in 1733. *Memoirs of the Twentieth Century* told the story of a guardian angel who travels back in time to 1728, carrying letters from 1997. Since then, other novelists have followed suit. Among the most famous: Charles Dickens' *A Christmas Carol (1843),* Mark Twain's *A Connecticut Yankee in King Arthur's Court (1889),* and H.G. Wells' (1895) *The Time Machine*. And the subject continues to enthrall us: Audrey Niffenegger's *The Time Traveler's Wife* (2009), Lee Child's Jack Reacher Series (1997-2014), and Mark C. Malkasian *The Chronomonaut* (2014). All imaginative and inspired perceptions of time and how manipulation of it could affect the human condition.

But what about real science? I thought it might be interesting to recount a few verifiable theories about time because compelling fiction contains elements of fact. And these theories and experiments are real—not something created in my author-brain.

Theory: The higher you live, the faster you age

Scientists placed two atomic clocks on two tables. One table was 33 centimeters higher than the other. What they discovered—the clock on the elevated table ran faster than the lower one. Not much—only 90 billionth of a second in 79 years. The concept is called *time dilation* and means that gravity warps time and space. The closer you are to the ground, the more affected you are by the Earth's gravity and the slower time moves. Does this mean that living in space with zero gravity could lead to immortality? I don't really want to live forever, but I wouldn't mind looking like I'm 20 when I'm actually 80. And do women outlive men because they wear high heels?

Theory: The faster you go, the slower time moves

Thanks to Einstein, we're all familiar with the concept that if you travel at the speed of light, time pretty much stands still. But this theory also holds true in everyday life on a much smaller scale. Scientists took those same two atomic clocks, put one on a plane and sent it around the world. When the clock came home, scientists found that it was missing 230 nanoseconds. So if I drive 130 mph to work every day, will I have more time? Those speed limits could be detrimental to invention and productivity. Just sayin...

Theory: Faster-Than-Light Neutrinos could mean Time Travel is actually possible

No, I'm not kidding, nor am I drinking or smoking something mind-altering. Laws of physics have held that nothing can travel faster than the speed of light... until recently. Scientists have discovered that under certain circumstances, subatomic particles known as neutrinos *may* sometimes travel faster! They theorize that it might be possible to send a message to the not-so-distant past. Which begs the question, those flashes of inspiration, intuition or déjà vu that we all experience—could those be messages sent back in time from our future-selves? If so, I could use a little more concrete information, like who's going to win the 2015 World Series.

Time travel, alternate universes, parallel realities, changing the past, changing the future. The possibilities are endless. *Then Again* offers them all.

We hope you will enjoy this journey into the fantastical and imaginative. Prepare yourself for a ride into the unknown where life isn't measured by hours, or seconds. Turn off those reminder alarms and hide your cell phones. Suspend yourself in a place where your mere existence is all that is required.

And, most of all…

Have a good Time!

—Sue Ann Culp, Editor
MiFiWriters

Purify

Sue Ann Culp

GREGORY LANGE WAITED for the ringing in his ears to subside before opening his eyes. Re-entry nausea was minimal now, or he'd just gotten used to it after so many journeys to the past.

He detected an unexpected sound—*splat, splat*—and looked down. Blood dripped from his clothes, forming Dali-like images on the white, tiled floor. His mouth stretched tight at the sight. He prided himself on killing cleanly, with finesse, but recognized that his recent penchant for good, old-fashioned hatchet methods provided a much needed outlet for his feelings of frustration and helplessness. Having a nine year old son struggling for every breath while hospital paraphernalia monitored the ebbing of his young life also made him impatient. He could hardly bear any time away from Julian right now.

"Don't give up, son," he prayed silently, staring at the blood. "Daddy can save you. If you'll just hang on for two more weeks."

A mechanical voice crackled through the intercom. "Strip, please."

Lange quickly disrobed, dropping his blood-soaked clothing at his feet. Bits of shredded flesh and muscle nestled among the folds.

"Step forward onto the disc."

He didn't really hear the instructions. His body slipped naturally into the routine. Only when he heard the barrier close behind him, and felt the heat of the inferno incinerating his garments, did he fully return to the moment.

A trickle of sweat slithered along his jaw line, and he wiped his hand across his face. He detected a sweet, copper taste on his lips and realized, too late, that his hand was painted in blood. Inferior blood. Revulsion burst in his chest. His skin crawled. He spat repeatedly, trying desperately to expel the foul substance.

"Cleansing. Now!" He coughed. "Now!"

Immediately, water and sterilizer swirled around him, as if he'd just stepped into a vintage car wash. He opened his mouth, letting the liquid bathe his tongue, not caring that it tasted like arugula, whose bitter, peppery leaves he despised. A favorite of his wife, she sometimes hid a few leaves in his salad, hoping he wouldn't notice. He did, but said nothing. He knew that this subterfuge pleased her, and seeing her sweet smile far outweighed the nasty flavor.

He missed her smile. Julian's diagnosis had killed it, much like Lange had just killed the inferiors.

Warm air spun around him like an April breeze skimming off the ocean, drying his skin and blowing his hair around his face. When it subsided, he checked his hand for any trace of blood before sweeping his blonde locks from his forehead. Standing in the silent, colorless chamber, he wondered if this was what awaited Julian. No sound. No feeling. No anything.

The panel in front of him opened revealing a short, pimple-faced technician whom he didn't recognize. The standard black jumpsuit didn't fit him properly and pooled around his ankles. The familiar "P" superimposed over the spinning bars blazed from the chest pocket in shimmering silver thread. He handed Lange a plush, white bathrobe embroidered with the same insignia and a bottle of water before raising his arm in the familiar salute.

"Purify!" he said.

Lange returned the gesture, noting the twinge of sore muscles in his forearm. Frenetically swinging an axe over a hundred times had taxed his body more than usual. *I'll ask for a longer Respite,* he thought. *They may not care about Julian, but they certainly care about my ability to carry out the Mission.*

"Must have been a great trip," the technician said. "Haven't seen that much blood in a while. I extended the cleansing, just to make sure we got it all."

Lange shrugged into the robe and only nodded, hoping to discourage further conversation. His desperation to get to the hospital made him impatient and irritable.

"Kills?" the young man asked.

"Twelve."

"Wow, good job. How many will that eliminate in our time?"

Lange shook his head. "Do I look like a computer?"

The sharpness of his tone seemed to cut through the technician's admiring smile, and the boy stepped backward. A pustule on the young man's nose oozed blood, and Lange's stomach heaved at the sight. His reaction unnerved him. He saw blood all the time, and it didn't bother him. But this was pure blood, which he revered, not the vile stuff he fought so hard to eradicate.

"Collateral damage?"

Lange sighed audibly. "None." He rolled his eyes. "Naturally." It had been years since anyone had asked him that question, and Lange felt mildly insulted.

The technician shifted on his feet. "Sorry, sir. I just transferred in from the southeast district. I'm trying to follow protocol."

Lange smiled slightly—a feeble attempt to apologize. He cracked open the bottle and drained the liquid.

"A car is waiting at the front entrance to take you to the hospital," the technician said, his voice quivering about the edges. "I'm... sorry about your son."

Lange didn't bother to reply but headed straight for the locker room where he quickly changed into khaki trousers and a sky blue polo shirt. He hurried through the front vestibule, then dashed down the steps to where a black sedan idled by the curb in the No Parking zone.

Gratefully, the driver did not try to engage him in conversation, which was unusual considering Lange's status as one of the Council's most renowned Purifiers. He often drew a crowd wherever he walked through the halls, and normally didn't mind answering their predictable questions.

"How far back did you travel this time?"

"How many inferiors did you erase?"

He could spend hours pontificating about how time travel streamlined the goal to purify their race. No more rounding up inferior bloodlines and hauling them off to extermination camps. One kill in the past erased multiple lives in the present, and didn't disrupt society. People couldn't notice what was never there. Plus, the Council soon discovered that rarely did an inferior-created invention or innovation disappear or cause much of a ripple in their daily lives. Nature, it seemed, really did abhor a vacuum, and a Pure Blood always created a similar widget at approximately the same time.

With the Yeshuites all but gone, and places like Israel and New York City cleansed of their presence, Lange now concentrated on his true passion—eradicating the Ebonites. He particularly despised their black faces and kinky hair which seemed much more suited to primates at the ecology reserve. Everything about them screamed inferior. He just wished that the technology could send him back farther than 1860, to a time before the race infected his home continent. Or allow him to make multiple stops along the timeline.

Traffic was light at this hour and in minutes, Lange breezed past hospital security. The guards instantly recognized him and waved him through. It had taken years, but Pure Bloods now occupied all positions of authority within the government. Lange chuckled to himself. When Universal Health Care required that everyone's DNA be mapped, it became almost too easy to identify those with inferior bloodlines. In fact, some Pure Bloods continued their lives unaware of the purification process. Those with misguided consciences even thought that the Purifiers were nothing more than urban myth, a conclusion that amused Lange and his colleagues. He unconsciously rubbed the insignia tattooed onto his inner arm and smiled. It was all so easy.

Lange punched the elevator button several times before deciding to take the stairs. Every new minute away from Julian became more unbearable than the last. He sprinted up five flights and jogged to the corner room, his boots cracking on the floor like pistol shots. He paused at the entrance to the room where he'd spent the majority of his non-working hours over the past month.

His wife sat by the bed, her face buried in the mattress, palm cradling Julian's hand. Only her thumb gently stroking his forefinger indicated that she was awake. The paleness of the boy's face and hair matched the white linens, almost as if his body had melted into the sheets. His shallow breaths echoed in ragged accompaniment to the ping of the hospital monitors.

Lange approached and kissed the top of his wife's head, pausing for a moment to breathe in the scent of magnolia and feel the softness of her chestnut hair against his cheek. "How is he?" he whispered.

Savannah raised her head, and Lange sucked in a breath of filtered air. In spite of the red puffiness under her golden eyes and the tears glistening on her cheeks, her beauty remained unmarred and startling. Her hair cascaded over her shoulders, like the mane of a champion Andalusian. He still regarded his successful wooing of the southern heiress as his greatest accomplishment. She could trace her bloodline directly to the Hamptons of the Carolinas. Her ancestry even included distant relative Wade Hampton, a Confederate general who was not only the wealthiest planter in the south but also owned the largest number of slaves. Her family considered the *Emancipation Proclamation* to be a blight on civilized society, an opinion that Lange wholeheartedly shared. He counted himself lucky to have a mate who not only shared his Purification ideology, but willingly accepted that traveling back in time was much more than fodder for fantasy novels and movies.

Perfect career, satisfying and meaningful. Perfect wife, exquisite and adored. Perfect son, promising and cherished. Lange, indeed, lived a perfect life. Until Julian's heart betrayed them all.

Lange took Savannah's hand and rubbed it between both his palms. "You're so cold, sweetheart. When was the last time you slept? Or ate?"

She shrugged as if concern for herself simply wasn't important. "He's not going to make it, Greg. The doctor says two weeks at most. But probably only a few days." Tears slipped down her cheeks, spattering onto her peach silk blouse in a shadowy pattern of impending death.

"Damn the Act! Whoever determined that life under ten years has no value should be exterminated, right along with the inferiors."

Sobs burst from her throat as Lange bent to fold her into his chest. Universal Health Care did not authorize transplants of any kind to children until they reached the decade mark. And Julian needed a heart. It didn't matter that he was a mere twelve days from his tenth birthday. Going back in time to harvest an acceptable organ presented no problem. Lange had already identified a group of possible donors—a school bus crash in the Appalachian mountains in 1958. Thirty elementary school children drowned in the Chattahoochee. Surely one of their hearts could save his son. But the Council would not authorize his trip until Julian met their criteria. And the law didn't bend, not even for a decorated Purifier.

Lange clung to his wife, his desperation matching hers. So close.

A growl resembling a bear waking from hibernation rumbled through the room. Savannah broke away and turned toward the door. "Daddy?"

A giant, barrel-chested man in an impeccably tailored, ecru suit filled the portal. He reached the bed in two strides, and Lange marveled again at how Savannah's father carried his three hundred pound bulk with such agility. He moved with the grace of a white Bengal tiger. And was just as lethal. Ezra Beaumont III smiled, flashing glistening white teeth from a smooth pink face nearly void of lines or wrinkles. His white blond hair curled about his collar. He extended a manicured hand to Lange who always felt a little small in the older man's presence in spite of his own, six foot, muscled frame.

"Governor," Lange said. "We weren't expecting you until the weekend."

Beaumont nodded and turned to gaze at Julian, lying so small and still. His ice blue eyes grew misty, and his voice thickened with emotion. "We're ahead of schedule in the Southeast District right now. Ebonite population down forty-seven percent. No reason my lieutenant can't handle things for a week or two."

Savannah rose then nearly collapsed into her father's arms, crying openly. "Come, child," he drawled as he led her to the door. "You'll wake the boy. Besides, I have a plan, and this is no place to discuss it."

A spark of hope flickered in Lange's chest. The Council had denied their request for an early transplant dispensation, even when Beaumont, himself, had interceded. Had they reconsidered?

"Sir?" Lange said.

Beaumont put a finger to his lips. "A car is waiting downstairs to take us to my hotel. Obviously, time is of the essence." He took a white handkerchief from his pocket and dabbed his daughter's cheeks. "It would be better if you stayed with Julian, my dear."

Beaumont spoke in a whisper but both Lange and his wife recognized his tone. He wasn't offering a suggestion. He was giving an order. Savannah smiled weakly as her father kissed her cheek, then returned to her son's bedside. Two men seemed to materialize out of nowhere to flank the governor. Fifteen minutes later, Beaumont ushered Lange into his suite at the Four Horseman Hotel, leaving the two bodyguards standing sentry outside the door.

Beaumont strode to the sideboard and dropped ice cubes into two crystal glasses. He filled one with sparkling water and handed it to Lange before pouring two finger's worth of single malt whiskey into the other. "I'd offer you a drink, but you'll be traveling tonight, and you know the rules—no alcohol for forty eight hours prior to a phasing."

Lange cocked his head, confused. "But I've only just returned, sir. I'm required to take at least three days Respite between trips."

Beaumont's bushy eyebrows rose. "Those are their rules, yes. Mine are a little more flexible." He took a swig from his glass, smacking his lips. "Our business tonight is about ignoring their rules. That is, if you want the chance to save my grandson's life." Lange nearly dropped his glass, and water sloshed onto the walnut sideboard. "I'll take that as a 'yes.' Come sit down."

Two seafoam, damask-covered sofas flanked a glass-topped coffee table, and each man took a seat, facing one another. Beaumont sipped his drink, looking too casual and relaxed for Lange's taste, while Lange struggled to control his wildly pounding heart. He knew better than to rush the statesman.

Beaumont removed a disc from the inside pocket of his jacket and slid it into a slot on the underside of the coffee table. Instantly, letters and numbers appeared on the glass surface arranging themselves into a standard family tree format. Beaumont pointed to the surface, moving names and numbers as he traced the lines. "This is Savannah's ancestry line. We can trace her lineage back to the 1400's, but I want to bring your attention to this point." He tapped an entry labeled 'Hampton.' "After three miscarriages and two still births, George and Emelia Hampton finally had two children—a set of twins, Matilda and Michael. Savannah is a direct descendent of Matilda on my wife's side."

"So?" Lange asked, wanting his father-in-law to move it along. Beaumont raised an eyebrow as if in reprimand, and Lange gulped. "Sorry, sir."

"On July 8, 1854, at the age of eight, Michael Hampton drowned in a creek which ran through the woods behind their plantation outside of Charleston, South Carolina." Beaumont paused. Lange didn't know if he was expected to comment and opted for silence as the safest course. "Medical science has come a long way, and I have a physician who believes that there is a good chance that Michael Hampton's heart could save Julian. If you leave tonight." A cold draft passed over Lange as the implications of what his father-in-law suggested registered. He shivered visibly. Beaumont nodded. "Now. Questions."

Lange took a deep breath. His hands ached from clenching, and he tried to relax. Even so, his voice sounded unnaturally high and barely controlled. "I'm assuming this trip isn't authorized?"

Beaumont looked at him in a way that made Lange feel as if he were a two year old. "What's the point in having power if you can't circumvent a few rules now and then? Travel and surgery arrangements have already been made. You just need to go get the heart."

The response was not surprising and not what bothered Lange the most. "Even if the heart is useable, we can only go back to 1860. Michael died six years beyond our capacity to travel."

Beaumont slammed a beefy fist onto the coffee table, and a web of tiny cracks slithered outward from the blow. "Your son is dying. He won't last until he's ten! Are you willing to take the risk or not?"

The risk was monumental. Perfecting the ability to travel farther and farther back in time came with a price. Scientists offered criminals the opportunity to earn an early release from prison by 'volunteering' as test subjects. Initial travelers often came back in pieces. As Chrono-Crashing for each new decade improved, one might only be missing a hand, or a foot, or a kidney. This trip could end Lange's career. Or his life. Even as the worst case scenarios played through his head, Lange knew he'd gladly sacrifice anything for a chance to save Julian.

"Everything is in place?" Lange asked.

Beaumont leaned back against the cushions, and the sofa groaned under his weight. "Your clothing is hanging in my closet. You'll pose as a doctor. There was an outbreak of scarlet fever around that time, and you'll tell George Hampton that his childhood friend, now a physician, has sent you to 'test' the children for the illness. You simply have to swab their gum lines with cotton. If the cotton on Michael's swab turns blue, then his heart is useable. You're taking a vial of crushed baby aspirin with you. Dissolve a bit in water and give it to the boy, telling Hampton that the medicine will keep him from getting sick. The next day, July 8th, pick your opportunity to harvest Michael's heart, and return immediately. The medical team will be waiting." Beaumont reached for his drink and drained the glass. He wiped his mouth with the back of his hand, smacking his lips. "Michael would have died that day anyway so future repercussions should be minimal. If anything, a slave will be accused of the killing and hung—an added bonus." He leaned forward and locked his eyes with Lange. "This is risky business. For all of us. You must believe, son, that I truly hope you'll return safe... and whole. Even if the heart isn't viable. My daughter loves you. You're a good husband and father. A credit to your Pure Blood heritage. You're also Julian's only hope."

A tremor of fear rippled up Lange's spine, and the hairs on his arms prickled. So much could go wrong. He could be mangled during the trip and stuck in the past, waiting for death to slowly finish its job. The heart might not be a match. If he did manage to survive and return with the organ, they could still be discovered before or during the surgery. Punishment would be swift. And final. Lange shuddered. Death lurked in every corner of this implausibly foolish mission. And Beaumont wouldn't risk exposure.

But then Lange pictured his son, and the future he fought so hard to give him. A world cleansed of inferior bloodlines where Julian could enjoy countless possibilities for success and happiness. He choked back his trepidation and set his jaw. "When do I leave?"

"My team will be in place at nine tonight." He glanced at the grandfather clock ticking softly in the corner. "You've got three hours."

Beaumont tapped the coffee table, and its surface filled with pictures and writing. Lange recognized the usual background information that he studied before every mission. "Read fast," Beaumont said. "Dinner will be here shortly. I hope you like steak and water—lots of it. You're not getting any Respite between trips. You need to hydrate and amp up on protein."

With that, Beaumont rose, went to the bedroom, and closed the door, leaving Lange alone to study.

At eight forty-three, Lange entered the portal room, dressed in pleated wool trousers, white shirt, vest and a knee length frock coat. He carried a wide-brimmed felt hat, a brown leather valise which contained the simplest of medical supplies, and a burgundy carpet bag with a bottle of water, a nightshirt, and shaving tools. The latter had been fitted with a special lining designed to keep the heart fresh and secure on the return trip.

The pimple-faced technician he'd met earlier handed him a gold pocket watch. "Your chronometer, sir. Press the timing stem when you're ready to return." Lange's hands shook slightly as he fastened the clasp to his belt loop before slipping the timepiece into his pocket. "And may I say, sir, it's an honor to serve this mission."

Lange looked at the young man with admiration. "You know we could all fry for this, don't you?"

The technician grinned. "Your father-in-law pays handsomely." His smile faded, and he lowered his voice. "And I have a son, too."

The men shared a nervous chuckle as a side door opened. Savannah flew to Lange's arms, her father following behind.

She clung to him, but didn't speak. Lange knew they were both painfully aware that this could possibly be their last embrace. He regretted not being able to visit Julian again, but time was short, and he didn't want to chance arousing any suspicion. Though he tried to act normally, he feared any subtle change in his behavior might somehow alert the Council's watchdogs that something was amiss.

He stroked Savannah's hair and breathed in her scent. She raised her chin, pressed her lips to his then stepped away. "I love you," she whispered. Lange mouthed the words in return, not trusting his voice.

"Any questions?" Beaumont asked.

Lange shook his head.

His father-in-law extended his hand, and Lange clasped it in return. "Good luck, son."

Encased in the white chamber, Lange listened as the mechanical voice counted backward from twenty. At twelve, the pressure started, as if he were sinking into the fathoms of a bottomless pool. At six, the temperature dropped to an Arctic level, his vision blurred, and his skin burned. As the chamber dissolved around him, Savannah's voice crackled through the intercom. "Purify!"

The air swelled with moisture, and Lange opened his eyes to a typical South Carolina, July afternoon—oppressively hot and humid. He struggled to sit and immediately shrugged out of his coat. His chest contracted, and searing pain sliced through his temples. He opened the carpet bag, extracted the bottle of water, and quickly guzzled all thirty-six ounces. In minutes the pain eased, though he still felt the air was better suited to chewing than breathing.

Beside him, a small, gray tombstone leaned to the left as if the sandy soil beneath it could no longer hold its weight. White hot pain shot up his leg, and he lifted the cuff of his trouser. Ugly red welts dotted his calf from the ankle to his knee. Travelburn. Not unusual, but this case was far worse than normal. He pulled the salve he always carried from his coat pocket and smeared it liberally on the affected skin. It cooled the area enough to make it bearable. Thankful to be posing as a doctor, he wrapped his leg in bandages from the valise so the scratchy wool of his trousers wouldn't further irritate the skin.

He took a mental inventory and breathed a sigh of relief. The intense burn seemed to be the only casualty of venturing further back in time. However, he also knew that return journeys held the greater probability of more extensive damage. An image of his body, covered in oozing welts, hung behind his eyes. He pushed it away, replacing it with a picture of Julian, running the bases after hitting a grand slam home run.

Besides, no amount of suffering was too great. As long as he returned with a viable heart. Luckily, travelburn only infected flesh fueled by flowing blood. The heart would journey to the future unscathed.

Thunder rumbled in the distance, and the wind picked up, blowing chaff around the tombstones. He ambled among the markers, noting that the name Hampton appeared on most. Family cemeteries were common on plantations. A spray of wilted daisies lay on the brown grass beside a stone bearing the name *Emilia Hampton*. Lange remembered reading that she had taken her own life, just a week following the birth of the twins. Post-partum depression at its worst. George had never re-married. Lange smiled, running his hand across the smooth stone in a gesture of understanding. He could never replace Savannah either.

He crested a small hill, and the manor house appeared like a beacon of hope. White stately columns stood like sentinels amid the wrap-around veranda. Lange wasted no time in heading straight for his destination. He ambled up the long winding driveway flanked by azalea bushes, whistling through his teeth. The Hampton plantation made Margaret Mitchell's *Tara* seem like a poor second cousin.

Dark clouds rolled in from the east and soon blotted out the late afternoon sun. He picked up his pace, the burning in his leg increasing with each step. By the time he reached the home's expansive lawn, he was visibly limping.

"Can I help you, sir?"

Lange turned to see a sprite of a girl with ebony curls and periwinkle eyes dancing toward him, swinging a basket of wildflowers in her hand. Her arms and legs were bare, and no hat shielded her face from the sun's tanning rays, which intensified the blue of her eyes.

"I'm looking for George Hampton," Lange said in his best southern drawl.

"Daddy's in his study," the girl replied, smiling widely between matching dimples.

"Tildy!" a voice called from the veranda.

Lange looked up to see a tall, waif-like woman in a grey, calico work dress approaching. Her white, starched apron rustled when she walked. She carried herself almost regally, and if it weren't for her milk chocolate skin and kinky black hair, Lange might not have assumed she was a slave.

"He's lookin' for Daddy."

"I'm Doctor Gregory Lange from Atlanta." He took a deep breath to steady his voice. Lange hated conversing with inferiors, but suspected that this slave acted as Gatekeeper to the family home. Much as she didn't deserve it, he adopted an air of civility and respect. "Doctor Jameson Westerfield sent me." The demeaning need to explain himself to an Ebonite nearly choked him, and he coughed to cover his disgust.

The slave's eyes raked over him, obviously assessing his trustworthiness. Lange pulled an envelope from the inside pocket of his coat. "A letter of introduction for Mr. Hampton."

He handed the letter to her, being careful not to come into contact with her skin. She flipped open the envelope and pulled the forged sheet from its sheath. Lange gasped at her pretentiousness. Pretending she could read! The woman seemed to sense his surprise, and she cleared her throat, a little warbling sound that reeked of nerves and embarrassment.

"Follow me, sir."

In minutes, Lange sat comfortably across the desk from George Hampton, sipping a cool lemonade, listening to the plantation owner tell stories of his escapades with boyhood friend, Jamie Westerfield, in Atlanta.

"So, this test you want to do," Hampton said, fingering his perfectly trimmed gray beard, "It won't be painful?"

"Not at all, sir. I'll simply wipe the inside of their mouths with a bit of cotton. If they've been exposed to the fever, the swab will turn blue. I've got the remedy with me." Hampton's blue eyes pierced like lasers, and Lange didn't miss the spark of suspicion. "I'll even take a dose myself, so they won't be afraid of the taste."

His offer produced the desired result, and Hampton's shoulders relaxed. Rain pattered against the window, and the room brightened as lightning flashed. "Looks like we're in for a drencher," Hampton drawled. "You can perform your test after supper. My nephew, Henry, is here for the summer. He just turned twelve. My brother, Grayden, and his wife are traveling abroad. Might you test him also? I'm sure his parents would be beholdin' to you."

"Of course. I have plenty of supplies."

Hampton nodded. "I'll write Jamie and thank him for sending you, though he should have let me know you were coming. I'd have had one of my darkies meet you at the train station. Now you've gone and aggravated that leg injury of yours."

"It's nothing, sir."

"Well, you'll be my guest for the next few days. I can't send you back to Jamie limping like a horse that threw a shoe." Hampton rose. "Willadean!"

The slave who had met Lange initially appeared at the door. She responded so quickly, he wondered if she had been listening from the hallway. The thought didn't surprise him. There was something odd about her. She seemed much too confident and well-spoken for her station, "Dr. Lange will be staying a few days," Hampton explained. "If you need anything at all, Doc, Willa will take care of it."

The evening could not have gone better had Lange scripted it himself. He rested on a soft down mattress, then enjoyed a dinner of quail baked with sweet potatoes and mushrooms, hearty brown bread, and peach cobbler swimming in cream. Knowing the food had been prepared by inferior hands marred his enjoyment somewhat, but didn't keep him from having seconds. Slaves in white, starched shirts served each course on plates of ivory bone china, their sleeves rustling as they kept the crystal water goblets filled. Willadean hovered in the background, orchestrating the service with slight flicks of her hand.

Hampton, obviously accustomed to being the center of attention, boasted about the success of his plantation, and his disdain for the political direction the country seemed to be taking. After dinner, Lange carefully swabbed the cheeks of twelve year old Henry and the twins, Matilda and Michael. Then he waited, nervously sipping a cup of tea, the three pieces of cotton laying side-by-side on a linen dishtowel. Slowly, one swab turned a clear, bright blue, as if a bit of the sky had fallen to earth. Henry. Five anxious minutes later, Michael's transformed as well.

You're going to be okay, Julian, he thought, a new surge of hope coursing through him. *Just a few more hours.*

Lange made a show of crushing the aspirin, mixing it with water and administering it to the boys.

Hampton clapped him on the back, relief glistening like sweat on his features. "You tell ol' Jamie I'm in his debt. I won't forget it."

"Glad to be of service, sir," Lange replied.

They retired to the porch to enjoy the cooler breeze which heralded the impending storm. Hampton talked politics and economics while Lange pretended to sip a glass of blackberry brandy. When Matilda and Michael appeared for their good night hugs, Lange dumped the contents over the rail into the begonias.

The household retired when darkness fell, and the storm unleashed torrential rain that rattled the windows. Wind groaned through the eaves while Lange tossed on the crisp, white sheets, anticipating tomorrow's kill. His leg throbbed, and the welts oozed a sticky, yellow substance that smelled like canned tuna. He needed to get some sleep and thought some water might help him relax. He padded to the door, the polished walnut floor cool against his bare feet, when a child's cry echoed in the darkness.

A door opened, followed by footsteps. He peered into the hallway and saw Willadean, carrying a candle. She disappeared into a room down the hall. A few minutes later she returned and met Hampton, emerging from his room.

"Is she alright?" he asked the slave.

"Don't you worry," Willadean replied. "That last clap of thunder woke her up. Just startled her a bit. It'll take more than a summer storm to scare that child. She's fearless."

Hampton leaned in and placed a gentle kiss on Willadean's forehead. "Just like her mama. Now come back to bed." The door closed behind the pair.

The next bolt of lightning shot straight through Lange's heart. His knees buckled, and bile rose up the back of his throat. He crawled to the chamber pot and vomited so violently he feared his ribs might shatter. He shook with cold and pulled his knees into his chest, trying to control the tremors.

The image of Hampton caressing the slave blazed into his brain like a white hot poker. It wasn't just the revulsion of seeing their intimate relationship, but the disgusting insight that accompanied it.

The twin's softly tanned faces weren't the result of playing in the South Carolina sunshine, but the manifestation of their inferior blood. The fact that they had their father's piercing blue eyes and rounded features made it possible for Hampton to pass them off as Pure Bloods. Lange pictured Matilda's smiling face, the dimples in her cheeks, and the way her eyes crinkled at the corners. So like her mother—Willadean. Lange struggled to suck air into his lungs. Emelia's suicide became even more macabre. Childless into her forties, Lange could only imagine the devastating effect of learning that her husband had betrayed her. With a slave. Even worse, that Willadean had given him what she could not. Michael and Matilda were products of their unholy coupling.

Lange's emotions cycloned out of control. Shock. Denial. Anger. Despair. He couldn't possibly put Michael's heart into Julian. It was half Ebonite. He couldn't defile his son's body with such inferior tissue.

The next realization hit Lange like a hurricane making landfall. Inferior blood. Savannah and Julian had *inferior* blood! Sure, time had diluted it. But why hadn't the standard DNA test detected it?

Lange pictured Ezra Beaumont, a man swollen with power, comfortably bending rules to suit his own purposes. He could have waved his family's impeccable pedigree in front of health authorities and insisted they defer the test.

Lange gritted his teeth until pain shot through his jaw.

It was more likely, however, that Beaumont's actions mirrored his wife's ancestor, Wade Hampton. Secrets required power and resources to survive. Beaumont had both.

Another wave of revulsion washed over Lange as he thought of the countless times he had held his wife, melting into her with passion and abandon. His skin crawled, as a torrent of convulsions wracked his body. The heaving purged his stomach. How would he ever purge his soul?

The pounding rain quieted to a soft patter as the thunder grew more distant. Lange huddled in the corner like a child, afraid of the dark. Hours passed. He couldn't find the strength to drag himself back to bed. Images swirled around him in a confusing maelstrom.

Savannah, poised, accomplished, and breathtakingly beautiful. Her voice rivaled any birdsong. Her mind, quick and astute, an equal counterpart to his own. He couldn't remember the last time he had beat her at chess. She simultaneously soothed him with her grace and challenged him with her intellect. Her blood ties to a house slave were incomprehensible.

And Julian. Reading chapter books by the age of five. Doing complicated sums in his head. Batting .350 on his little league team.

No one with inferior blood, no matter how infinitesimal, could be so accomplished.

Could they? Doubt seeded his soul like larvae waiting to hatch into questions that could shake the foundation of all Lange's beliefs. He covered his face with his hands, trying to ignore the misgivings burrowing into his brain.

The first rays of dawn crawled through the lace curtains like roaches, scattering light across the floor. Lange opened his eyes, realizing he must have fallen into an exhausted sleep. His night shirt twisted around his legs, damp from sweat or humidity, he didn't know which. Sunrise bathed the room in a soft pink glow, and he struggled upward to peer through the window. The wet lawn glistened in the morning light under a cloudless sky streaked with violet and fuchsia.

The muscles in his stomach groaned. He splashed tepid water on his face from the basin on the dresser, and caught a glimpse of his face in the mirror. The night's revelations had ravaged his chiseled Aryan features. His aquamarine eyes glowed brightly above gray half-moon shadows, giving him a gaunt, specter-like appearance. He combed his hair, shaved, and changed into his day clothes, thankful that the welts on his legs had healed considerably during the night.

He sat on the bed, feeling the sun caress his skin. So like Savannah. He just couldn't reconcile the fact that inferior blood ran through her beautiful body. He still craved her. Needed her.

Loved her.

Lange's body felt clammy as he broke out in a cold sweat. Could the Purification Doctrine be flawed? Was inferior blood no different than his? Savannah and Julian were perfect in every way.

No! He couldn't entertain such a wild notion. Generations of Pure Blood mating had simply diluted the inferior, making its contamination inconsequential. No one need know. George Hampton had taken the lineage of Michael and Matilda to his grave, letting history write their futures. Lange's love for his wife and child dictated that he would do the same.

Still, he could not allow Michael's heart to beat in Julian's chest. The inferior infection would be too great. But he also couldn't bear the thought of burying his son.

The physician's valise sat open beside the bed. Two blue cotton balls lay in the bottom where he'd tossed them.

Henry.

Lange knew that harvesting Henry's heart directly violated their core commandment; Effect No Collateral Change. The result of his untimely death would ripple into the future, changing things. But nature had a way of righting itself. In a generation or two, adverse affects would barely be noticeable, if at all.

A wave of guilt hit Lange like an earthquake aftershock. Henry's death would be murder. Pre-meditated. Despicable. Lange never thought anything could compel him to spill Pure Blood. He clasped his hands, like a supplicant seeking forgiveness as he pictured his son struggling for breath in a sterile hospital room. His heart swelled.

Ethics be damned! Two boys would die today. And one would live.

The household bustled with activity as Lange descended the stairs. House slaves scurried about, dusting, sweeping and polishing every surface from the floor to the chandeliers. The humidity seeped into his shirt, pasting it to his skin, and he wiped a trickle of sweat from his temple. His foot had no more than hit the main floor when Willadean appeared with a silver tray laden with fresh fruit, bread, preserves, and a carafe of coffee.

"Good morning, Doctor Lange," the slave said. "Breakfast on the veranda?" Lange nodded to avoid having to thank the slave verbally. After witnessing the exchange between her and Hampton last night, his revulsion had grown to the point where he didn't trust his voice.

"Massa Hampton is out in the fields, but he said to tell you he'd come in about noontime to take you on a tour of the plantation."

She set the tray on a wicker table and poured Lange a cup of steaming coffee. His stomach growled. Hunger beat his feelings of disgust into submission as he slathered berry preserves onto a slice of thick, brown bread. Fields spread out on either side of the mansion beyond the slave quarters. Cotton, tobacco, corn, pole beans. Knobby black heads bobbed among the plants, tilling and weeding, and the low, dulcet tones of their songs wafted on the breeze.

A laugh like delicate wind chimes drew his attention and Lange turned, half expecting to see Savannah round the corner of the house. Matilda skipped into view, Michael following closely on her heels.

"Willa, can we go pick some blackberries?" the girl asked.

"I bet Doc Lange would love one of your pies," Michael added.

The slave's eyebrows rose, her fingers thrumming gently on the porch rail. "Are you really interested 'n berries, or are you sneaking into the woods to go swimming? I already tole you, that creek will be rushin' from all the rain last night. It's too dangerous right now."

The children's eyes grew wide, faces serious. Lange saw the lie hovering on their tongues.

"Just berries." A quartet of dimples dotted their cheeks. "We promise."

The day flowed out before Lange like a moving picture. Michael would drown in that creek today. Obviously, he didn't heed his mother's warning.

His death meant nothing to Lange now. Of greater concern was Henry. Julian didn't have much time, and he needed that heart as quickly as possible. Still, Lange must kill inconspicuously, secretly, so he could safely harvest the organ. His nerves quivered. At the moment, Henry was nowhere in sight.

Then, blessed destiny intervened. Willadean said, "Alright. But you take Henry with you."

The children's smiles faded, and their shoulders drooped. "Henry's no fun," Matilda said, thrusting her lower lip forward in a pout. "He'd rather read a stupid ol' book than play outside."

"Then stay here. Makes no nevermind to me."

"I'll go get him," Michael said. "Meet me out back." He scampered into the house.

"Now you be careful, missy," Willadean said. "Come give Willa a hug."

The little girl flew into her arms. Lange's breakfast threatened to reappear at the sight, though he'd made enough trips to the Civil War South, to not be surprised by slaves taking maternal roles in the lives of plantation children. Mother and daughter shared an inferior bond, but Lange's sensibilities still reeled at the affront to Matilda's Pure Blood lineage.

With the opportunity to catch Henry alone looming before him, Lange stuffed a strawberry into his mouth and gulped down the last of his coffee. "I think I'll take a little walk," he said. "My leg is much better today, and a little exercise will do it good."

"Yes, sir," Willadean replied. Her eyes narrowed even as her mouth edged upward in a polite smile.

Lange looked upward, shielding his eyes from the morning sun. "I'd better go get my hat."

Lange stepped past the slave and sprinted up the steps. Moments later, he slid out the back door, empty carpet bag in hand, a sleek, thin hunting knife sheathed in his pocket. He spotted the children, about to disappear into the woods. Michael and Matilda laughed, running circles around Henry who carried a book and shuffled along, obviously not sharing his cousins' enthusiasm for the outing.

The air cooled considerably when Lange slipped into the trees twenty yards south of the children. The scent of moss, loam, and Queen Anne's lace melded into a heady perfume. Birds flitted through the leaves, and squirrels scurried up trees, their claws scratching against the bark. Water, flowing fast and torrid, hummed in the distance.

Lange followed the sound of laughter, carefully stepping over branches and disturbing brush as little as possible. His talent for stealth enabled him to kill cleanly, with minimal disturbance or warning.

Through the trees, Lange spotted the twins, pulling berries from bushes, more ending up in their mouths than in the baskets. A few yards away, the creek, swollen from last night's deluge, lapped at its bank like an angry tongue. Just like the slave had warned. Its swift current carried debris with such force that branches shattered into splinters against the rocks.

Henry sat under a tree, his nose buried in a book. Michael and Matilda drifted closer to the water's edge. As soon as they disappeared from Henry's sight line, Lange would strike. Snapping the boy's neck would take seconds. Then he'd disappear into the trees, harvest the heart, and be home in a matter of minutes.

Blood surged through his veins, spreading the adrenalin-high that preceded a kill. The tips of his fingers tingled. He crept closer. Watching. Waiting. The roar of the water drowned out the tinkling of the twins' laughter.

When he lost sight of the pink ribbons fluttering from Matilda's hair, he pounced. Henry's life ended abruptly, without pain or distress. He carried the body away from the creek, deeper into the woods. As he laid the boy on the moss-covered ground, another wash of guilt wracked his chest. He'd never killed a Pure Blood. Then he pictured Julian's face, flushed from the sun, eyes bright above an angelic smile.

Lange tore open the boy's shirt and raised the blade. As the steel slipped past flesh and bone, Matilda's scream echoed through the air. *Poor Michael*, he thought.

With Henry's heart safely encased in the carpet bag, Lange punched the stem of his pocket watch. Trees dissolved, and he gasped for air as fire spread throughout his limbs.

"I'm coming, Julian. I'm coming."

The ringing in his ears seemed louder than normal, and he opened his eyes too soon. His stomach lurched from the nausea. He dropped his clothing without being told. As he stepped forward, blistering pain shot up his left leg. The skin from ankle to knee glistened with blood, and it took a moment for him to realize that it was his own.

A small price to pay, he thought. *I'll heal.*

"Welcome back, sir," the mechanical voice crackled through the intercom. "Commence cleansing."

The water and sterilizer soothed his seared flesh, and soon the chamber doors slid open. Two men in white jumpsuits, standard issue for medical personnel, rushed forward. One grabbed the carpet bag and disappeared. The other tossed him the familiar white bathrobe and proceeded to dress his burns.

The pimple-faced technician handed him a bottle of water as he exited the chamber, and Lange drained it without a word. "Congratulations, sir," the tech said, admiration evident in his voice. "A five year Chrono-Crash with only some minor burns to show for it."

"Six, but who's counting?" Lange replied.

"Too bad we can't tell anyone," a voice boomed.

Lange turned, and Ezra Beaumont clasped his hand. "Nice work, son. Julian's new heart will be beating in his chest within the hour. I don't know how to thank you."

"No thanks necessary, sir. You know there isn't anything I wouldn't do for Julian."

Beaumont's eyes widened slightly. "I trust everything went as planned."

The image of Hampton kissing Willadean floated behind his eyes like storm clouds. "Like clockwork."

"And young Master Michael experienced no pain?"

Lange paused. Lying to a Pure Blood violated his personal code of ethics. He pictured Julian, struggling for every breath as his heartbeats grew more erratic. "It was a clean kill."

"Good, good," Beaumont said. "Well, I'm sure you're exhausted. Get some rest. I need to get back to my grandson."

He turned to go when Lange reached for his arm. "Wait! Let me change. I'll ride with you. I don't know where the surgery is taking place."

Beaumont frowned, obviously impatient at being detained. "Understandable. Like to see things through, don't you?" He clapped Lange on the back. "One of my men will bring you."

With that, he turned and thundered out the door.

Lange headed to the locker room where khaki pants and a black polo shirt waited for him. Twenty minutes later, two men ushered him through the back gate of an expansive estate and lead him to an octagonal room overlooking gardens flanked with flagstone walkways and wrought iron benches. Cherry trees in full bloom sweetened the air.

Beaumont reclined on an ivory settee, his bulk dwarfing the piece. Savannah gazed out a window, her chestnut hair flowing like a waterfall down her back. Lange reached her in three strides and touched her shoulder.

"Savannah," he said.

She turned to him.

Lange gazed into her face, his voice catching in his throat. "When did you get contacts?" he blurted.

A frown crossed her delicate face, her blue eyes creasing at the corners. "Excuse me?"

Lange studied her. It was definitely Savannah, but her forehead seemed higher. Nose slightly narrower. Voice a tone or two deeper. He blinked several times. He'd just pushed the limits of time travel so a little disorientation wasn't totally unexpected. No matter. He breathed in her scent and reached to fold her into his arms, needing to feel her body melt into his.

Savannah stepped backward, pushing both hands against his chest. "Mr. Lange, please!"

Beaumont appeared at his daughter's side. "Here, here, Lange. I know you've just been through an ordeal, and we're extremely grateful, but let's not forget ourselves."

"Is there a problem?" a voice called from the doorway.

A man with a strongly muscled frame carrying two glasses of pale, pink liquid strode into the room. Ice clinked against the crystal like little bells as he set the glasses on a side table before approaching Lange.

Recognition dawned on the man's face, and he extended his hand. "Mr. Lange," he said. "Julian is expected to make a full recovery. We can't thank you enough for your bravery. Rest assured, you will be handsomely rewarded for your service."

Lange opened and closed his mouth several times, as his words cowered on his tongue. "Who… who are you?"

"Chase. Chase Reardon," he said. Looks bounced among the quartet like a silver sphere in a pinball machine. "I'm Julian's father. Savannah's husband? I know we only met once, but surely you remember."

Lange's fist connected with Reardon's jaw without warning, hurling the man's body backward into the side table. A china lamp etched in roses crashed to the floor. Savannah's screams became one with the roaring in his ears. "*Your* wife?" Lange screamed. "She's my wife, you asshole. Mine!"

Lange lurched forward, arm poised to strike another blow. Two beefy arms circled his chest and lifted him from the floor. Beaumont's bellows echoed throughout the room as navy-suited men stampeded through the door.

"Please take Mr. Lange home," Beaumont ordered. "He's suffering some ill effects from his recent trip."

"No!" Lange screamed. "I need to see Julian. I need to see my son." Two men flanked him, each holding his arms in vise-like grips. "Savannah, please! This isn't funny. Tell them. Tell them!"

His voice broke as sobs burst from his throat. The men dragged him from the room, his shoes screeching against the hardwood floor. They forced him into a waiting sedan, still restraining him in the backseat. For the next ten minutes, he tried everything in his power to convince them of the mistake. He recounted his first date with Savannah. Their wedding on the beach at Kitty Hawk. Julian's birth. His first day at pre-school and how he'd quickly re-arranged the classroom chairs into the shape of the Purification emblem.

His captors shook their heads, exchanging glances similar to those passed among mourners at a wake. By the time they reached his home, Lange had managed to calm himself.

Two men escorted him to the door. Lange pressed his code into the keyboard, fearing, for a moment, that it might not work. The lock disengaged, and he stepped inside.

"You'll stay here, won't you, Mr. Lange? Governor Beaumont is sending a physician. He should be here shortly."

Lange growled at the man's condescending tone and slammed the door. He watched from the window as the car pulled away then caught sight of the two men standing sentry on either side of his door. He slammed his fist into the wall, and pain shot up his arm. At least he knew he wasn't dreaming.

His home looked sparse, naked even. No flowers on the dining room table, no baseball equipment dropped by the door. No family pictures, except for the one of his parents at their twenty-fifth wedding anniversary party in Niagara Falls ten years ago. Gone was the lavender chintz bedspread and matching curtains in the master bedroom, and Savannah's side of the closet held a three piece luggage set and some wrinkled silver and black wrapping paper. He wandered down the hall to his son's room, leaning on the wall for support. Only a cherry desk and matching chair stood in the space usually strewn with games, books, and crumpled popcorn bags.

Lange sank to his knees. The room tilted like a carnival funhouse. He felt trapped inside a tornado, unable to stop the spinning.

What happened? What had he done?

He crawled to his desk and pulled himself into the chair. A touch to his computer filled the screen with color.

"George and Emilia Hampton," Lange said.

New images flickered across the monitor. Lange recognized the veranda of the Hampton mansion immediately. George Hampton stood next to a woman in a dark-colored dress. Its skirt billowed out from the hoop underneath and seemed to act as a barrier between the couple, keeping them from touching. The woman's dark hair was pulled high atop her head in a tight bun. Her eyes seemed sad as she stared away from her husband. Lange wondered if the couple had ever been in love. Or had their relationship died alongside their stillborn and miscarried children?

Several Ebonites sat on the grass in the foreground, dressed in the starched shirts and aprons of house slaves. Hampton's hand rested on the railing, his eye gazing downward. On Willadean.

Lange skimmed the history of the family. Hampton's early years in Atlanta, his eventual success as a planter, and the growth of his plantation. The section titled "Hampton Heartbreak" recounted Emelia's miscarriages and stillbirths, and her suicide only days after delivering Matilda and Michael.

The section concluded with the tragic drowning on July 8, 1854.

Lange gasped. On that day, the waters of the swollen creek behind the manor house claimed the lives of both Michael *and* Matilda.

Lange's spine turned to jelly, and he slumped down in the chair. Matilda Hampton, Savannah's ancestor, perished that day along with her brother. Consequently, Savannah, the wife that he knew and cherished, had never been. The son he saved was not his own. Not the boy he loved. That boy was gone forever.

A sidebar noted that Hampton's nephew, Henry, who had probably been watching the children, was also found dead in the woods, the victim of an animal attack.

The tremor started at Lange's toes, shimmied up his legs and out his arms, until his entire body shook uncontrollably. Had Lange not interfered, Henry would have rescued Matilda that day. But Lange had clung to his Purification ideology.

And he had lost everything.

He crumpled into a mass of grief and guilt and slipped out of the chair, landing in a huddled heap on the carpet. He laid there, too cold and empty to cry, his spirit desolate. Memories spun through his mind. Savannah's laugh, light and lyrical like a flute. Her touch, soft and sensual. Julian's smile, disarming and engaging. Pictures of the past that was no more wound through head like gossamer strands, too delicate to remain unbroken.

A door opened, closed. Boot steps on the polished wood floor. Lange's head felt like an anvil, and he just didn't have the strength to raise it. Voices in the hall.

"Ever seen Millenium Madness?" a man said in hushed tones.

"No, sir," another replied. "Is there nothing that can be done?"

"Afraid not. Too many trips to the past can break a man's psyche. Taints the blood."

Three pairs of shiny black boots came into view. He caught the muffled word "inferior" and his head shot up. He pushed himself into a sitting position. "What? What! I'm not inferior."

Two men knelt beside him, their faces blank. Lange looked up into the countenance of an elderly man. Kindness glowed in the man's eyes even though his mouth was set in a hard line. He wore a navy jacket with a medical pin affixed to the lapel.

"A tragedy, really," the physician said, sighing. "You've served the Council well, Mr. Lange." He clicked his tongue. "Such a shame. Were you in your right mind, you would understand and agree."

Lange tried to rise, but the two men firmly grasped his arms and pinned him backward onto the floor. Light glinted off the hypodermic needle in the doctor's hand.

"Wait! Wait!" he screamed. "I made a mistake. I killed the wrong person. I changed history. It was just a mistake. That doesn't make me inferior. I'll live with it. You don't have to do this!"

The doctor sighed and shook his head. "Please, Mr. Lange. You've dedicated your life to the purification process. Do not abandon your beliefs now."

Lange screamed as the needle pierced his neck. The room faded in fog, and he felt himself falling. Down. Down into a dark tunnel filled with swirling faces. Faces framed by ebony, kinky hair. Faces with large, flat noses. Faces with slanted eyes. Yellow faces. Red faces. Brown faces. Their mouths distended in endless screams of horror as their life's light faded from their eyes. Lange recognized every one.

His Kills.

Sobs bubbled from his lips and mingled with a strange, unfamiliar sound. The peals of their exuberant laughter.

Three men stood over Lange's still body. No sound disturbed the solemn countenance of the room. They slowly raised their right arms in a salute of respect and spoke as one, their tones hushed and reverent.

"Purify."

Sue Ann Culp has been writing professionally for over twenty years. Her fiction has appeared in such magazines as *Wee Wisdom* and *Kaleidoscope*, nonfiction in *Urban Street Magazine*, and her stage play, "The Lies That Bind", won national recognition in the 2009 *Writer's Digest* annual competition. Her primary focus is on fiction for middle grade and young adults and she also writes for English Language Arts standardized testing for the state of Michigan. She has completed a middle grade novel the first book in a series of young adult, romance novels with a paranormal twist (however without any witches, werewolves, vampires, fairies, or other fantastical creatures!). An active member of the Society of Children's Book Writers and Illustrators, she is also a professional nonprofit development executive. Her appeals, newsletters, and marketing pieces have raised millions of dollars for a variety of worthy causes across the country. She is also an accomplished musician, actress, and fabric artist. Sue Ann and her husband, Michael, reside in Zeeland, Michigan with their 100 lb. Collie, Percy, whom they rescued. Visit her website at sueannculp.com.

Time Enough

Matthew Rohr

A VOICE IN HIS HEAD. Not his own. *"You must kill Hannah Bradley."*

He opened his eyes to find himself standing on grass under the night sky with no memory of a time before this moment. A long, complex equation hung suspended in his mind, white chalk on blackboard—a familiar image? Maybe. In that instant, the world went mad.

A memory of chaos and violence shattered his consciousness. Bullets thundered into the street, a counterpoint to the metallic rhythm of the machine guns themselves. Dust thickened the air that smelled of grease and death. Fleeing pursuit, protesters scattered through the ruined hulks of buildings. Wilson wasn't part of the skirmish. The protest simply provided cover, so he could reach his goal. There was something... something important he had to do. He checked his watch. Past two in the afternoon, it looked like twilight here in the downtown sector. A vast, orbiting platform blocked out the sun, growing larger each day. Wilson hated it, but he couldn't remember why.

The memory spun out of his control, like a dream. Part of him wanted to stop, to understand, but the larger part of him focused on getting to the subway entrance. He surged forward, crossing the cratered street as quickly as possible. Two men in sunglasses and black, military uniforms came jogging around the corner at the end of the block. Shades.

"Stop, citizen! In the name of the Transitional Authority, stop and submit to questioning!"

Wilson willed the uniformed soldiers to see him as a fleeing protester, too far from the main group to be worth the effort. He didn't pause when he found the stairway. The steps flew by faster and faster until he lost his balance, crashing to the unforgiving landing at the bottom. He held his breath and listened for sounds of pursuit. He had something important to do.

Wilson knelt on the ground, gulping down air. Where had that come from? The memory of running from the shades was clear and crisp and utterly out of place. He knew his name—Wilson Gabriel Andrews—but nothing else. With each breath, the dry cold shocked his lungs. His memory was a blackboard, the contents hastily erased. Hints at what had once been written remained. He knew the names of common things, but many memories were just gone. The equation scrawled in their place dominated his thoughts. Instinct told him it meant everything to his continued survival. And yet, it carried an implicit threat. He existed within it as just a small variable, an unnecessary complication. Equations didn't tolerate imbalance. So, it would search for him and remove him as it would any irritant. Trying to solve for x. Trying to solve for Wilson. The fear of teeth, claws, and darkness - an echo of memories more ancient than the human species - personified it with consciousness and malice. The equation was a Monster.

Fear knew the sprint, not the measured run, and it couldn't continue to push him. Confusion overtook fear and demanded answers. Wilson put aside his personal condition to look around. Carnage and devastation surrounded him. Mangled corpses, bones, and piles of steaming organs poked out of a small pond of blood and viscera. He knelt within the only clear space in a vacant lot at the end of a block. Splashes of red arced across the house next door, and the head and torso of a man leaned out of a tree as if they were merely another branch. In a moment of clarity, he realized that the man fused with the bark was his mirror image. Even though he had no specific memory of looking in a mirror, he remembered the *feeling* of recognizing his face. He had that same feeling now. He and the man were identical.

Wilson touched his cheeks in a rush of horror. He was identical to all the corpses scattered about the lot. They were all Wilsons, all him. Fear cracked through him, ready for another run, and Wilson had to clamp his hands over his mouth to suppress the scream that echoed through his mind. Of all these Wilsons, only he survived. What happened? Why couldn't he just—

Remember.

He recalled a room with a blackboard in it. Someone had tacked pictures to the wall all around the blackboard. He thought about taking down one of the pictures - a picture of a blue house - and when he imagined himself doing so, suddenly there was a voice in his head.

"Hey, Wilson. This is Tony." The equation on the blackboard seemed to strain to break free. *"I won't spend any time explaining who I am. Just understand that we're friends. We're co-workers and co-conspirators, too. A little bit of everything."* A memory of a conversation played in Wilson's head like a recording. He recognized Tony Sizemore's voice without remembering what he looked like. *"The images you're seeing are of the Safe House. This is where we anchored the bridge and where you're sitting right now. Stay out of sight."*

Images cascaded through his memory, showing a modest looking house in the lot where he crouched. Wilson frowned. The Safe House wasn't here. As comforting as it was that someone had a plan, it seemed to have gone seriously wrong.

"The Safe House was built in July of 1985, but remained unoccupied for seven months. It has a full basement and should be an ideal base of operations. From the Safe House, you'll have access to the tunnel system

just fifty yards away." An aerial view of the neighborhood flashed into his mind with an overlay showing the location of the tunnel. *"Right here."* Wilson looked toward the hillside, but the streetlights didn't extend far enough out to see anything. Shadows painted the hillside, obscuring details.

Tunnel system? To where?

"I'm sure you have plenty of questions. Just stay in the Safe House for now. You don't want to get picked up by the shades. In a few moments, you'll hear from Laughlin and some of the others. They'll fill in the blanks."

Wilson scrambled up, staying clear of the gore as it seeped into the space where he had been kneeling. Tony had mentioned shades, and the memory of running from them was still fresh in his mind. Hurrying into the darkness, he first thought to make for the tunnels. Bushes and trees covered the rise ahead, and he dove into the underbrush. Wilson wanted to replay the memory from Tony, but when he tried, something else entirely answered his effort. Looking into the emptiness where his memory had been, he saw the Monster. It moved like a massive snake. It coiled on itself, turning and turning in an unending pattern of white on black. Once again, fear lagged and this time, fascination surged forward. Intuition pushed Wilson toward the coils. He knew they held some kind of meaning, if he could just put it together. The blackboard returned.

Every time he tried to figure things out, his mind conjured the room with the blackboard. This time, it had been erased. He shuddered at the thought of the Monster, no longer constrained by the frame, free to hunt him. A picture tacked above the blackboard caught his attention. A beautiful young woman. Blonde hair. Half smile. Blue eyes touched by sorrow. Wilson had it in his hands before he realized he'd reached out for it.

"Testing. Testing."

The voice belonged to Doctor Walter Laughlin. Wilson struggled to remember anything else about him, but there were no details, nothing but his voice.

"If you're hearing this, then I was right. Wiping your memory was the key to getting you across the bridge and having you survive the trip.

Ross must be getting tired of being wrong all the time."

Ross. Ross Trevino. Another familiar name with nothing attached. In the empty lot, a person—another identical Wilson—appeared and then exploded, bits of flesh raining down with the horrific sound of a wet whisper. Another Wilson materialized half submerged in the ground. He moaned for several seconds before his cells lost cohesion, and he melted into the dark pool of blood and gore.

"Now give me just a moment, I have a script to read here."

Another Wilson popped into existence fifteen feet above the ground. He hovered for a moment, drew in a deep breath, and then fell apart. One second, a man hung suspended in the air, the next, a fine, pink mist drifted to the ground.

"Okay. Here we go." Laughlin, again. *"Wilson Gabriel Andrews, that's you. You've just crossed a Campbell Bridge. What? Who wrote this? He doesn't have time for this. Technical details about Campbell Bridges? He's the one who discovered how to cross them."* Laughlin's voice took on an edge. *"And why would I spend time going over any of this? The man has no memories, no context. Elsa will handle all that. Christ, Johnson, this is your idea of a debriefing script? Like everything else you do, it's crap."*

The nightmare happening in the vacant lot seemed to be over. No more Wilsons appeared.

"Here's what's important. You've gone back in time about 87 years, to late 1985. Travel into the past involves movement to a temporal reality of higher necessity." A pause. *"Oh, that's brilliant. You have no clue what that means. I'm starting to sound like Johnson."* Laughlin's voice got louder. *"Johnson! I think your stupid has rubbed off."* He went on, quietly again. *"Look, the past is more real, more solid than the present you came from. The past always is. Think of it as Nature's defense mechanism against people messing around with causality. The universe runs over any intruders from a future reality and destroys them. But don't worry. We figured out how to cross the bridge. Well, you figured out how to cross the bridge. I figured out how to beat the universe."*

Wilson wanted to think, but the memory pounded on, disrupting his efforts. He couldn't think. He had to think.

"How wonderful it must be for you, standing there in our past. One giant step backward for mankind. You may be seeing flashes in the air. Those would be other timelines like our own attempting what we're attempting. We've included countermeasures to ensure that you'll have priority. If we've done everything correctly, they'll be returned to their timelines, and you'll remain. We couldn't risk ending up with an infinite number of Wilsons in a limited space, mucking about in the critical moments."

A momentary pause hung ripe with the implied criticism. *"Enough about that. You have a job to do. You're there to kill Hannah Bradley. Whatever happens, remember: You must kill Hannah Bradley."*

A line of headlights came sweeping down the road toward the vacant lot. Wilson pulled back, deeper into the bushes. Laughlin's voice chased him relentlessly.

"We preserved and encoded everything you need to know as symbolic icons in your memory, Wilson." The empty blackboard image appeared in his mind, again. Pictures hung all around it, tacked to the wall. *"They should be obvious. Just access them to remember the information you need. Hannah's picture is the icon that raised this memory. We're all counting on you, Wilson. When you do this, you won't just be saving our world, but countless other worlds that have been lost in our fight."* His voice hardened. *"I'll let one of the idiots wish you good luck. I'm just going to tell you to do your damned job."*

Black military vehicles pulled into the intersection and surrounded the vacant lot. Soldiers piled out of the cars with cold efficiency, and in moments, several groups had established a high perimeter wall of plastic sheets, blocking Wilson's view. Some patrolled outside. All wore sunglasses, even though it was night.

The sunglasses reminded him of the shades in his memory, and his stomach lurched. The overwhelming desire to run sent him into a panicked sweat. Fighting for control, Wilson slowly crept backward up the hillside, unwilling to lose sight of the soldiers. The uniforms they wore differed from the one the shades in his memory wore. These had stylized eagle insignias, names, colorful patches. He closed his eyes and thought back to the memory of being chased. Those shades wore all black, no patches, just gray bars on the chest and back to indicate rank. Without warning, bright spotlights panned down the hillside, nearly exposing him. Overhead, silent helicopters hovered, visible only because they blacked out the stars. A cold dread snatched at him. They stalked him like predators. They wanted him. They would find him.

He heard the shades creeping hesitantly down the steps after him. Fear opened a pit in his stomach.

"Lord, why today?" whispered Wilson.

Wilson waited. He could have put distance between himself and the shades. As a savant, protocol deemed him too important to hazard, but Wilson knew he wasn't going to put Forty Below in jeopardy. There were other protocols. One, take the pursuit past the entry point. Two, get the pursuit back to the surface level and go to ground. Wait three hours and then return. Jesus, but Laughlin was going to ream him out for this.

Wilson checked his weapons. His pistol held only three rounds - all that could be spared from the rapidly dwindling armory. He had a single ROC, a random, oscillating Campbell point. Not a weapon for close quarters, but effective. He wasn't military. He'd had some training, but running always came first. He'd have to do that now. He'd run, but not until he was sure that the shades' attention was fixed on him.

The shades advanced slowly to the bottom of the stairs. Close. Wilson picked up a chunk of the brickwork and hurled it toward the sounds of his hunters. As he turned to run, a shout of pain rang out behind him. He smiled. He'd just intended to get their attention. Well, mission accomplished. He turned the corner a heartbeat before the shades opened up with their automatic rifles. Ricochets echoed in the tunnels. He sprinted past the men's room door and the hidden entrance to Forty Below. Ahead, he saw the next stairway climbing out of the darkness back to the street level.

Too far away. Not enough cover. No time for indecision.

He threw himself down and forward, turning over in the air to land in a backward skid. Before he stopped, the shades came into the concourse, framed by the faint daylight behind them. Wilson fired one shot. He didn't want to actually hit them. If he killed one of them here, the Transitional Authority would send a team in to sweep the whole area. He fired high, hoping to drive them back for a moment. He rolled to his feet and ran again, hugging the right-hand wall. He covered about half the distance he needed before the shades returned fire. That was his cue. He spun around, crouching, allowing his momentum to carry him further away. His arm came across the passage in a swift arc, and as before, he fired high. Two shots this time, doubling down. They'd retreat from their exposed position if he sold it.

In a single breath, he completed the turn and bounded onto the stairway. No more bullets. His legs burned from the exertion, but he forced them to push him upward, two and three stairs at a time. The shades sprayed indiscriminately, now. The tiles and bricks exploded around him, showering him in stone fragments. He reached the top of the stairs and didn't stop. He ran across the open street, crashing through an abandoned storefront. He heard the screams of the homeless behind him. Other rabbits to chase. Without looking back, he plunged through the building, an old laundry, looking for a back door. An escape route. A way home.

"Remember. Kill Hannah Bradley."

Wilson opened his eyes. Darkness. Something had broken his mind. Some of his few, remaining memories delivered planted messages. Others offered only jumbled images of armed conflict. No sense of context or purpose. If he believed the messages, he had traveled back in time to kill a woman. He shook his head. He didn't know what being a killer felt like, but the hollowness inside hinted he was capable of it. Some basic part of his humanity made him want to believe he wasn't a killer, but without his memories, he could be anything. Anyone.

The helicopters moved away, perhaps expanding their search, and

Wilson crept further up the hillside, shrouded by bushes and the moonless night. He closed his eyes to shut out everything and pulled himself along. With images of maps in his mind, he crawled toward the promised tunnel access. Before he could find it, a sudden burst of sound drew his attention. A team of shades trotted over the hilltop, flashlights slashing through the air. Wilson slipped over a fold in the hill, away from the shades but also away from the tunnel. With the shades out of sight, he hurried to the thickest stand of brush and trees he could find. The path took him close to several houses. No lights glowed from any of them. He had to operate, literally and figuratively, in the dark.

Searching for a clue, Wilson re-examined his small collection of memories. He remembered Laughlin saying he could access more information.

Wilson envisioned the blackboard again, surrounded by pictures—symbolic icons—in a room partially collapsed to rubble. He heard something moving, something digging through the mound of debris. The Monster hunted for him. He thought back to the horror just down the hill, and he knew. That was what the Monster did, what it would do to him if it found him. He grabbed at the first image he saw, a picture of a radar dish on a tower. Wilson touched it, and memories washed over him. He stood in a room with a glass floor—no, a floor made up of computer screens. Below him, tactical markings covered images of an installation.

"That's Montauk. It used to be a military base, home to several black ops projects." Wilson couldn't identify the speaker, despite the certainty that he knew the voice. In the memory, he paid attention only to the floor. *"They were decommissioned in 1984 when a Congressional committee got cold feet after some kind of accident. But you don't just shut down black projects, do you? Not these kinds of projects. This is where the Transitional Authority gained entrance to our reality. Once that happened, humans weren't really in control of Montauk anymore. That's where you have to go."*

In the memory, Wilson walked to another edge of the floor and used hand gestures to pull up a detailed map of the base. The voice spoke again. *"Even before the Transitional Authority took over, the Montauk Group was working with teleportation. They were able to seal the lower* levels, the project levels, off entirely from the main base. By 1985, they'd re-purposed old entry and exit tunnels as storage. One of them terminates under the hill, here. You'll be able to get in undetected."

Wilson ground his teeth in frustration. The info was probably important, but he still didn't understand why. It gave him no insight into what he needed to do.

Kill Hannah Bradley.

He wanted to understand the whole plan, but he had to understand at least that part. He found the idea of simply being a weapon unacceptable. He had to know why. He dug his fingers into the leaves and dirt, taking a moment's comfort in anchoring his physical presence to the world. Time. He needed time to go over all the memories left to him by Laughlin and the others. Together, they might provide him with a wider understanding of what was happening.

Less than a hundred feet away, a slightly open door to a garage beckoned to him. That would make as good a hiding place as any. Wilson gathered himself to move as quickly and quietly as possible.

The laundry had seen better days. Looters and the desperate had gutted the place long ago. Doors were broken or missing, and garbage had collected in corners around the front desk and in the hallways. Once past there, Wilson found himself in a big space where rusty chains and hooks hung from the ceiling. Industrial sized washers and dryers had once stood here alongside presses and dry cleaning machines. So much had been lost in the war and even more in the time under the Transitional Authority. Wilson saw the over-sized loading bay doors and headed directly for them. The back alleys would provide enough cover to go to ground and hide out. He saw one dock with the door jammed open enough that he could roll under it.

Once through, he sprang up to continue running, but tripped on something and sprawled to the pavement. He looked up, and all the strength left his legs. Terror gripped his heart. A drone stood over him, the edges of his black suit writhing like a fringe of tiny snakes. It was difficult to look at where the face should be, because when you stared right at them, there was nothing there. Wilson forced himself to see the drone as it was. Seven feet tall, thin with long limbs, long fingers. Too many fingers. Angular. Alien.

"You are citizen Wilson Gabriel Andrews," it said. "Singularity. You will come with us. We will correct your flaws. Your service to the Transitional Authority is appreciated."

Wilson scuttled backward, but he knew he was already dead.

Wilson realized he had pressed himself against the ground in the dark, cringing away from the creature in his memory. Shouts drew nearer, and he tore himself away from the cover of the hill. He made it to the open door, slipping inside the garage and quietly closing and locking it. No lights. He felt his way around the station wagon that was parked in the middle of the space. Once he had put the vehicle between himself and the door and window, he allowed himself to breathe deeply. His exhaustion came as much from the strain of trying to understand as from any physical exertion. He wanted rest, but he'd be vulnerable while he slept. He didn't dare risk it.

Instead, he envisioned the blackboard and the pictures. This time, he concentrated on looking for a picture of a drone. There, a man in a black suit, standing in shadow. While the white shirt and black tie were clearly illuminated, the edges of the suit seemed to bleed into the darkness. He reached out and touched it.

The sudden brightness surprised him. This memory was different. It didn't seem staged like the others; it felt more personal. He sat high up in the stands, waiting for a parade. To his right sat a man in a dirty lab coat. Laughlin. Wilson remembered. Balding, with a black goatee, and constantly fidgeting with his glasses. Beyond him sat Tony. Curly, red hair. Enthusiastic.

The emotions weren't right. A parade ought to conjure up pride, or at least happiness. Wilson felt only dread. The sun shone down through bitterly cold air. Then, the shades marched past. Black uniforms and sunglasses. After several minutes, one of the uniformed men climbed up to a podium on the opposite side of the street.

"People of New York, you are the truly fortunate. Many sacrifices have been made and many loved ones lost to bring us to this day. The loyal among us have suffered willingly, given what was asked and more, because we knew that we looked forward to a shining day of glory. This is not that day, but it is the first step. We will be rewarded, and from the ashes of our self-destruction, we will rise like the phoenix. Today, we trade the light of the sun for a greater light. Today, we step into the shadow of our benefactors and step closer to our own destiny. Behold!"

The bright light began to fade. Wilson looked around and saw everyone else looking up. When he raised his eyes to the sky, Wilson gasped. Something was blotting out the sun. Something massive in orbit. He remembered the despair and felt it all over again. Central Authority, they called it. He wanted to run, but there was nowhere to go. He turned away from Laughlin and Tony, but when he turned to the left, something went wrong. The memory blurred and jumped.

In a moment, he sat across a table from Laughlin. The dirty lab coat had been exchanged for a cleaner one.

"That was the day we call Sunset. You were there, and we thought it best to let you remember it as you experienced it." Laughlin took off his glasses and wiped them as he continued. *"The Transitional Authority are creatures that do not belong in this reality. We aren't sure if they're from another timeline, another dimension, or another universe altogether. They seduced the leaders of the world, turned them against one another in a horrific war. When we were at our weakest, they took control and merged all human government into one puppet regime that exists to further their agenda."*

Photos and video clips dominated the room. The Transitional Authority looked human-shaped, although too tall and thin. They all dressed in black suits, white shirts, and thin, black ties. The distilled essence of authority. In the pictures, they had unremarkable faces, blank expressions.

"*We don't know what they want, but we think they may be looking for something or someone. They take people, and those people never come back. The rumors of hybrids, alterants, and experiments are just that. Rumors. We know that some wavelengths of visible light burn them. That's why they're putting that monstrosity into orbit. Some of us decided to do something about it. We have to stop Montauk from letting them in. We have to stop the person who made it possible. Hannah Bradley.*"

Another person stepped into view from Wilson's right and walked around behind Laughlin. Ross Trevino.

"*There's more. You need to know what they're capable of, just in case,*" Ross said. "*They aren't bound by time the way we are. They move forward and sideways through it, and they can manipulate reality. They aren't building that thing in orbit; they're bringing it here from somewhere else.*"

"*None of that is relevant,*" Laughlin said. "*They can't go into the past. Not any further back than their own personal present.*"

Ross addressed Wilson directly. "*If they somehow find out about what we're doing, it would be foolish to assume that they can't reach you. It's possible that they'll be waiting for you in 1985. They've managed to outmaneuver us at every turn up until now. You have to be ready for anything. If you see them there, don't let them see you.*"

"*He won't see them there, and we shouldn't waste his precious memory space with unsubstantiated rumors—*"

"*You're right, we shouldn't waste his time, so we'll have this argument later.*" Ross turned his back on Laughlin. "*Wilson, listen to me. The reason we wiped your memory will be covered in another recording, but you need to know that memory isn't an exact science. It imprints itself in some hard to reach places. You'll experience it as intuition. As deja vu. Or maybe just a feeling. Trust yourself, because that's your own memory echoing back to you.*"

Wilson remembered being in the room. Uncomfortable. The argument. Something... something else. A moment of blank, white space. The memory shifted. Ross was gone, and Laughlin had put a few pictures of the Transitional Authority on the table between them.

"*We were supposed to give you a detailed briefing on them, but now* that's out of the question." Laughlin rested his head in his hands, his voice quieter, more subdued. "*You shouldn't have to worry about them, because they don't invade until almost a year after you arrive in the past. Contrary to some claims, there is no evidence that they have discovered how to travel backward in time. This is our great advantage. You are our great advantage and our only hope. Focus on the goal. Kill Hannah Bradley.*"

Wilson opened his eyes. The garage was still dark. He replayed the memory several times, trying to focus on the blurs and jumps that took him from one scene to another. Each time, it replayed the same way. Missing pieces. His memories had been edited. The thought filled him with rage. Laughlin had ordered him to kill, but not allowed him to know the whole story.

The door clicked. A delicate, barely audible sound. Wilson held his breath, stilled himself to silence. Click. Someone testing the lock. Quietly. A slight creak. Pressure on the door, trying to force it past the lock. Quietly.

Wilson looked around for anything that might serve as a weapon. The best he could do was a large screwdriver. He picked it up from the workbench, gripping it like a knife. Holding something in his hands gave him some confidence, and he slid down the side of the car to the deepest part of the garage, where he would be least likely to be seen. Waiting in the darkness, Wilson felt his heart racing. How long had he been listening? It seemed like forever, but no more noises came. They must have moved on.

Straining to see, he could not be sure if the sky outside the window was beginning to lighten. Everything remained quiet, so Wilson closed his eyes again. He returned to the staging area of his memories, the blackboard surrounded by pictures. This time he scanned the photos before him and found a picture of a woman next to a blackboard. Intrigued, Wilson took it down.

A new memory activated. A older woman stood opposite him, smiling. She wore a lab coat with a name badge. Elsa Campbell. Between them stretched a blackboard. "*Hello, Wilson. Look at me! This is really happening, yes? I'm a memory. Oh, I suppose that's not a terribly professional way to begin, right?"*

This memory was warmer than the others. He felt a deep friendship for Elsa.

"So, how to explain the most complicated aspects of your situation in five minutes or less, eh? Let's start with why you keep seeing this blackboard and this room."

Elsa's energy was contagious. Wilson felt the urge to pace as he listened. *"This blackboard is special. You and I found it in storage when we first moved into the school, yes? All the smartboards had been stripped for metals already, but this relic escaped the looters. You don't remember, but we used it to discover the source of the drones' power. That was the key, yes?"*

Elsa seemed to be organizing her thoughts as she spoke without a script. *"But what are the drones? The drones are the individuals of the Transitional Authority. They are able to manipulate reality by merging other realities into our own, yes? Imprinting a small portion of the incoming reality over ours, they sublimate the rest. Infinite realities mean infinite potentialities. If they want a bolt of lightning, they bring one in from a universe where a bolt just happens to hit right when and where they need."*

Wilson remembered the feeling of anticipation. He knew that Elsa had something very important to tell him.

"So, yes. We did it. We unlocked that ability." She began scribbling with chalk. *"It comes down to a very, very complex set of equations, right? The first idea was to build machines that could harness this power. We knew from the start that they'd be unstable. Dangerous, really. But some of us wanted a weapon, yes?"* She stopped for a moment, her eyes closed.

Wilson recognized the Monster on the blackboard. For now, it remained dormant. Elsa continued writing and talking.

"That was a bad idea. Very bad. Then, quite by accident, we discovered that a math savant could manipulate the equations mentally and generate the same effects as the drones. Being a mere genius isn't enough, right, or I'd be standing there with you. We change what we observe, and savants use parts of the brain that most humans never use to

observe and change the equation. We made several attempts to have our savants act directly against the Transitional Authority, but they were miserable failures. Savants aren't combat troops, and they're too rare to risk, right? We quickly turned our few savants to defensive missions. Honestly, we almost gave up hope."

Elsa stopped writing and looked directly at Wilson. "You brought in quantum entanglement. Time as an emergent property of the universe, not a dimension, yes? Everything fell into place. We could go somewhere the Transitional Authority couldn't. We could go back into the past and change everything, eh? You said that the answer was in my work from the beginning, so you named the connection a 'Campbell Bridge,' but you're the one who saw it."

Elsa looked at her watch. "Never enough time, eh? Okay, short version. We ran a few proof of concept bridges, but our savants died before they could act. Temporal necessity, yes? How to explain? A timeline has a lot of temporal momentum, and popping into the past is like jumping in front of a truck on the highway. Laughlin figured it out. So, how did he solve it? We opened up more of a savant's brain to manage the nuances of the math, and we conditioned the savant to run the equations continuously. This lets the savant pop into the cabin of the truck, and it stops the driver from throwing him out."

She scowled, and Wilson remembered smiling. "That's such a horrible metaphor," she said. "But it doesn't matter, right? You volunteered, but really, you were the only savant we had left." Elsa smiled, but the smile didn't reach her eyes. "We couldn't have stopped you if we wanted to." Elsa reached out and took Wilson's hands in hers, and Wilson felt a deep sadness, although he had no idea why. "So here's the big thing, yes? You still have access to their powers. You can do what they do. Nobody can stop you. Do what you have to do. Afterward..."

Elsa's eyes filled with tears. She looked away from Wilson, but continued. "You've already lost so much. It's unfair, right? I know, I know, I'm out of time. Afterward, you won't have a home to come back to. Not one that you recognize or belong in. The world will be a better place, but you'll be a copy of that world's Wilson Andrews, severed from a universe that never was. You'll have to decide what to do, yes? Will you *travel into the future you protected, a future you won't recognize, or stay in the past? Either way, everything you know will be gone. Laughlin didn't want me to tell you this. He assumes that it will make you weak. I know you, Wilson. It makes you stronger, yes? Yes. Good luck. I hope you find what you're looking for."*

In the memory, Elsa turned and walked out of the room. Wilson examined the equations. Without warning, the edges of the blackboard grew in all directions, creating an infinite surface. The equation written on it became the Monster. It broke free and surged toward him. Wilson dodged and felt the impact to his side as the numbers and symbols slid past. He could smell the chalk dust, and he coughed as it burned the inside of his nose. He ducked under the equation and sprinted for the door, slamming it open and hurtling into the hallway beyond.

He opened his eyes and found himself huddled in a corner of the garage. Light streamed into the space past the person standing over him.

"Hello," the stranger said. Thin and wiry. Gray hair poked out from beneath a ski cap. The older man held a shotgun.

Wilson sat up, but didn't speak.

"That must have been some nightmare, son, the way you were carrying on." He sat down on a bench opposite Wilson. "My name's MacCreary. Alan MacCreary. And this, as you might surmise, is my garage." He seemed to notice the shotgun in his hands. "Don't mind the gun. I believe in being prepared, even though we don't get many thieves or vandals out here." He set the shotgun down on the bench.

"I'm not a thief," Wilson said.

"I never said you were." MacCreary smiled.

"What day is it?"

"What? It's Sunday, of course. That's what normally follows Saturday around these parts."

"No, the date. What's the date?"

"It's March 24, 1985. Are you alright, son?"

A few of the pieces slid into place. The Safe House hadn't been built yet. "No, I'm not alright. It's supposed to be October. I'm early."

"Well, then you might as well come inside and get some food in you. If you're waiting until October, you've got some time to kill." He stood up and turned to go. The shotgun remained on the bench.

Wilson stood up but hung back, unsure. "Aren't you curious about why I'm in your garage? Who I am?"

"Are you going to tell me?"

"Well, no, but—"

"Then what's the use of me being curious? Come in, sit down."

"Look," Wilson said, "I don't know you. I don't know what's going on. Why should I trust you?"

MacCreary gestured to the shotgun on the bench. "You're closer to it than I am. If it makes you feel better, you can hold onto it. But really, son, I just want to offer you some breakfast and a chance to clear your head."

"But you don't know me," Wilson protested. "Why would you want to help me? Maybe I lied. I could be a thief." Wilson brandished the screwdriver as evidence.

"Your name is Wilson, and I don't think you're here to steal my screwdriver," said MacCreary as he opened the door to the house.

Wilson surrendered to the surreal and shook his head, handing the tool to the strange man as he walked past him. "No, but this is weird."

They entered the small, bungalow style house through the kitchen. A woman managed several pans on a stove that looked like an antique. She glanced up at Wilson and quickly looked away.

"Norma sure can cook, son. Breakfast is just about ready." MacCreary pointed to a table in a small dining area. "Why don't you sit down? Would you like some orange juice? Coffee?"

"Coffee, please." Wilson noted that there were three places already set.

MacCreary poured two cups and sat down with Wilson at the table, opening up a newspaper. Norma brought the food to the table—scrambled eggs, bacon, toast, and country gravy—while MacCreary reached behind him to a counter and pulled a bowl of oranges over to add to the spread. They ate in silence. Norma never looked up from her plate.

When he had finished, Wilson looked around at the small but comfortable home. "I hope I didn't take someone's breakfast. Do you have children?"

MacCreary and Norma held hands and shared a smile. "We raised a child a long time ago," MacCreary said, "but it's been just the two of us for a while now."

"Then why did you have three places set?"

"Remember what I said earlier about curiosity? Well, there are some things we're not going to talk about." MacCreary turned to Norma. "But it's okay to talk to him, dear. I'm sure small talk won't be a problem."

"I hope you liked breakfast," she said.

"It was great." The words came automatically, surprising Wilson. He felt relaxed, more relaxed than he could remember, and that surprised him, too. "Thank you, Mrs. MacCreary. You've been very kind."

"Oh, just call me Norma. Everybody does." She seemed somewhat more at ease and began clearing the table.

Silence threatened to return, and Wilson felt the need to fill it. As a mostly empty slate, he didn't have much to talk about, and he wondered if that intensified the feeling. Just as he was about to remark on the weather, MacCreary spoke.

"Take as long as you need to put things together. When you're ready, we'll answer the questions we can. Until then, you're safe."

"Thank you," Wilson said. "I need this. Something normal, I mean. A minute to think."

"Go on in the living room, and we'll leave you to it," MacCreary said.

He got up from the table and left the kitchen. In the living room, the stiff couch barely seemed to register his weight. Elsa had mentioned powers. They were likely to be the key to carrying out his mission. Maybe even to survival. He looked at his hands, turning them over. Training. He needed training.

A sudden realization struck him. His hands. The blackboard image surged forward as soon as he closed his eyes. He scanned the pictures arranged around it. There, a picture of his hands. He snatched it down.

A memory activated. In the memory, he stood in a huge, open space. A series of floodlights arranged in a rough semi-circle provided the only illumination. Outside of their sharp halos, absolute darkness reigned. A rock ceiling glinted above him, maybe forty feet up. Likewise, the side walls were only visible in a small area.

Opposite Wilson stood a young woman. Grace. Grace Ramakrishnan. Her name came to him out of the void that had been his memory. Her slight frame radiated flexibility. Brown skin and long black hair provided a sharp contrast to marbled white-and-gray eyes. Wilson remembered that Grace tended to ignore her blindness.

"Wilson, we don't have time for much. These memories have to be kept short. We'll cover the basics, and you'll have to work the rest out for yourself." She tilted her head to the side slightly, as if listening. *"The preparation for going back has disoriented you. Good. It will help. Get ready."*

She exhaled and relaxed her stance, as if finding her balance. Wilson felt himself doing the same.

"The most important thing about working the equation is to let it flow through you. Your conscious mind wants to understand it. You don't have time for that. Envision the flow, and let it be. Do it now."

In the memory, Wilson followed her instructions. A portion of the equation materialized before him, rising from the ground like the coil of a sea serpent breaking the surface of the water. It coruscated and shimmered like a waterfall made up of variables, matrices, constants, and operators. It washed over him, through him. Then he heard it, the scraping in the darkness. Just outside the range of the lights. The Monster. How could that be? He bent his mind on the equation that was flowing around him.

"No, Wilson. You are considering. You are studying. You must let go!"

He ignored her voice. Grace used the equation without fear. And then he realized. Grace worked the equation through the machines. Of course she did. She wasn't a savant. Also, Wilson saw that Grace worked only part of the equation. The Monster didn't seek her because she didn't displace through time. Time.

A vortex opened before him like a gateway to hell. Screams echoed through the darkness. Glass shattered, machines sparked. Grace remained serene. A small gesture, and the vortex disappeared.

"That brings us to the second most important thing. Focus. Not on

the equation, not on the power. Focus on what you want. Find the universe where it's waiting for you. Reach through, and own it. Then bring it back with you."

Grace's form shimmered, becoming unreal in a stark light that demanded definition. Shadows wavered, and then it was over. She held out her hand. A flower lay across her palm, wet with the dew of another world. He took it from her, solid and real.

"The third, and last lesson. Always balance the equation. Envision the flow tied off. If you don't, you'll destroy the universe you opened just like the drones do. It makes the work harder. It takes more out of you, but you have the added benefit of knowing that you haven't just damned an entire universe to a hell where natural laws and the rules of physics can no longer be counted on."

Grace touched his arm, and suddenly, he could see the equation as she envisioned it. She folded it, over and over and over. Each time more difficult than the last. After the sixth fold, Grace gripped his arm tightly and strained, pushing against the equation. One more fold, and it suddenly collapsed down and away into nothing. Grace sank to the floor, gasping. Wilson knelt with her.

Out of the darkness, the Monster struck with a roar, ramming Wilson in the chest and throwing him through a brick wall. He sprawled on a tiled floor and looked around. It was the space in his mind where the blackboard and pictures waited. The hole in the wall - the one he had just created - had vanished, but he could hear the Monster coming for him. He let the memories go and opened his eyes.

He sat in the living room. MacCreary stood in the doorway. From the sounds of things, Norma was still doing dishes in the kitchen. His ribcage hurt like he'd been hit by a train. The idiom had risen from the fog of his erased memories without context, and though he knew what a train was, he had no context for understanding why a train would hit a person. It felt strange, but he couldn't help thinking that understanding the idiom in context would be stranger yet.

A flash of insight struck Wilson. "You knew my name. In the garage."

"That's right."

"But I have no memories of you or Norma. No memories of this place."

MacCreary nodded. "You will."

"There's a problem," Wilson said, looking up at MacCreary. "But then, you already know that, don't you?"

MacCreary nodded. "And I trust that you've figured out why there are some things we won't talk about."

Wilson smiled. "Because I told you not to."

"You did, and you will."

Wilson stood up and began pacing. "Then let's talk about my problem. I can't do what I need to do. There's a thing, a Monster that keeps getting in the way. This Monster will kill me if I try to do what I need to do."

"That may be," MacCreary said, rubbing his chin. "But then, why would you go to all the trouble of having me help you get this far? Why not warn yourself, through me?"

"It doesn't make any sense." Wilson stopped pacing and turned to face MacCreary. "Let's go for the obvious. Tell me how to use the equation without the Monster killing me."

MacCreary chuckled. "Even if I knew what you were talking about, I doubt I could answer that."

Wilson took in the whole puzzle. "I did this. I mean, I will do this. Deliberately. Knowing I need your help, I'm going to go back into the past and ask you to offer it when I arrive. All so that I end up here, in your living room, now. And it all worked out. So far, so good."

"Okay," MacCreary said. "What does that mean?"

"It's a loop. I set up a loop as a guide. I have to assume that it was the best I could do. But that means that I'm here early on purpose." Wilson frowned. "Maybe I had to be here early, and there wasn't time to adjust the plan. My gut says that I need to hurry."

MacCreary ran a hand through his hair. "What if you're here early to give you more time? Maybe plan A didn't give you enough time."

"I've been pushing myself to stay ahead of this thing, this Monster, since I got here. It just doesn't feel like I have time. It feels like I'm late. Like, if I stop or slow down, I'll be caught."

"So what are you going to do, son?"

Wilson looked MacCreary in the eye. "Since I can't get around the Monster, I'm going to spit in its eye and see if it kills me. It might be best if you take Norma and go for a walk. I wouldn't want something to happen to either of you accidentally. If I'm wrong, things could get pretty bad."

Norma brought MacCreary his coat. She had already put hers on.

"Thank you, again, for everything you've done for me."

MacCreary leaned in to speak quietly. "You're going to be alright, son. You just be careful, now. We'll be back in ten minutes."

Norma rested her hand on Wilson's arm for a moment. Wilson bowed his head slightly, grateful for the gesture. "Thank you," he said.

The two of them left. In the silence, he thought he could hear the Monster scrabbling inside the walls. His subconscious was constantly unbalancing the equation to keep the Monster at bay. He had been operating under the assumption that it would destroy him if it caught him. But that had to be wrong. He had to use the equation, or he would fail.

Seeking focus, he calmed himself, emptying his mind of distractions. It took several minutes. Images of the bodies in the vacant lot continued to surface every time he thought about using the equation consciously. Finally, he settled his fear, and his mind slipped into a state of detachment almost as if by habit. He was ready. He could feel it.

Without hesitation, he began working the equation. Grace had worked a small part of the equation with the aid of machines. This time, it wasn't just a single coil of the Monster that came to him. The whole infinite, eternal entity spiraled around him. He saw everything. Not just the universe, and not just the future. All universes. All futures. All pasts. Each and every present. His mind somehow perceived them all without overwhelming his ability to process his thoughts. Then, something shifted, and he realized that the Monster—the sum total of all realities and possibilities—had seen him. The vastness exposed him as small, insignificant, and out of place. Interfering.

The primal nightmare descended on him without mercy. The Monster did not come from any particular place. It came from everywhere, striking at Wilson with the full force of its fury.

In that moment, he remembered Elsa, what she had said. Time is an emergent property. He felt the Monster tear through his continuity, severing the motes of his consciousness and being from each other and scattering them into an infinite void.

"You will come with us." The drone repeated its command but didn't advance toward Wilson. It merely stood there, darkness steaming off into the artificial twilight under Central Authority.

The slight odor of ammonia coming off the drone cut through the dust and stung his nose. Wilson had the fingers of his left hand wrapped through the chain link fence behind him. Bits of gravel from his fall had stuck in his right. As he brushed it off against his coat, he felt the bulge of the ROC. Ross had created the weapon based on an early failed attempt to open a Campbell bridge. It created a portal with an unstable endpoint that was continually shifting through possible target universes. Randomly oscillating. Everything inside the portal's range of effect experienced the conditions of those universes. A good number of them were fatal. The portal also interfered with the drones' abilities. Reaching into the pocket, he ran his fingers over the smooth, aluminum casing and pressed the button. Three seconds.

"You can't have it," Wilson said, throwing the ROC as hard as could down the alley away from the drone.

The drone teleported, materializing in the alley with a buzzing sound, and caught the metallic sphere. Twenty feet away. Too close.

Wilson threw himself backward, away from the drone as the ROC went off.

Wilson landed just beyond the range of effect. The boundary of the portal zone shimmered, almost touching his feet. It cycled at slightly more than two shifts per second. Though he couldn't track all of the changes, he saw that at one point, bedrock filled the entire portal. Another split second showed the earth from orbit. The whole thing lasted no more than fifteen seconds. When it was over, the drone—and *everything organic that had been within the portal—collapsed to dust. Wilson wanted to rest, but although the Transitional Authority was blind to ROCs, it would only take them minutes to realize that a drone was missing. Wilson put the minutes to good use. He got up and walked away.*

As he turned the corner, he tried to remember what his plan had been. He had to do something. Something important. Whenever he concentrated on it, his mind seemed to slide past, unable to make sense of it. If he just walked, he seemed to know where to go and what to do. Cold realization struck him. The memory had been altered. There were other memories. Altered memories. Wilson had known what the plan was. So why couldn't he remember it now?

Wilson opened his eyes, but the living room had vanished. When the Monster attacked, he had dodged somehow. Shifted. Perhaps his blank mind afforded him this preservation, although he doubted that his friends and colleagues in 2072 had intended for it to save him from direct interaction with the equation. The blankness was meant to prevent him from interacting with the full equation at all. And it had, until he tried to use it consciously. That had taken him here.

Here. Wherever that was. He hung naked in a cold, dark, emptiness. No movement. His senses registered the faintest aroma of ozone. Impossible. No atmosphere existed to carry a scent, and here, time wasn't something that passed so much as something you passed through. Wilson needed to figure out where he was, but he didn't want to risk another direct confrontation with the Monster. There might be nowhere else to dodge to. What would happen to him then? Again, the destruction in the vacant lot rose through his memory. How could he manipulate the equation without waking the beast?

Grace had done it. She worked the equation with cool serenity, teaching his memory to make sure Wilson would later be able to do the same. She remained invisible to the Monster because she only used a part of it. The rest canceled out, masked by her anchor point in the native time and space she shared with Wilson. Since he no longer occupied his native time and space, he required the full equation. He needed the Monster. There was no other answer.

Even without the flow of time, he could still think. A causality of thought remained. One idea followed another. After what may have been a second or a lifetime, a flash of insight sparked in the darkness. Wilson was surprised to see light actually shine from him as it happened. It was cold lightning, crawling slowly away from him. A slim chance remained. Something he could do to shield himself.

There was no point in waiting. He relaxed, searching for the Monster. He was shocked to find it unimaginably far away. It should have been everywhere. He shut his eyes and willed the distance to close. He felt the vertigo of rushing toward it, although he felt no external sensation. The weight of his dread grew as if he was standing on train tracks, terrified by the blinding light of the oncoming train. When he could reach the equation, he immediately thought of what he wanted. The memory of the encounter with the drone caused a momentary slip of focus, but there was no time to make corrections. He shifted.

Wilson stood on a circular piece of asphalt maybe three yards wide, cut from a sidewalk, curb, and street. He had ripped a portion of his own native time and space away from its reality to create a haven. After the time he had spent in the clean air of 1985, he could taste the grit in the atmosphere of this small piece of home. A shimmering curtain bordered the sphere of his haven, courtesy of the untimely memory. A small portion of chain link fence confirmed that he had taken the area where he had killed the drone. From here, he could work with the equation. He could return to 1985.

Beyond the coruscating boundary, the truth glittered. The Monster didn't exist, not really. His mind created the Monster as a context he could grasp. Beneath that, a more complicated view revealed itself. Wilson unbalanced the equation. The equation sought balance. The totality of the omniverse lay before him, enormous beyond understanding. Dimensions and subdimensions extended all the way down into an infinite abyss of existence. All of it balanced. Time and space, all of what his limited humanity had once comprehended, all of it was an emergent property of the omniverse. Simultaneously, his subconscious saw the reality, while his conscious mind struggled to interpret it. Wilson decided that it looked like layer upon layer of sparkles caught in glass, each shiny, reflective grain of reality an entire universe in itself.

The effects of the Transitional Authority were here, too. A stain. A void. His mind interpreted the intrusion. Sections of the glass blackened and curled like paper, smoldering and slowly turning to ash without ever bursting into flame. They destroyed everything, consuming the omniverse like a blind, ravenous cancer. When the Monster had found him sitting on the MacCreary's couch, in the moment of that failure, he had translated himself into that darkness, for moments or millenniums. That is what awaited his reality if the Transitional Authority succeeded.

From within it, Wilson's perceptions had understood the void to be nearly all that there was. From outside, he could see the true extent of it. His world, his universe, was a flaring ember at the edge of the darkness. If he had been destroyed, his reality would have soon followed. He realized that it wasn't about just saving the world. It was about saving worlds. Universes. Everything.

Defeating the Transitional Authority would be an overwhelmingly complex task. It might be impossible, but he would try. He would work his way back across the omniverse, pushing them out of his reality first. The Laughlin in his memory remained silent, but that was fine. He didn't need Laughlin to tell him what he already knew. Wilson had to stop them from invading, at all costs. He knew who was responsible. He had to kill Hannah Bradley.

The pale green of the living room wall snapped into existence. Wilson returned to 1985, to the MacCreary home, several seconds before he left it. He reappeared behind the old but still serviceable couch. His previous self began to work the equation, and Wilson opened himself briefly to the omniverse. He shoved his previous self off into the only place where the omniverse wouldn't destroy him, out into the void created by the Transitional Authority.

Immediately, he began folding the equation away. Technically, he was solving parts of the equation in sequence, balancing his actions by allowing other variables to absorb the changes. He began by canceling the variables related to his displacement in time. It was much more difficult than he'd expected. Like forcing two strong magnets together, positive to positive. It resisted for a five count, and then suddenly fell away. The other folds came easily by comparison.

When he finished, he nearly fell to his knees. He was hungry. Starving. He could still smell the bacon from breakfast in the air, but how long ago had that been? Stumbling into the kitchen, he saw a large, open box of donuts sitting on the counter. He devoured several. Delicious. He could not recall a specific memory of ever having eaten a donut before. His memory contained no reference to them at all except as a name for a thing. But they were perfect. Almost instantly, his energy returned. Half a gallon of orange juice remained in the refrigerator. He drank most of it, washing down the sticky meal. The oranges at breakfast had been sweet, and the bitterness of the juice surprised him.

In his mind, he considered the plan as it had been presented to him. An access point to the Montauk base waited nearby. Though it was sealed in this universe, he would be able to change that easily enough. From there, a long corridor separated him from a stairwell. The stairwell ran from the top of Montauk all the way to the depths. He would find Hannah Bradley there, in the depths, and kill her. He would have liked to transport himself directly there, but if each use of his power drained him so, he might arrive in no shape to do anything but lie on the floor. He would have only one chance, and he must not fail.

While he was reluctant to move himself there, there were other options. He calmed himself, and the essential focus answered him immediately. He stepped into the equation, seeing it as a doorway. For a moment, it splayed out before him like a million doorways. All doorways. He concentrated on his goal and kept himself blank to everything else. Enough rank to be left alone, not enough to draw attention. The right size. It was... there. He reached out and grabbed a package wrapped in plastic. Exhaling a breath that he didn't realize he was holding, he stepped back out of the doorway. The Monster howled its rage, but Wilson had carefully constrained himself to this reality, this universe, this time. Small actions with minimal impact. He folded the equation, closed the door. It collapsed away immediately, without resistance.

His hands held a uniform, wrapped up in plastic. One of the Montauk uniforms. His legs felt a little unsteady, so he ate another donut. Quickly, he stripped off his clothes and put on the black clothing. The package contained boots, socks, everything including the sunglasses. When Wilson held up the sunglasses to look at them, he saw that they had integrated displays. The left side had an ear piece attached to the temple. Dressed as a shade, he walked into the little hallway. At the end, a full length mirror revealed his new look.

He stared at the image before him, intimidated. He set his jaw and raised his left hand to the ear piece.

He walked along nearly deserted streets, coming at his destination indirectly. He spiraled around it, surveying the area and ensuring that nobody followed him. Hours had passed since his confrontation with the drone in the alley. He dared not go back there. The site probably crawled with shades and drones, even now. Instead, he went up the line, looking for the entrance to the old Monroe platform. The acrid tang of burning tires scratched at his throat. The cold of night stalked him, gaining fast. Nameless, faceless anxiousness gnawed at him. Impatience demanded that he run. He needed... there was something... something important. He was already late.

This memory seemed to work differently. A distance buffered him from the full experience, forcing him to watch rather than ride along. The Wilson in the memory knew why he had to hurry. The Wilson watching the memory couldn't see it. The blind spot constantly irritated him, kept him from settling into the memory.

He finally approached the stairway that led beneath the surface. He descended without hesitation, trusting that no one followed. At the bottom, he found two squatters. A good sign. Nobody had rousted them. The shades and the drones had not been here. Wilson kept clear of the squatters and their small fire, heading deeper into the darkness of the old subway system. He held a flashlight with rechargeable batteries. It barely worked anymore, but he had nothing else to keep the darkness at bay. Now, he moved as quickly as he dared, heading down the old tracks toward Harrison and Forty Below. Ahead, a cave-in blocked the tunnel. Wilson climbed the slippery rocks, flashlight held in his mouth, and found a way through. Descending the other side, he slipped and tumbled headlong into the black. The flashlight fell, spinning through the air. Fortunately, he landed without sustaining more than a few bruises. The flashlight smashed, and the weak light snapped out. In the dark, he couldn't find it. Wilson used the tracks and the rock fall to orient himself. Once he faced the right direction, he could see a tiny light glowing in the distance.

He made his way along the tracks, moving slowly to keep silent. The light grew brighter as he approached the next platform. Harrison. Wilson heard voices now, as well. Low, mumbling voices. Echoes tumbled over each other, obscuring the words.

He could come no closer to the platform. Shadows shielded him, but another five feet would have him directly in the light. On the platform stood two shades. One of them raised his hand to his ear piece and motioned for the other to be quiet. After conversing via radio for several seconds, the first shade signed off. Within moments, a portal opened in the air above the platform. The two shades stepped into the portal, and it closed. Wilson jumped up, ran across the tracks, and flung himself up the rusted rungs to the main platform. He scooped up a chemical light stick that the shades had left behind and hurried toward the turnstiles. With a practiced move, he hurled himself over them, hitting the floor beyond without losing his momentum. He turned the corner and pushed open the door to the men's restroom. He picked his way through the room. Debris camouflaged it to discourage the curious. He waited in a small space behind a barricade of stall walls, still and quiet.

A section of wall swung back in silence. Wilson stepped through and waited for it to close behind him. He found himself in a small room. In a steady voice he said, "Forty below." Another wall slid aside, revealing a hallway. A small boy careened out of the corridor and wrapped his arms around Wilson.

"Dad, you made it! I knew you would. I knew it!"

The dissonance between the Wilson of memory and the Wilson watching grew. The memory faded, but just before it winked out, Wilson remembered the feel of running his hand through his boy's hair.

"Connor," he heard himself say, but the widening gulf robbed the moment of its original emotion, leaving Wilson unexpectedly unsure of how to feel.

His son.

Wilson snapped out of the memory at the sound of the opening front door.

"Wilson, it's Alan and Norma. Wilson, are you here?"

He took the sunglasses off and turned away from the mirror. "I'm here. I'm okay. Close the door."

He walked into the living room and saw the older couple standing in the kitchen. They didn't seem surprised to see him in the uniform, and that comforted him.

"Looks like you're ready." MacCreary's voice was solid, a wall he could put his back to if he needed.

Norma crossed the kitchen, and stood in front of Wilson. She reached up and adjusted his tie. She didn't make eye contact.

"There," she said in little more than a whisper. "You be careful, now." Tears began to fall down her cheeks, and she rushed out of the room, down the hall to the bedroom.

"Don't you worry about her, son," MacCreary said. "She'll be fine. You go do what you have to."

Kill Hannah Bradley.

"You and Norma, I don't know what I would have done without you. I felt so alone." His own tears threatened to spill down his cheeks. "Whatever happens, you've helped me in ways I can't begin to explain. Stay in the house. Hopefully, you'll know when it's all done."

The older man nodded, gripping Wilson's arm. "You let yourself out. I'm going to see to Norma. Good luck, son."

MacCreary followed Norma to the bedroom, closing the door gently.

Wilson wiped his face and put on the sunglasses. He left the ear piece out. After a moment of consideration, he left the house the same way he had entered: through the garage. He closed the door behind him and squared his shoulders. He filled his walk with a confidence he didn't feel. The beauty of daylight nearly stopped him. He wanted to stand in it, drinking the golden warmth into his heart. With each step, he pushed memories of constant twilight under an alien threat further away. No memories of joy under the sun rose to replace them, but a general feeling of contentment and rightness radiated through him. That would have to be enough.

He saw no sign of anyone else as he crossed the MacCreary's back lawn. Daylight made the paths through the hills much easier to see, letting Wilson move quickly across the rise, back toward the vacant lot. He was surprised to see a construction crew breaking ground. No sign remained of last night's horror, except for the patrols. He disciplined himself to maintain a steady pace. He knew he would be seen. The hillside access was too exposed to think otherwise. He had to trust his disguise to work long enough for him to get into the base.

"Hey, what are you doing up there?"

His heart thundered in his chest. He turned, standing as tall as he could. One of the patrolling shades broke away and jogged toward him. Several others watched, faces impassive. Wilson just waited.

"Did you hear me? What are you—"

"As you were," Wilson said, trying to keep his voice hard.

"Sorry, sir. I didn't realize, ah, right away, sir." The shade hurried back to the construction site, and the others returned to their posts. Wilson relaxed and picked his way a little more slowly now. In the dark, he had found no indication of any tunnel access.

He closed his eyes and saw the blackboard, surrounded by pictures. So many pictures. He needed more time. On his left, a picture of an analog clock caught his eye. He took it down, and another picture slipped out from behind it, fluttering to the floor.

"Wilson, this is Max. You need to understand the timelines. You're probably confused already, but this information might save your life."

Wilson remembered a series of sketches. Lines with loops on them, indicating events where the team had attempted to send someone into the past.

"Originally, the Transitional Authority came out of nowhere, it seemed. We fought back. The straight line here."

Wilson remembered Max. Dependable. A big man, but gentle. He also remembered Max's legendary presentations. "Come on, Max," Wilson talked to the memory. "I haven't got all day."

"We believe that we captured some of their technology. Adapted it, just before they took us out in 2080. With it, we disrupted the straight line with a series of messages back to 2070." A dotted line made a loop back to 2070, and from there, the original straight line split.

Wilson nearly tumbled headlong into a large drainage ditch that sliced through the hill. This had to be what he was looking for. He descended a few feet to find a place where he could jump down into the ditch without risking injury.

"In 2071, we sent some preliminary missions back to stop the Transitional Authority from ever invading, but they failed. We did uncover valuable information, though. The key to the whole thing is a person named Hannah Bradley. You kill her, and the Transitional Authority never invade. We can erase them from the timeline completely."

Wilson shook his head. The people from the future, his people, had no idea how bad the problem was. They barely thought beyond their own timeline. The corrugated tunnel had room enough that Wilson could crouch in it. He started in, carefully keeping clear of the small stream of water that flowed in the bottom. After about ten feet, the tunnel widened abruptly, and gained a ledge on one side. On the platform, new, uniformly gray cinder blocks replaced the moss covered bricks of the tunnel. He ran his fingers along the bricks, feeling the roughness. The cinder blocks were smooth.

Wilson stared into Connor's thoughtful brown eyes. Only six, but already so smart. Having two genius parents probably helped. Whenever he thought about Connor's potential, Wilson longed to set fire to Central Authority. The boy should have had a childhood full of joyful summers in Grandma and Grandpa's cabin. He should be going to school, astonishing his teachers, making friends—all the things bright little boys were supposed to do. As always, the frustration and anger twisted quickly into a knot of helplessness that Wilson swallowed down to keep it from showing.

"Connor, what's that in your hands?"

"I made it for you." Connor held out a piece of paper. Scribbles, equations and notes covered one side. On the other, Connor had drawn a colorful scene. Wilson felt that he should have recognized it.

"What's this?" Wilson asked.

"Look, it's a green field, and that's a tree."

"Well sure, buddy, I can see that. But what's this?" Wilson pointed to an angular, brown blob.

"It's a house. Our house. After we win, we're going to live where we want. In a real house. With a tree."

Wilson smiled. As good a reason as any to fight. He took the picture from the boy, careful not to fold it.

"I'm so glad you made it for the party, Dad."

"Of course I did. Nothing could have kept me away."

"Not even a drone, Dad?" Connor's voice was a taut bowstring, full of the awe and wonder of a boy in the presence of his hero.

"Especially not them. Not a hundred of them. Not tonight. We have to be here for…" Words failed him. Suddenly, everything got jumbled, mixed up. He didn't know where he was. Empty, blank areas dotted the room. Blind spots. They slowly grew, pushing everything else away.

Wilson gripped Connor's shoulders, and the boy gasped.

"*Dad, what is it? What's wrong?*"

"*Connor, tell me. Why are we here?*"

"*What's wrong, Dad? We're here because everything is going to be okay. We're going to win.*"

The room spun, and Wilson felt the memory pulling away from him. He stared at the picture in his hands, uncomprehending. "*Why, buddy? Tell me what's happening.*"

"*Dad, don't you remember? Mom—*"

Everything went black.

"You must kill Hannah Bradley."

Wilson snapped back to the present with a headache. The voice still echoed in his mind.

"*You must kill Hannah Bradley.*" Laughlin's voice.

Understanding that it needed to be done didn't make it any easier.

"I'm working on it," Wilson said under his breath.

He stood in front of the cinder block wall. On the maps he remembered, a door had been here. The cinder blocks probably hid it. He breathed in and out, calming himself. An idea struck him. He had pulled things to him from elsewhere. Surely, pushing would work the same way. He envisioned the equation, saw it flow past him with his mind's eye. He canceled the variables for time displacement. That would give him a few seconds. He reached out for a version of reality where empty space waited. When he found it, he pushed the brick wall and whatever else was just behind it out of his own reality and into the other.

It felt like stretching after sleep. Muscled uncoiled. With a satisfying pop, it worked. The wall disappeared. He stepped forward into a wide tunnel that had been converted into a storage bunker.

With each use of the equation, the consequences came quicker and hit harder. The Monster would wait no longer. It descended on Wilson from all sides. Just before it hit, Wilson reversed what he had done, returning what he had removed. The Monster struck a glancing blow, and the impact drove him to the floor. Groaning, Wilson balanced the equation.

Not a hundred feet away stood a shade holding a clipboard. He stared at Wilson, mouth agape. He dropped the clipboard and drew a pistol, screaming orders. Something distorted the words and made them sound far away.

Wilson raised himself to his knees, held up his hands. Empty.

The shade put the pistol away and reached behind his back for cuffs.

Wilson remembered. MacCreary's house. On the bench. This time, the shift happened almost instantaneously. He reached through the omniverse, from here to there. Wilson smiled.

"I believe in being prepared."

The shotgun appeared in his hands. He fired. The shot echoed through the tunnels ahead. Instead of just the one shade he expected, three bodies lay on the floor. Fatigue kept Wilson from expending the effort to figure out where the extra bodies had come from. They weren't a threat, and that was all that mattered at the moment.

Since he had taken the gun from this time, from this reality, the equation balanced easily. He felt the Monster raging just out of sight. Didn't it know that he wanted to help? It felt like a consciousness, an awareness, but vast on a scale that he could not even comprehend, let alone communicate with.

His vision blurred and refocused, shimmering lines and ghostly images floated across his normal eyesight. He dropped the shotgun and clawed the sunglasses from his face, but it didn't help. Then, he realized what he saw. Possibilities. He had broken something in his mind, removed some barrier to fuller perception. He could see layer upon layer, possible futures, the past, and alternate nows. It was as if he were floating in the omniverse again, but this time, immersed in a single shining point of light, seeing the way that each particular moment connected and could connect with others.

He lurched down the tunnel. His objective waited for him, but he hurt. His whole body ached, and his lungs burned as if he had been holding his breath for minutes. He consumed the rest of the training memories as he walked, pulling picture after picture from around the blackboard. Each of them became a stabbing finger from Laughlin, goading him, demanding that he do his damned job.

Kill Hannah Bradley.

As he neared a juncture, visions revealed that he would confront two shades. No choices, no path offered a way to avoid them. It was simply a matter of when and where they would meet. Wilson stopped and waited, working through layers of possible futures, trying to find a solution. Footsteps closed in, loud and menacing. Fear scrabbled its way up Wilson's spine. If he depended on these glimpses of possible futures, he might miss something in the now. He ripped the equation forward in his mind, tearing through it, spinning it around the pivot points of constants to highlight variables and unknowns.

Then, he saw it. He could factor the equation, simplify it, and do something different with it.

He braced himself, and connected the present with the past, this place with that place. The approaching shades saw Wilson through the connection point, kneeling on the floor ahead of them, hands upraised. When they ran through, Wilson balanced the equation and let the connection collapse, but not before the sound of the shotgun echoed through the tunnels again.

The Monster slipped past his defenses and refused to negotiate. Pain shot through him, bursting his nerves, clenching random muscles so tightly that he couldn't even cry out. Welcome darkness swept him away from his consciousness.

In the darkness, Laughlin chided him.

"You must kill Hannah Bradley."

"I can't. I'm dead," Wilson croaked, his voice broken and hoarse. "You're not real, anyway."

"You're not dead, you useless excuse for a scientist. You're giving up. Work it out."

"The programmed memories are botched, and there's nothing in them about the omniverse. Whenever I try to use it, it tries to kill me."

"Excuses! I figured out how to keep you alive, Wilson. I did. And you're wasting it. You're not dying, Wilson. We are. You're killing us."

"No."

"What? Did somebody say something? I can't hear you over the sound of your son dying."

Impotent rage flickered. "Leave Connor out of this."

"Why should I listen to you? You're dead, remember? Now, we all die, too. Including poor Connor."

"No!" His anger became an inferno that consumed and purified him at the same time.

The light scoured his eyes, but Wilson opened them and forced himself to sit up. He fought his own muscles, willing the bones to move. He couldn't breathe. He tried to inhale, but like his muscles, his lungs refused to respond. He wanted to breathe so badly, but nothing happened. His chest tightened, and he could feel another blackout coming. Panicking, he slammed his hand down on the floor, but his respiratory system seized up. The horror of suffocating to death summoned a scream, and Wilson lost control. Something in his throat responded to the attempt, and without thinking, Wilson reversed the action, sucking in air. The aborted scream twisted into a harsh gasp. He panted and wheezed, and slowly, he stood.

"Work it out," Wilson said to himself as he stumbled toward the stairwell door, still coughing.

The equations held the key. He had figured out how to buy time, how to postpone the backlash, but that had only protected him temporarily. Like his early attempts to use the equation, something important eluded him, and he had run out of time to discover it.

Emergency lighting dimly illuminated the stairwell, augmented infrequently by bare bulbs on the landings. Twice he fell, both times crashing onto the hard metal of the stairs. The second time, he rose more slowly. After that, a fog descended, and he had no concept of how long the rest of the descent took. Eventually, he stood at the bottom of the stairwell before a door. Before The Door. The door to the room where

Hannah Bradley waited.

Kill Hannah Bradley.

Wilson tried to find a calm center, but exhaustion intervened. He couldn't maintain his focus. The surroundings distracted him. Being so close to the end distracted him. Closing his eyes, he envisioned the room with the blackboard. Empty, because he had taken down all the pictures and experienced the associated memories. He could start there; the quiet held the promise of success. He began writing on the ebony surface, scribbling out the equation. The first line ran from the left edge to the right, and as he returned to the left edge to continue, he saw something lying in the rubble on the floor. Another picture.

Wilson reached up to put the chalk in the tray and saw the equation writing itself in neat script. White lines appeared on the blackboard as if by magic. He heard something scrabbling inside the walls.

Wilson was tired. Tired of missions. Tired of dodging the Monster's attempts to erase him. He watched the equation grow. Before long, the blackboard could no longer contain it. The blackness deepened, and Wilson saw that the frame of the blackboard now held a window that looked out onto the void. In the void, the equation coiled on itself. Infinite, bone-white coils.

Stalling would accomplish nothing. He turned to go, but remembered the last picture. Carefully, Wilson shifted a broken brick. Unlike the other pictures, this one had no glossy sheen. It didn't look processed. The hand-drawn crayon artwork showed a green field under a blue sky. The sun shone, innocent and yellow. The frame of a simple house dominated the center of the picture, an angular brown blob. Square on the bottom, triangle on top. Windows. Flowers. A door. Connor. With an anguished scream, Wilson broke out of his memories and back to reality.

Still screaming, he pounded the door with his fists. His voice gave way, and then his strength. Unfamiliar hardware on the door spoke to security concerns, as did the signs posted alongside. *High Voltage* and *No Unauthorized Entry*. Ghost images crowded before him. Using the power of the omniverse as he had before would be lethal. Another direct strike from the Monster would kill him. He needed another way.

Concentrating, he filtered out the possibilities that included his death.

A promising future floated ethereally in the dim light. Before he could change his mind, Wilson stepped into that future. He brought up the equation and used it to displace the door in front of him inward by just a centimeter. It barely caused a ripple in the omniverse. Wilson reached out and pushed on the door with his left hand. It fell inward and clattered to the floor. Balancing the equation brought on a splitting headache, but at least he was still alive.

Something in the room threw a painfully bright light everywhere. He waited for his eyes to adjust. There, in the midst of equipment and crackling energies, a frail, female form hung suspended in some kind of frame. Though she looked beaten and half-starved, he recognized Hannah Bradley.

"Wilson," she croaked in a voice that overflowed with relief. "Thank God." Her throat seemed to tighten as she spoke, her next words squeaks and whispers. "You have to kill me."

He wanted to. He wanted to kill her. It would all be over, then.

"You must kill Hannah Bradley."

Laughlin had made it crystal clear that there was no other option. But something inside of him, like a shadow, whispered that he couldn't kill her.

"What are you waiting for?" Hannah asked. "Just do it. My God, Wilson, if you ever loved me, just kill me."

That was it. The missing piece. Hannah raised her head, and her eyes locked onto Wilson's.

"I knew it would be you," she said, her voice barely audible above the electrical hum of the machines. "It had to be. You have to stop them. You have to kill me."

Overwhelmed, Wilson retreated to his programmed memories again.

He found the room unchanged. The equation still writhed out in the void, and Connor's picture still lay in the rubble. Wilson sobbed uncontrollably, his voice barking out gasping cries of pure, miserable agony. He couldn't hold it in any longer. The insanity of the situation pried at his rational mind like a crowbar. Laughlin had sent him back in time to kill the woman he loved.

He sank to his knees in the dusty debris, snatching up the last picture.

Without warning, he was on his back, looking up at lights. A medical facility. An operating room. It smelled of antiseptic and chlorine. And blood. He wanted to move, but leather straps restrained his head, arms, and legs. He heard a commotion nearby, but he couldn't see anything.

Footsteps. Someone running toward him. He heard the doors open, and the pressure wave hit him. He braced himself, not knowing what would come next.

"*Professor!*" The voice. He recognized it. Johnson. Johnson's face loomed into view. Jeremy. Jeremy Johnson. His friend.

"I'm not," Wilson began, but words were hard to form. He felt drugged. He strained mentally for the syllables. "Not your professor anymore."

Johnson's brows furrowed, and he frowned. He put a comforting hand on Wilson's shoulder. *"That's right. It's been quite a while, hasn't it?"* He checked a stopwatch that he held in one hand. *"You have to listen to me. We don't have much time. I'm going to talk as long as I can, or until they realize what's going on."*

He heard the sound of a chair being drawn close, and after a moment, Johnson lowered Wilson's bed.

"They lied to you. Christ, Professor, I lied to you. We told you you'd be going back to save Hannah. Laughlin wanted you to volunteer. Then, we wiped your memories and replaced them with the training you'd need. But the mission we gave you was to kill Hannah. I was a part of it. I believed it was necessary."

A crash rumbled outside the room, nearer than before. Wilson felt the truth in Johnson's words. The young man continued.

"Laughlin made it sound so perfect. Sure, we had lost Hannah, just like all the others. And buying her time only allowed them to capture her and stabilize her. But we had created a pinch point. The timeline adjusted around her, but she was so potent, it had to include her. History had changed slightly. Now, it depended on Hannah being the source of the invasion. If we killed her, we'd win."

Johnson looked around, but his narration never paused. *"But yesterday, when I was triple-checking the telemetry, I found a discrepancy. Something else had changed. I'd checked the figures twenty* times. Laughlin said it was just a temporal pre-quake. Nothing to be worried about. But, the same thing happened when we sent Hannah back. Adjustments. The timeline was adjusting to you, before you even arrived, just as it did with Hannah. It reacts like some kind of living creature, and something is tipping it off."

Shouts. Threats. The words "living creature" shot through Wilson, conjuring up images of monsters stalking him in the dark.

"I decided to throw a quantum monkey wrench into things." Johnson held up Connor's picture so that Wilson could see it. "Remember, Professor. When it comes time to make the decisions that will save us or damn us all over again, remember that you love her. Remember your little boy, Connor."

Wilson felt Johnson releasing one of his arms from the restraints. The young man pushed the picture into Wilson's hand.

"Maybe, our collective intent gives the timeline an indication of what we're doing, and because Laughlin is too worried about temporal contamination, he cuts it too close. We can't react. People aren't like equations. You can't just solve them with an equal sign. We need time to understand why. Besides, we owe you that much."

Wilson heard Laughlin shouting outside the door, his words unintelligible. He could only focus on Johnson.

"While they're busy getting me out of here and making sure that you're okay, they aren't going to notice that I've reprogrammed your bridge. You'll be early, have time to understand. You'll make it. You have to."

More running footsteps, lots of them. Johnson snatched the picture away, and the doors burst open. Wilson heard the sounds of several people tackling Johnson to the ground.

"What the hell?" Laughlin's voice. "Get him out of here."

"No! No, no, no! You have to let me tell him! He deserves to know! It's not right!" Johnson's voice faded they dragged him from the room.

Laughlin's face appeared. He held a syringe. "You shouldn't be awake, Wilson. Time to go back to sleep. Remember, you must kill Hannah Bradley."

The memory ended, and Wilson returned to the room with its

window. The equation of everything roiled and sinuated, growing larger and larger. Nobody could hope to understand it all, control it. Not even with a mind mostly blank. Suddenly, Johnson's words came back to him. "Equal sign." The equation swelled, breaking the frame of the window, expanding into the room. Equations could be solved. All the variables. You put in values. He saw the coils, rolling past each other. Rows of characters. What if they had nothing to bind them? The coils would slide through each other, becoming more and more dense, all the way down to the single point at the center of the spirals.

In that instant, he knew. Everything vanished. The room, the blackboard, the equation, all gone. He floated in the void, looking out into the omniverse. His mind stubbornly clung to the visualization, labeled it "reality." But reality was something much more elegant than the construct his mind had chosen.

The omniverse disappeared. In its place shone a single light. Wilson felt its warmth. He knew that warmth. Transcendent unity. A singularity.

Wilson opened his eyes and found the ghosts gone. He no longer needed them. Hannah hung before him. Wilson could see now that the energy surrounding her was an open portal. A Campbell Bridge.

"The shades captured me," Hannah said wearily. "Reprogrammed my ROC to open a doorway. They didn't care where. But I was deteriorating. Disintegrating. Until they put me here, in this field. Then, I was able to hold together." Her gaze took on a haunted look. "When I realized what was on the other side, I didn't think. I just, I don't know. I did something with the math. Somehow, I put myself in between. Nothing can cross unless I allow it."

"The Transitional Authority," Wilson said. "They're on the other side, just waiting. If I kill you, it closes the doorway, and they can't cross."

Hannah cried out. "Yes, yes. Kill me, please."

"I could go back, try to help you avoid this."

Hannah shook her head, looking into Wilson's eyes. "You'd risk losing this containment. If one little thing went wrong, we might not get this chance again."

Wilson's whole body shook as he suppressed his tears. "No, you're right, of course. But we have time." Wilson stepped into the light and put his arms around Hannah's thin shoulders, holding her to him. "I don't remember much, but I'm going to fix that now."

Wilson envisioned the singularity. Every time, every place, every thing, all of it one and the same. No here, no there. There was no Monster, just as there was no Wilson, and no Hannah. Nothing at all. Just one continuous point of existence. Wilson found himself in the future, and recovered his memories from that Wilson. He no longer needed to close down the equation. The equation held no meaning, now. He saw beyond it. In a rush, he remembered being with Hannah in the parade stands on the day of the announcement of Central Authority. He remembered her going away party when they had sent her into the past. The holes in his memory made sense, now. Laughlin had stripped away all his memories of Hannah to turn him into a weapon Laughlin could use to kill her. He remembered a weekend spent out in the country. Green grass, blue sky, and the sun. He remembered everything.

"What was that?" Hannah asked. "What did you do? I saw stars, galaxies, things I have no words for."

"I love you, Hannah. I love you so much." Wilson's throat ached with tears that wanted to overwhelm him. He held them back, willing himself to believe what he said next. "I'm not giving up. I've only just learned what Campbell's equation is for. I have to let you go for now, but I'll find a way."

"You can't risk letting the Transitional Authority into our universe."

"I'll do it without endangering the path that brought us here, but I'm not going to give up."

Hannah looked at him with hope. "Don't forget Connor. If you do this, he'll be gone forever. Save him, if you can. Tell him... tell him how much we love him."

"I'll save him. And I'll find a way to save you, too. Tell me you believe me." He centered himself, listening to the rhythm of her breathing. He saw the singularity.

"Wilson, you're glowing. Shining like the sun! I believe. I love you." Hannah buried her head against Wilson's shoulder.

In a heartbeat, Wilson stepped into the future, to the very second he had first journeyed from. With a thought, he froze time, holding the scene before him in perfect, silent stillness. He froze the whole crew in place, gazing at the empty pod that had just sent him back in time. He froze Laughlin's hand in midair, caught it in the motion of descending toward Connor's shoulder.

"As if," Wilson muttered. He strode over and knelt before the young boy. Gently, he took Connor's hands and nudged him out of the timeline with a moment of concentration. Connor hugged him tightly.

"Dad? What happened?" Connor asked, looking at the figures frozen around him. "Did you make it? Did we win?"

Wilson held his son close. "We're about to. But it wouldn't be worth anything without you. Come on, buddy. Let's go."

The next breath, they were back in 1985, at the bottom of Montauk Base. Alarms screamed. Doors opened, and black-clad soldiers with assault rifles swarmed into the room, surrounding Wilson, Connor, and Hannah. With a thought, Wilson erased their weapons.

"Come any closer," he growled, "and you'll find out where I sent your weapons."

Connor hugged Hannah's legs, and she smiled down at him.

"You're a brave boy, you know, and I'm so proud of you."

"Mom, when this is over, we'll live in a house."

A man in a lab coat shouldered his way past the soldiers. "Just stop. Just think about it," he said, holding up his hands to show that he was no threat. "We're this close. Alternate realities. Unlimited, clean energy. The ability to travel through time. Just imagine what waits for us beyond that portal."

"I know what waits beyond that portal," Wilson said. "It's probably everything you've ever wished for."

"Connor," Hannah said, "let me go now. Don't worry. It'll be okay."

The boy reluctantly disengaged and returned to Wilson's side.

Wilson looked into Hannah's eyes. "I can't take you down. I can't risk—"

"Wait, just wait," said the man in the lab coat. "We've been looking for a way to get her out of there without compromising the portal we've created. We just need time."

Wilson ignored him. "I can't take you down, and I won't kill you. That leaves just one option."

"I believe you."

"Hold onto that. I'll find you."

He found the edges of the portal and plucked at them like the strings of a guitar. The vibration resonated with a clear, deep sound like a bell. Hannah vanished through the portal, and it closed behind her.

MacCreary scratched his head, confused. "So, what did you do?"

"I sent Hannah through." Wilson took a deep drink of his Coke. "Then, I needed a place where Connor would be safe. For some reason, I had a hunch that a younger Mr. and Mrs. MacCreary might be willing to look after him for me." Wilson swallowed a bite of his grilled cheese sandwich. "After that, I went back to the facility. I rescued a few other people who were being held there. Then, I sealed it up completely," he said. "Cut off their communications, destroyed their teleporters."

"And then?" asked Norma.

"Velociraptors."

Norma choked and coughed on her lemonade.

"That was Connor's idea," Wilson said. "It was better than what they deserved. Later, I filled the whole thing with lava from under Yellowstone. Nobody will be coming back to their work there. Never again."

"Are you going to go after them?" asked Norma. "The aliens, I mean."

Wilson nodded. "Eventually. First, I'm going to do what I promised. I'm going to get Hannah."

"Do you know where to look, son?"

"I have a few ideas," Wilson said. He stood up from the table. "Now that I know what you did for me, looking after Connor while I bring Hannah back, I can never repay you for all the kindness you've shown. But you already know that part."

MacCreary put an arm around Norma, pulling her close. "Son, it was the decent thing to do."

Wilson regarded them gravely. "I know there's more you aren't telling me, and that's okay. I have to do this. Short cuts won't work. I already know that you'll be there, no matter how long it takes, no matter what happens."

Wilson prepared to leave, and MacCreary said, "There's more, but just remember, son. There's time enough for everything."

Matthew Rohr is a writer and editor who dreads writing about himself in the third person. However, since he has to, he might as well tell you the important details.

He's a little odd. He loves to write short stories and novels. His preferred genres include urban fantasy, historical fantasy, science fiction, and post-modern pre-industrial retro-futuristic steampunk haiku-funk fusion. Okay, that last one totally doesn't even exist. But it should. If he drops hints that he has an incredibly important secret to tell you, he's more than likely making it up, but it's best to be sure, so you probably ought to listen. He has lived a thousand lives, each more adventurous than the last. A thousand more await.

He's been an elven child, imprisoned by demons along with the remnants of his race in the breeding pits. He's been a private detective killed and raised from the dead to solve his own murder. He's been an angel, a half-breed, and a normal, everyday guy willing to sacrifice it all to save the world. For as much as reading shows us places and things we never thought we'd see, writing creates those places and things, It puts us in them and them in us forever.

He tried to tell you. He's a little odd.

Look Forward to Tomorrow

Haley Brown

MY LOVE,
It has been so long.

If I were to count the hours since I last saw your face, they would outnumber the stars that hang in the night, scattered into an ocean of oblivion. An ocean where everything falls, lost beyond hope. I am closer to despair than anyone anywhere. And I'm so afraid of being alone. I'm so afraid to move and even more afraid to try. Days and nights go by, like slowly ticking hands of time. I kick and scream and thrash and plead. How am I to live without you next to me? I needed you then, the way I need you now, to take away the suffering that's painfully loud.

Don't be mad. I found a way, a way to finally see your face, retrace every step like one two three, three two one. And every day I promise, I'll be there by your side, take your place again then again, until you come back to me. It's the only way I could find you, and tether you and I together. So wait for me my Love. I'm on my way. I'm coming.

Always yours.

Forever.

Folding the letter over at the edges, I put it inside the envelope and place it on the shiny surface of the mahogany desk in our room, a desk that has been in your family for several generations, and I wonder who it will pass to when I'm gone. A half bottle of whiskey sits just inches away, my drink of choice these days, and I stare at the white envelope in the middle of the desk, wondering how long before someone comes and finds me. An hour? Two? Four, or more? When they do, it will be too late. I will be long gone away. So far that there will be no coming back.

It has been one year today since you died, leaving me behind to pick up the shambles of what my life has become. And what a life it is. Bleak. Desolate. Hiding out in this room, waiting for the sun to set once again on another wasted day without you. I cannot do it anymore. I cannot be here another day, breathing in the same emptiness until I am smothered by my despair like a pillow down my throat.

If I had not left you that day to embark on a new chapter in my life, would you still be here? Could I have prevented what happened? Been your knight in shining armor and saved you? Every night I lie awake, envisioning what would have happened had I come back, had I listened to the intuition that urged me to turn around and run back to you, fall into your arms and never leave. If so, I would have found you, there at that place we first met, there where the winds blew your hair away from your face, and I saw that haunting expression full of loneliness and pain. That look that made me want to know you, made me want to erase all your sorrows, however many there were. And there were many. I remember the day you finally opened up, telling me about your past, about the childhood trauma that would surely scar anyone into hiding away from the world. And you hid. You bottled up your memories and tried to forget, tried to run away, but didn't get very far. Your wounds were like weights attached to your ankles. They held you encased in a tomb of iron that left you cruel and isolated from the world and everyone in it.

Until that day. That day we met under that tree, silently connecting our hearts, like we were the only two people in the world.

I should have gone back.

I was leaving you for a while, going off to fulfill my dream of going to college and becoming who I was meant to be. I had my scholarship. I had my road laid out and paved. You said I could do it, and I believed you because I believed in you, the way you believed in me.

I would have worked hard and then worked harder. I would have struggled, fallen, then picked myself up and crawled if I had to. I would have graduated with honors at the top of my class. And you would have been proud. You would have rewarded me with the embrace of your arms and the prize of your lips against mine.

I can feel them still. Soft. Wet. The first lips I ever kissed that will also be my last.

Just a little bit longer. My fingers tap an irregular rhythm on the desk. *I need to remember you just a little bit more.* Feeling the sudden need to walk, I quickly stand, swiping up the letter and shoving it in my front pocket. I leave our room with two things: a jacket, and the half bottle of whiskey.

The driveway is long, and before I venture into the street, the whiskey is gone along with the bottle as it is thrown onto the lawn by my arm that has a mind of its own. The night is chilly, and the winds are howling like wolves for the moon. I zip my jacket shut with unsteady fingers and feel the welcome effects of the alcohol as it burns through my veins, setting my mind at ease.

Come with me. Be by my side. I begin my journey to town, traveling down the street in the fog of a drunken stupor. We do not live far, so it does not take me long, and before I know it, I am wandering into town like a lost pup. People crowd the streets, remnants of the annual fall festival, but I only note the mass of color like a rainbow spinning on a spindle. All the lights and the movement blur before my eyes, and it's a wonder I do not pass out right in the middle of the street. Somehow, I wander into a bar, pushing and shoving my way through the mass of patrons, and end up sitting in the back, digging my thumbnail into the rubbed wood of the table. A thin waitress with bright crimson lips and limp hair comes up and comments on my age and how I do not look old enough to be away from my mother. I tell her what she can go do with herself. The thin waitress is soon replaced by two rather large men I want to name Tweedledee and Tweedledum, who hand me a one-way ticket out the back door. *Thrown* out the back door.

A blessing in disguise.

The alley behind the bar leads me into another world. One that is dark yet comforting. I stumble around for a minute before nearly colliding with a man who introduces himself as Mr. Abberforth. He wears a cloak that is tattered where it brushes the ground and a top-hat, scuffed and gray like smoke from a chimney. His eyes gleam in the moonlight, deep orbs of midnight blue that seem to look right through me.

After I stare at the man for an awkward moment, he offers me a drink, and I take it. Water.

Water leads to conversation, which leads to secrets, which leads to tears. He listens with grace, nodding every few seconds like he understands the ins and outs of my sorrow. How I don't care if I live, and care even less about dying. After I am done crying, we say our goodbyes, and I begin walking away.

"Hold on a second," he says, the flick of a lighter sounding behind me. I turn as he lights a cigarette, takes a long drag, and blows a puff of smoke out that clings to the air like a low cloud. "I shouldn't be telling you this but, damn, I can't pass up the opportunity. I believe we were meant to meet." He takes another drag and scratches his forehead. "If you could have the chance to be with your Love again, even if it meant risking your life, would you?"

Before I am aware of it, my hand rubs the pocket that houses the letter. Without another thought I nod. Yes.

"Then you will meet again," he says, this time grinning a little. "That much I can promise you."

With that, his hand disappears inside his cloak and re-emerges with a small leather pouch. It dangles from his hand by twine that is wrapped tightly around the top, sealing it shut. He holds the pouch out, and I take it gratefully, but with curious fingers that shake with apprehension and need.

"When you are ready," the man says, "take this." He points to the little bag in my hands. "And you will find your way."

I want to know. What is inside? A ray of hope? A joke? I want to trust the man but find him a mystery. A mystery that I want to ignore, because he's too good to be true.

I don't.

Instead, I look at Mr. Abberforth like he is my good-luck charm. A piece of sunshine I can cling to long enough to brave a try. I can only try. Even if it be only once. I must.

If it really works, there won't be enough thank you's in the world to express my gratitude, but for now, I thank him once and turn to leave.

"One more thing," Mr. Abberforth calls out. "When you return, come and see me. I'll want to hear about your trip. Just follow the bread crumbs and you will find me."

Like the fading light of a sunset, he disappears within the shadows of the night, and I run back to the house wide-eyed and alert, the alcohol in my system gone, my heart beating faster than it has in over a year. When I am safely in our room, I sit in the desk chair and open the leather pouch. I turn the pouch over, and the contents fall out onto my hand.

A little golden pill. I stare at the pill, the size of an almond, feeling confused and conflicted, as if what I have been planning all along—to end everything once and for all—was staring me in the face. *What is this? What will it do? Will it really bring me back? Can I really see you again?* I close my eyes and take a measured breath. I see you in my mind, steady and true. You invade my thoughts like an all-consuming fire. There is no other choice. Soon, very soon, I will be with you, see you again, and all this waiting will come to an end. I will hear you laugh and hear you cry. How I'd die to hear the sound of your voice, and lived for this very moment.

My decision made, I take a deep breath and, with no further thought, swallow the golden pill.

Seconds tick by that turn into minutes. I sit with my back against the desk chair, twining my fingers together and squeezing like they might fall off if I were to let go. Suddenly, my vision starts to blur, and a violent cough overtakes me. Clutching at my throat, I fall out of my chair ending up on my back as the attack subsides. Tears leak from my eyes and run down the sides of my cheeks in great streams. My breathing returns to normal as I stare at the ceiling, at the particles of dust floating suspended in the air. The dust turns into stars that twinkle brighter than the morning's dawn, bright like the light I saw reflected in your eyes every time you stood by that window in the morning. I am flying. Falling. Floating. Because if I were soaring, I would know it.

Darkness falls around me like the collapse of time and space, as though there were no meaning, and there never had been. It feels like I'm standing in a room, with four walls of pitch black, silent and empty. No air. No reason to breathe. But my chest moves anyway, expanding like a balloon with each breath.

Then, I feel your hand. I know it's your hand because I can feel the scar cutting the horizon of your wrist. You curl your fingers around mine and squeeze like you're afraid to let go. Like the world might fall apart and toss us around until we are fragmented and dying with our eyes covered, hands hiding sight, and enveloped in a wooden box buried six-feet under.

Squeezing your hand in return, I see you. Your eyes are the exact color that I remember. Deep rivers of hazel flecked with traces of gold. Gold like the color of your hair. We lie in our bed, you on your back, me on mine, hands firmly clasped, and stare. I watch the corner of your mouth turn up in the start of what I know will be a smile that makes my heart beat faster. Like all your smiles do. They capture my heart. Like when we first met, and I thought I was having a heart-attack. You were so mesmerizing. So captivating, yet sad. Haunted. And I found myself wondering what I could do to make you smile. That's all I ever wanted.

Now I have you before me. Smiling.

"We should probably get up," you say without conviction. The statement more a point-of-view than a suggestion.

I shake my head no. "Don't want to just yet." I want to stay like this forever. Freeze time and never leave.

You smile, knowingly, then lean over to kiss my lips, a reminder of our long night together. Your free hand reaches up and strokes the side of my face leaving a trail of fire down my cheek.

"If we could lie here forever, I would," you say, "but there's a world waiting for us outside that door, and as much as I'd like to stay here with you forever, you are not mine to keep."

"But I am." I look as deep into your eyes as I can get. "I'm yours."

I feel my brow furrow and my throat tighten. I cannot leave. If I leave, something will happen. Something bad. I want to warn you of it but do not know how. How do you tell someone they are going to die? How do you warn your most beloved of their impending doom?

You just do.

So I'm going to.

Any minute now.

Before I open my mouth, I'm distracted by the nearness of you. By the rise and fall of your chest and the smell of sandalwood coming from your skin like you'd been dancing in the forest at twilight. You crush your mouth into mine, and we fall into a world where no one but you and I exist.

Some hours later, I wake up and you are gone. The bed is cold where you'd lain, and a shiver runs though my body at your absence. I know this scene. I've walked it before. I know if I get up, dress, and leave the room, I will find you downstairs in the piano room, sitting on the bench playing Beethoven's *Moonlight Sonata* with a look of finality on your face. You will tell me to go fulfill my dreams. And I will go.

Before I can even think to move, the world turns black, and I'm suddenly standing in the room with four walls, suspended over time and pulled away from you, blinking through a series of what appears to be images, flashcard memories that flicker like a light burning out. I feel my chest heave, and I suck down a breath that pulls me from the darkness back to the present into the dim light of our room.

My eyes fly open, and my heart feels like the running footsteps of a child, pounding erratically this way and that. Stiff and cold, I realize I'm lying on the floor, arms stretched wide, fingers digging into the wood floor as if it were dirt. Willing my arms to move, I peel them slowly off the floor, lifting my hands up to inspect a throbbing in my fingers.

Sure enough.

They're bleeding.

How I survived this long without you is a mystery. And some mysteries are just too painful to relive. But I want to. I have to. If I don't, I will not survive the night.

On a mission that seems impossible, at an impractical hour in the dead of night, I hurry into town and find the bar I'd been thrown out of. All the lights are off, and a "closed" sign hangs in the window, but I do not care for I am in search of something so much more important. The back alley where I was tossed like a bag of trash.

Rounding the corner, my eyes begin to adjust to the darkness, an eerie, colorless ambiance that creeps along the back alleyway like a prowling snake. Tents made from boxes are clumped together along the right wall where the homeless have set up a shared community, their refuge from the world around them. And even though it is the middle of the night, the alleyway is moving. Someone coughs. A group of people huddle around a fire and whisper words inaudible. I hear someone laugh loudly and bang on something that sounds like a metal trashcan. I look around, wondering why I've come here. He'd told me to follow the bread crumbs in order to find him. But all I am doing is retracing my steps, and then continuing to walk because walking is all I have. It keeps me moving forward toward something, when all I want to do is go back.

My head spinning, I stop. Leaning back against the alley wall, I look up toward the heavens. The sky is dark, a spread of gray clouds obscuring the moon and stretching out over the sky attempting to paint the stars away. I close my eyes briefly, picturing those stars and how they reflected in your eyes. How they twinkled and glistened like the waters of a brook.

"Hey you. What you be here fer?" A voice asks from right next to my face.

My eyes spring open, and I stare into the face of a gruff looking man whose dirty blond hair is pulled back into a messy pony tail, and who stands too close for comfort. His bearded chin bobs up and down and a bit sideways, his squinting left eye blinks rapidly, and his breath smells like he's fallen into the bottom of a barrel of whiskey and decided to drink his way out.

I back up, and the reflex puts some distance between the man and myself.

"I'm looking for someone," I say, deciding to divulge some information. Perhaps this bystander will have seen the man before. Perhaps he will know. What harm could come from asking for a little help?

"Someone's a lot o' people to be lookin fer down Caster Alley. Ain't seen the likes o' you round here before." The man scratches his head and looks me up and down.

"I'm... just visiting."

The man laughs, and the sound echoes through the alley like a rushing wind. "Nobody visit Caster Alley widout want'n somethin. What you be want'n?"

"I want to find a man named Abberforth. Mr. Abberforth. Have you heard that name?"

"Abberferth. Abberferth," the man thinks out loud and then shakes his head, "Don't know no Abberferth, but dere's a Mr. Abby what lives up in da top o' dat dere bidness buildin' down Crooked Lane wit da big windows and such."

"Which way is Crooked Lane?" I ask, grabbing the man's arm. It's him. I know it is.

"Few block down on da lef," the man says. I let go of his arm and start down Caster Alley. "Cain' miss it. Juss be lookin for da sign."

"What sign?" I call back, turning around.

"Bread Crumbs."

With a word of thanks to my helper, I hurry down Caster Alley almost tripping on the cobblestones in the dark.

Like a yellow-brick-road for me to follow. My path is laid out. My bread crumbs. I'm on my way.

I'm coming.

After a few blocks and more than a few wandering homeless, I come to Crooked Lane and take a left like the man said. Several rundown buildings line the road and look like they should be condemned. A shiver runs down my spine as a gust of wind blows past stirring up a cloud of dust. Bad things happen down roads like this. I know it, but I still walk.

My attention is distracted momentarily by a wooden sign hanging on a brick building to my right. Bread Crumbs Bakery. The dilapidated sign is faded with long cracks in the wood. Underneath the bakery's name, an arrow points down to a doorway, confirming I've reached my destination.

It's a two- story building with dark shingles and butter-cream shutters—most which are hanging askew—and as I get closer, I notice all the windows are either broken or missing. In the storefront, another sign reads "Bread Crumbs." It dangles crooked on its post, informing the passerby of the obvious, that the bakery is officially closed. The building looks more like a condemned house than a place of business. The kind of place you would expect to find rats living in the walls and stray animals making their homes. I should feel scared. I should turn around right now and run home with my tail between my legs.

I don't.

Walking up the short walkway to the building, I lift my hand to knock on the door before realizing it is already open. I push the door in just a little, and it rocks on its hinges with a slight creak before I push it the rest of the way. "Hello," I call and hear my voice echo somewhere beyond my sight. With no outside lamp or light, it is very dark.

As I contemplate going inside, a figure emerges out of the darkness like a corporeal ghost. A gaunt looking Mr. Abberforth saunters slowly toward me with a slight limp that I do not remember him having before. Instead of the tattered cloak and top-hat, he wears a simple white t-shirt and trousers.

"Well, well," he says, leaning against the door frame. "Look who we have here."

Suddenly finding myself lost for words, I swallow my nerves and start, "I need you to help me."

The man's chin lifts as he regards me. "Then it worked."

"Yes, it did." I shake my head feeling a shiver run through me.

"Fascinating." He pushes away from the door and holds it open for me.

I stare at the dark entryway for a moment feeling the weight of the darkness settle somewhere behind my eyes. I will my eyes to adjust and hone in on my destination. What I need. What I came here for. What I could not leave without.

I don't even hesitate to walk through. I need to see you again. The need is so great, it is pulling me with a force stronger than nature itself. And I'm so close. So close that I can almost see you waving at me from across the street. So close I can smell the musk of your skin, like sakura and sage. I'm intoxicated by these overwhelming feelings. So wait for me my Love. My one and only. I will see you again.

"Please," I openly beg, fixing my eyes on the man who has now become my savior. "Please give it to me again."

"First time's free," he says. "Anymore and there will be a price."

"I have money," I say, reaching around to my back pocket and pulling out my wallet. "Name your price. It doesn't matter how much."

"Well, now we're talking business," he says, and waves for me to follow. "I knew we were meant to meet."

I follow Mr. Abberforth down an unlit hallway where our steps stir up smells of dirt and mold. Someone has pushed the remnants of the old bakery into a large room on the left. Old tables, broken chairs, and a smashed display case gather dust. We pass a set of "He" and "She" bathrooms on the right as he leads me to the back of the building. Pulling a set of keys from the belt-loop of his pants, he unlocks a door on the right and enters, holding the door open for me to follow.

Once again, I know I should turn around and run. There's a voice in the back of my head, warning me not to do what I'm about to do. But I do it anyway.

I enter the room and immediately notice the smell, like chemicals and alcohol and the faint residue of burning wood along with something sweet I have a hard time placing. Like a cherry sucker. Mr. Abberforth switches on a lamp next to the door, then walks to the back wall to turn on another. The light is low and cascades an eerie glow about the room. It looks like it had once been a large office. A long table against one wall and a short bookshelf lining the other. A square counter sits in the middle of the room, littered with an array of items. A couple of microscopes.

Thermometers. Cylinder tanks. Glass vials. Chemicals labeled with warnings.

My senses on overload, I feel panic surge. But then I think of you, and my feet remain firmly planted, determination winning over fear.

"Here we are," Mr. Abberforth says, stretching his arms out then letting them fall to his sides. "I must say. You found me a lot faster than I predicted." He pulls out a chair from the table and sits down. "Now tell me, did you find your Love?"

I don't feel like talking. I don't feel like a heart-to-heart. But the man is helping me, and at the end of the day, he is my only hope. "Yes, I did," I say, giving a quick nod.

"Then you saw the past?"

Again, I nod, and the man smiles. "Splendid. That's wonderful." He regards me curiously. "It is what you wanted isn't it?"

"It is," I say, suddenly at a loss for words. "It's just... I need..."

"You need to go back?"

"Yes." The word flows out of me like a rushing current.

He drums his fingers against his knees, then bobs his head. "Okay. If you think you know what you're doing." He gets up and moves over to a small safe against the left wall, grabbing the keys from his waistband. He crouches down, shielding the safe from my view. A lock clicks, a door screeches, and after a minute, he shuts the safe door and locks it. "I believe these are what you're looking for." He stands, holding out a handful of golden, almond-shaped pills. "These should do the trick. They will get you where you're wanting to go."

"I'll take all of them," I say, needing to get there.

After I pay the man, he places the bunch in a small bag and hands them to me. I snatch them away like they are a vital organ, the key to keeping me alive.

"A word of caution my friend," he says as I turn to leave. "Never too much fun. Just so much and no more. Never more than one."

Staring at the man unblinking, I can't think of anything to say. I bow my head in thanks and hurry along. Out of the building, down Caster Alley, and through the sleeping town until I am safely back in our room, gripping the small bag as if it is more valuable than gold.

It is.

No longer caring about the day, the time, I open the bag and take out a single pill and swallow it, feeling it scrape down my dry throat.

Minutes tick by, and I feel drowsy, so I lay myself on the bed. I close my eyes feeling my vision swim, and I squeeze the blankets under me with my fists, opening and closing my fingers as I cough. I can't breathe. I'm a fish out of water. Suffocating. A whimper escapes my lips as I feel myself falling, and my head feels as light as air. I want to breathe, but there's no need. So I open my eyes and find myself surrounded by darkness once again. I'm weightless in a room filled with the colorlessness of night.

"What are you still doing here?"

I whip around, and I'm standing in the piano room. You hold my eyes and stare at me intently, your hand resting on the piano's frame. I don't remember this moment. From before. And I don't know when in time we are.

"I... came back for you," I manage to say.

Your head cocks sideways as you regard me despairingly. "Why? When you could so easily walk away."

"Because I can't be without you." Tears choke my throat.

Your eyes fall to the floor and dart back and forth. "But... I let you go. I thought it would be best that way. That if I released you, you'd go your way. Be free of me."

Tears are flowing now, and I shake my head. "I don't want to be free of you. I want you to take me with you so that I will always be by your side."

"No," you say, stepping back. "It's not right. It isn't right of me."

"Yes it is." I take a step closer. "I'm telling you. I'm okay."

"You're okay?"

"That's right." I fill the words with as much meaning as I can, hoping they get through to you. "I don't care about anything else. I've already forgotten the past. The only thing that matters to me is right now." Your lip quivers, and I see the tears as they slide down your cheeks. "All I want... is to be with you."

After what feels like forever, you nod. Yes. "Alright," you whisper.

"Alright." And I'm there. Wrapping my arms around your neck. Pulling you near. "I missed you so much," I murmur into the crook of your neck.

"Missed me?" You chuckle. "You just spent the whole of last night with me. Did you forget?"

My face flushes, and I know that if I were to look in a mirror, I'd be blushing. "That's... not what I meant." But I can't keep my breath from hitching, can't keep you from noticing.

Your hands twine in my hair, and I feel tears on my cheeks. You hold my face mere inches from yours and trace the outline of it with your eyes. "How about you get some rest and when I come up, we can continue with what we started last night?" You say it so naturally. The easiest thing in the world.

Unable to speak, I nod my head in agreement, and you wipe the wetness from my cheeks with your thumbs. "Now go." You give my forehead a kiss and release me. "I'm going to play a bit more then come up." I hold onto your hand, unwilling to let go, but you do. "Be sure not to fall asleep," you say with a grin that plays on my heartstrings like your fingers on the piano.

"See you soon then," I say and back toward the door as you sit down at the piano and start playing *Nocturne in C Sharp Minor*. How many times now? How many days and nights have I sat and watched you play? Listened to the song of your heart as it was played and expressed so beautifully through your hands. I want to stay and watch you but decide it is best to get some rest as a wave of exhaustion sweeps over me. Quietly closing the door behind me, I lean into it and close my eyes for a moment listening to you play. The song flows through me like a trickling waterfall, reminding me of your gentle touch and your tender soul, a soul that I will forever be a part of.

Pushing away from the door with the song in my heart, I make my way up the stairs and into our room. The covers are bunched, your pillow is half-falling off the bed, and our clothes from last night are strewn on the floor like our honeymoon night that we live over and over. I pick up your robe and tears fill my eyes remembering how you look in it. For you it has been but a few hours, for me over a year, and the thought of you being downstairs feels too far away.

Rest suddenly sounds like wasted time. Time that I could be spending with you.

Leaving your robe draped over the foot of the bed, I exit the room, resolving not to return without you. My feet take the stairs two at a time, and I almost trip over the pants that are too long for my short legs.

I reach the landing and turn toward the piano room on my left, but I stop short finding the door open. I am certain I closed it, and you are no longer playing.

I am certain of two things: one, you never stop a song midway through; you always play through its entirety. Two, everyone you have employed in this house knows not to ever interrupt you while you are playing. Something is wrong. I don't hear your song.

Shouldering the door aside, I hurry into the room. You are gone.

A hand squeezes around my heart when I look down and see droplets of blood on the floor next to the piano. Like a fist to my gut, I realize during the few minutes I was gone, it happened. You were stabbed. This was where it happened. And this must have been *when* it happened. Foolish. Foolish me. Why did I ever leave you? I should have known. I am here to save you, but I let you die. I should have known something like this could happen. How could I have known when in time we were?

Cold fear rises in my chest, choking me like hands around my neck. My heart pounds, and my breath comes in shaky gasps. I need to find you. Fast.

With blinding panic, I hurry from the room, searching the floor for more drops of your blood and following the direction they lead. Out the front door. If I find you quickly enough, I can save you. I can take you to the hospital, and they will fix you up like new, and we will go home not one but two. Not just me, but me and you.

As I hurry over to the doors, my vision darkens, and our world is ripped away from me like a page being turned. I'm spun around, suspended in the black room with walls I can't see but feel them closing in upon me, trying to push me out. My eyes blinking, light and color flickering, and I sit up in bed as if being shocked back to life. Shortness of breath stretches me thin, making me feel lightheaded. My chest aches, and I cover it with a fist and press. I need to go back and find you. I need to stay longer and not come back so fast. I don't have enough time. Every trip is a whirlwind, happening so fast that I can't think, can't move, can't do anything, can't save you. Before it's too late, I must find you again before then.

Scrambling for the pills, I'm frantic as the bag is missing. After tearing apart the bed, I find the bag has fallen onto the floor. I dump the remaining pills into my hand and swallow them together. Unable to relax, I stand for several minutes, shifting my weight from one foot to the other, breathing fast, running my fingers through my hair, biting nails that I bit off long ago, when it hits me.

I double over, coughing and clutching at my throat. Feet carry me backward, and my back hits the wall where I thrash for a moment. My head sears with lightning bolts of pain. I can't see. I can't open my eyes. White hot static crackles behind my eyelids, inside my head, inside my ears, and I cover them with my hands trying to shut out the noise. Unable to stand, I collapse onto the floor in a heap of agony, crying out from the suffocating pain. And just as it is too much to bear, when I'm begging for the torment to end, the pain suddenly disappears. Like the snap of fingers, it is gone, and I'm left unsteady, wary, and afraid.

I blink several times, waiting for my eyes to adjust to whatever they are seeing. But I can't see. It is so dark. All around me is an abyss of black waves that bend and move like the waters of the sea. Like the waters that swim in your eyes, and are now swimming in mine. Where are you? I need to find you. It hurts so much, and I don't know what to do. Any more living won't be living without you.

"Shh, it's okay. I'm here," you say. And I search and search to find you but you're so far away, like the sound of your voice. "Hear my voice. Find me. I'm right here."

I feel a hand on my cheek—your hand—and rapidly blink my eyes as your face materializes like a warm light in the darkness. Your hair. Your eyes. Lips. Finding your eyes again, I stare, falling farther than I ever have before. They are so deep, so full of swimming emotions that echo within me. Sorrow. Fear. Longing. Love. A connection only we can understand. I think if I can just stare at you forever, I'll be okay. I could ride the winds of change and move on with the sea, forget all of my pain and just remember how to breathe. Because you'd be next to me.

I feel my heart beat now, throbbing in my chest. It slows with every breath I take. In and out. Thump, thump and repeat. My eyes water, but I keep them fixed upon yours, afraid that if I blink, you'll be gone, and this will all have been just a frightening dream. You. Me. Just a dream.

You hold me tight, then pull me tighter.

<*Does it hurt?*> I say with my eyes.

Your eyes respond. <*No.*>

<*What does it feel like then?*>

<*Like going to sleep.*>

<*Will I... be able to find you?*>

<*You already have.*>

Your lips curve into a radiant smile. A single tear slips from the corner of your eye, runs down your cheek and drops onto my face as a brilliant glow emanates around you, enveloping your silhouette with a colorless light that steals my soul.

The beating slows even more, and I struggle to take ragged breaths. Something that once was easy has become increasingly difficult, and I wonder how many breaths I have left. One? Two? Or perhaps two times two? Your muscles tighten around me, wrapping me in a cocoon of comfort. Using all my strength, I reach up with shaky hands and touch your face, your eyes, your lips, and feel the softness under my fingertips like you are made of silk. You smile at me again, and I think I smile back.

"I love you," you say, then lean over to kiss my forehead.

I want to tell you too, but I can't. My strength is all gone, whisked away along with my resolve. Instead, I close my eyes, and tears fall uncontrollably. A cough escapes my lips, then another, and I feel your arms shake. We are shaking together. My heart is so quiet now. No longer pounding an erratic beat. No more pain in my chest. Only a shortness of breath. Not enough breath to tell you how much I love you, how much I miss you, how I can't live without you. How every second of every day I was suffocating slowly. Miserable with despair. I searched for so long to find you. And now that I have, I can't let you go. I can't let you go where I can't follow. Maybe one day we'll wake up and find this has all been a dream. Maybe we'll realize the truth isn't in changing what was, but in living through what is; the reality of now, instead of yesterday's tomorrow, accepting today and feeling the sorrow.

Then hopefully, one day we'll be able to look forward to tomorrow.

Haley Brown is a full-time and part-time employee. She fully and timely spends her days as a mommy to a beloved son, and part-times at the bookstore where she buys all her books. And coffee. She spends her free time listening to music, writing stories, reading good books, watching international dramas, taking pictures of the sky, and climbing trees whenever she can. Which isn't as often as she'd like.

Saving JFK

Brion Scheidel

Washington, D.C. — April 19, 2157

DEAN SHELDON WALKED through a sub-basement laboratory deep below the White House, periodically scanning the surroundings with his augmented senses. The scans were not really necessary, he knew, with his MACH set to alert him to any change in the environment. But as the only agent protecting the president at the moment, he could not help but be over-cautious.

Still, Barlow is far safer down here with one bodyguard than he ever would be in public, even with a full security detail. Especially with the latest rioting.

Isolated as they were, the only possible danger to the president was the other member of the trio, James Roth. Not that the president's chief science officer could actually pose any physical threat to Martin Barlow—the president was just over two meters tall, a good ten centimeters taller than Dean, and he positively towered over the old scientist. With heft to match his height, the president's weight was probably more than twice Roth's. Dean smiled. *Well, Roth could be a danger, but only if you consider the possibility of being buried alive in quantum physics minutiae.* The scientist had no hair, wrinkled skin pasty from too much time below the surface, and a slow, shuffling gait that forced Dean and President Barlow to stop every few paces and wait for the old man. But the scientist's mind showed no signs of weakness, nor did his voice, and he wielded both as they made their way slowly into the depths of the laboratory.

"Martin," Roth said, "this is my last-ditch effort to talk you out of this foolishness."

"Look, Jim—" Barlow began, but Roth cut him off.

"Just let me say what I have to say, then you can tell me why I'm wrong, and then we can all get back to work."

Roth stopped his shuffle. Dean and the President turned and faced the scientist as he resumed speaking.

"I know our country, hell, the entire world, is in the worst condition it's ever been in. You are the historian, not me, but I know we've never before had such devastation. The population boom at the beginning of the century, the collapse of the global economy twenty-six years ago, and the horrible cycle of natural disasters that increases each decade, the resultant food shortages; they have all combined to bring this country to the breaking point. But this is not the solution. The cost of the enormous amount of energy we will waste sending Dean into the past will likely be enough to push us past that breaking point. And for what? You cannot alter history. What's done is done. If your quest is successful, you'll alter history, and we won't be in the situation we're in today. But look around you. We're here. We're in it. You did not succeed. You will not succeed. You can not succeed."

Barlow removed a bulging wallet from his pocket, unfolded it, and extracted a small folded document. "But we can succeed, Jim—you've shown me yourself. You sent a note in my own handwriting, through one of your wormholes, back in time thirty minutes. I saw it appear twenty minutes before I wrote it. I carry it around as a symbol of what we can accomplish."

"A piece of paper, Martin. Thirty minutes. It changed nothing—it had no impact on the course of history. And they're not my wormholes, they're space-time's; I've just developed a way to find them, track them, and use them."

Roth fished a rubber band out of his pocket and held it up, looking like a professor about to deliver a lecture. "Look, the space-time continuum is like a rubber band. It always keeps its shape. You can stretch it and distort it, but it's self-correcting. It will always return to its natural state. It will let you make small, insignificant changes that don't affect the overall structure, like your time-traveling note. But all my theories and experiments show that it is impossible to make significant modifications to history. For every significant change you attempt to make, the continuum's built-in defense mechanisms will cause an equal and opposite reaction to counteract that change. I can pull it out of shape, but eventually I have to let go, and when I do, it will take whatever actions are necessary to return it to its natural state."

Roth went on, "And what if all my theories are wrong, and Dean is able to somehow alter the past? What happens to us? Where does this chunk of space-time go? Do we still exist in some alternate reality? Do we disappear, because we never were? But if that happens, we won't be here to send him back to alter things. It's a paradox. Don't you see the impossibility of the entire enterprise?"

Barlow closed his eyes, looked down, and slowly shook his head. When the president looked up again, he frowned deeply and narrowed his eyes. "All I see are the last vestiges of humanity choking on itself," Barlow spat. "Look at our world. We're on the brink of humanity's extinction. At the current rate, we will be nothing but animals within the next one hundred years. What do we have to lose? If we are successful and it wipes out our own existence in order to save mankind, so be it."

Barlow's expression shifted slightly, showing a hint of pride. "John F. Kennedy was one of the greatest presidents ever. And I'm not saying that just because he's my ancestor six times removed. But as part of his legacy and as the current president, I do have access to information the rest of the world does not. I know for a fact that his vision for the space program included far more than just some trips to the moon. He had plans for colonies on the moon, and then Mars—achievements that would provide the scientific advancements that would eventually take us to the stars.

"The only way to fix our ruined economy, the massive overpopulation, the thousands of people dying of starvation every day in what's left of our country, is to get people off the planet. But it's too late for that, because not a single country in the world even has a space program.

"Society is disintegrating. Human civilization will die unless we save Kennedy and allow him to make his full space program dreams come true. If he had lived to do so, we would not be a dying race on a dying planet today."

Barlow pointed a thick finger at Dean, but kept his eyes locked on Roth's. "Dean is our only chance. With all the data we've stuffed into his mind assist chip, along with the advantages that it and his nanos will give him over twentieth century humans, he will have no problem stopping Oswald."

Barlow turned to point that finger at Roth, and Dean could hear the challenge in the president's voice. "Assuming, of course, you can send him through like you say you can."

Roth slumped a bit, looking resigned. "I can get him there, all right, but I have no illusions about his chances of success in altering history. They are zero. The space-time continuum will not allow it. His MACH and nanos won't make a difference.

"Don't misunderstand me. I may talk about the continuum as if it is a living, intelligent entity, but it is not. It's a complex, closed system that cannot be modified on the macro level. It contains all of history—past, present, and future—with all significant events and inflection points fixed and immutable. Small alterations can be made because they do not affect the overall structure of the system. It's related to the difference between classical physics and quantum physics—quantum particle states and events and interrelationships are flexible and in fact not completely knowable. But at the macro level, states and events—cause and effect—are fixed and hard, predictable. The unpredictability of the quantum world does not affect the predictability of the macro world. Just as alterations to minor events in space-time do not affect the overall structure of the system."

The scientist sighed, apparently realizing his lecture was being wasted. He turned to Dean. "All right. The most recent calculations show that in just under forty-eight hours, a wormhole will be optimally positioned to place you outside Dallas, Texas on October 2, 1963. That will give you over seven weeks to stop Oswald. This is likely the best geo-temporal position we will get."

Dean heard the old man add softly, "For all the good it will do you."

Washington, D.C. — April 21, 2157

Due to the tremendous energy expenditure required to push Dean's mass of eighty kilos (plus ten kilos of gear) through a wormhole, there had been no opportunity for practice runs. Trusting completely in Roth's theories and calculations, and using every joule of energy they could siphon off the grid, they plunged most of the East Coast into blackout for the insertion. The wormhole inserted Dean at what Roth had calculated would be three kilometers above and ten kilometers northeast of Dallas on October 2, 1963. Roth had explained that a certain amount of error was unavoidable when calculating the wormhole insertion point over such large quantities of space and time. They deemed it safest to attempt to insert Dean when the endpoint was estimated to be in the vast vacant space of the atmosphere, thus reducing the chances of an unfortunate insertion into the wall of a building or under the ground.

Fully outfitted for skydiving and prepared for freefall, Dean was not prepared to appear a bare three hundred meters above the ground, nor in the midst of a flock of pelicans. As soon as he appeared, his MACH screamed altitude and impact warnings, but not quickly enough to allow him to deploy his chute before one of the large birds slammed into his head and sent him spiraling out of control. Dazed, he reached for the ripcord. Before he could grasp the handle, he saw another pelican spin into view. The bird smashed into the right side of his face as he spun; his head snapped back and all went dark.

Dean left his eyes closed as he regained consciousness, too exhausted to open them. Grateful to find himself still alive, no longer spinning, and no longer being pummeled by huge birds, he took inventory of his condition. The area all around his right eye throbbed painfully to the beat of his heart, as did the base of his skull. Beyond that he could detect no real injuries. He queried his MACH for a detailed analysis, realizing as he did so that he should not have to actively query it—the MACH should be proactively providing him information. The MACH replied with a simple "repair mode" message that he had never seen before. He finally opened his eyes and found himself face-up on the floor of an oak tree forest. Nylon cords lead from somewhere under his body up to the camouflaged automatic reserve chute tangled in the branches above him. Dean used his hands to explore the areas of pain on his face and head, and discovered an enormous welt at the base of his skull, obviously caused by the log he found supporting his head. And probably the source of the damage to the MACH; Dean knew the chip had been inserted into his brain in that general area. Further inquiries revealed that much of his stored memories on Oswald's history and whereabouts leading up to the assassination were inaccessible.

Score one for the pelicans, zero for the time-traveler.

Dean pushed himself into a sitting position, then stood, careful to move slowly and allow himself time to regain his equilibrium. He removed his harness and jumpsuit, pulled down the chute, and stuffed it all under a nearby fallen tree, covering it with leaves and sticks. As he went through this bit of military protocol automatically, he contemplated what to do next.

With no real idea of his location and no GPS satellites for his chip to connect to, Dean decided to use the basic compass functions of his partially working MACH to hike southwest, based on the hope that, in spite of the altitude being incorrect, the insertion point was still northeast of Dallas.

As he hiked, Dean could feel the exercise improving his physical and mental state. He envisioned the increased blood flow propelling the nanos on to where they were needed most. He chuckled at himself as he imagined he could feel them working on his injuries while he walked.

Although with the MACH malfunctioning, I have no way to get status reports to know how repairs are progressing, and no way to give the nanos direction. I hope to hell they're up to something good. Dean knew the nanos did not need the MACH or his direction—they could operate autonomously and perform their programmed duties just fine without any outside interference. He'd had the nanos since shortly after birth, like most upper-class children of his generation, and they had never let him down. The implanting of the experimental MACH, however, had made him different. It had given him some incredible advantages, such as the ability to monitor and direct his nanos, and the augmentation of his natural memories and senses.

He increased his pace, working up a sweat, eager to get into Dallas and track down Oswald as the first step in his mission. After a few hours, he encountered a small road that ran roughly parallel to his course. He followed it until he found himself in the small city of Hot Springs, Arkansas—yes, northeast of Dallas, but about four hundred fifty kilometers off course. In addition, Dean discovered that Roth's calculations had also been incorrect on the date—it was October 14, 1963, and he was nearly two weeks behind schedule.

Dallas, Texas — October 21, 1963

Dean paused to look into a pawn shop window in a less-than-reputable section of Dallas. The shop was closed, as were most businesses at this time of the evening, with a metal gate between Dean and the window.

Dean was not window shopping, however; out of the corner of his eye, he watched Oswald enter a bar across the street and a few store fronts away. As Oswald disappeared into the bar's doorway, Dean took a real look at the merchandise on display. Dean made a mental note to come back during the day and purchase one of the handguns he could see in a display case. He had spent the past week making his way to Dallas and finding Oswald; now Dean was going to need a weapon in order to stop the would-be assassin.

Tracking Oswald down was supposed to have been the easiest step, but with most of his stored knowledge of Oswald locked away in his malfunctioning MACH, Dean had essentially begun from scratch. He had been tempted to simply contact the Secret Service and give them all the information he had—rely on them to take it from there and stop Oswald. But he had been explicitly warned not to do so; Barlow had proof that several Secret Service agents had strong ties to anti-civil rights groups, and secretly supported efforts to remove Kennedy by any means necessary. While no proof existed that any of them had actively participated in the president's assassination, it had been proven that credible assassination attempt warnings had been selectively ignored by the Secret Service. With no way to know who he could trust, Dean had to stop Oswald without help.

With the basic facts he still recalled in his natural memory, he had finally been able to find Oswald at a boarding house on Beckley. Over the past few days, Dean had also trailed him to the Texas School Book Depository, Ruth Paine's house in Irving, and now this bar on Commerce Street. Dean planned to establish Oswald's patterns and haunts in order to devise a plan to prevent him from assassinating Kennedy.

Dean crossed the street to a newspaper box on the corner, still watching the bar. He picked up a discarded copy of the previous day's paper and carried it over to a narrow alley between two buildings. Dean leaned against one of the buildings so he was looking up the street at the bar, opened the paper and pretended to read it in the light of the corner streetlamp, observing the bar entrance over the top of the paper.

A few minutes later, Dean heard a hissing voice from the alley's shadows. "Your wallet, now, or I shoot."

Dean whipped his head around to the right to see a young man with a dark stocking cap step up to the edge of the glow cast by the streetlamp. The man stood about two meters away, pointing a handgun at Dean's abdomen.

Dean cursed his MACH for not warning him about someone so close, especially someone with a weapon. The chip was obviously still damaged and had been unable to fully repair itself. Then he berated himself for his lack of awareness. The MACH had been acting erratically ever since the wormhole insertion, and he should have known not to rely on it.

Dean dropped the newspaper, raised his hands to head level, and put a look of fear on his face. "D-Don't shoot," he said, adding a tremble to his voice.

The man took a step closer. "Just shut up and give me your wallet."

"Okay, okay, don't shoot. I have about a hundred dollars here. You can have it all…" Dean continued spouting a stream of placations; as he talked, he turned his body slightly and lowered his right hand in an exaggerated move to reach toward his back pocket. Continuing his slow movement, Dean stared at the thief's eyes, which were focused on Dean's right hand as it neared the promised cash. Dean accelerated the turn of his body while taking a step toward the mugger with his left foot. At the same time, his still-raised left hand shot forward and grabbed the wrist of the mugger's gun hand. Continuing his turn, Dean jerked the startled man closer. Dean brought his right hand up, grasped the gun, and ripped it from the mugger's grip. His left hand still locked around the mugger's right wrist, Dean completed his turn while the man struggled to keep his feet under him. Dean propelled him head-first into the wall of the building now to Dean's right.

Dean rolled the unconscious thief up against the wall and covered his bloody face with the newspaper. He checked that the revolver was loaded and snapped the cylinder back into place just as Oswald emerged from the bar. Oswald turned and started walking down the nearly deserted street directly toward Dean.

With his sooner-than-expected gun ownership, Dean decided to move up his time-table. *No need for more surveillance or a fancy plan; just shoot Oswald now—mission accomplished.*

Dean squatted next to the mugger's still form, doing his best impersonation of a hunkering homeless man until Oswald walked by. As Oswald passed the alley, Dean stood and stepped out onto the sidewalk, bringing up the weapon. He aimed at Oswald's back and squeezed the trigger twice in quick succession.

At a distance of only about three meters, Dean knew he could not miss, even with an unfamiliar weapon. When the first shot fired, however, and even as he was automatically squeezing the trigger for the second shot, he realized something was not right. A bit of smoke drifted from the cylinder, and he heard a soft thump instead of a blast, so quiet that Oswald did not notice and kept walking, oblivious. By the time he had processed the fact that the first shot was a misfire, it was too late to stop himself from firing the second. The second round fired with the normal sound of a gunshot, but the bullet did not hit its target. Instead, it impacted the first bullet that had lodged in the barrel, blowing the barrel and cylinder off the weapon, leaving Dean holding the smoking remnants of the wooden butt and the trigger guard.

The few people on the street, including Oswald, all dropped to the pavement at the sound of the shot. Before anyone could recover, Dean raced down the alley. He tossed the remains of the revolver down the first sewer grate he encountered and made his unsteady way back to his motel, shaken by what had just happened.

Sitting on the bed in his room, Dean analyzed what had just happened, and he began to suspect that something more than bad luck was working against him. *What are the odds of a revolver malfunctioning like that? Is this proof of Roth's theory that the space-time continuum will prevent significant modifications to history? And if it is protecting Oswald, why didn't it just do the job right and make the gun completely explode when it misfired, taking my hand off, or even my head, and be done with it?*

It dawned on Dean that this was likely the continuum's second move preventing him from altering history. *So, instead of score one for the pelicans, it's score two for the space-time continuum. But if that was the continuum interfering with my insertion, why let my reserve chute deploy successfully? Why not one more little snafu and leave me a mysterious smear on the Texas countryside?*

Dallas, Texas — October 24, 1963

Oswald's movements tonight had been erratic. Dean suspected that

Oswald's recent behavior had been influenced by the gunshot three nights earlier. The man had kept a low profile for the past few days, doing nothing more than staying holed up at the boarding house and reporting for work each day at the Depository. Tonight, Oswald had finally broken that routine and left the boarding house after dinner. Dean had followed him through a series of cab rides, bus rides, and rambling walks, looking for an opportunity to strike.

Now midnight approached, and few people walked the streets, but enough pedestrians remained to allow Dean to stay just four paces behind Oswald without detection. Dean started to close the distance, planning to drag the would-be assassin into the nearby parking structure and strangle him—no weapons to possibly malfunction in that plan—when Oswald abruptly turned ninety degrees and dashed across the empty street. Another example of Oswald's unpredictability. Dean followed and picked up his pace, resolving to overtake Oswald as he reached the far side of the street and finish him there.

Two steps into the street, a movement to his left drew his glance. Less than three meters away, a northbound Dallas Transit Company bus raced toward him. The huge front window and shiny chrome bumper filled his vision. He saw his own reflection, a distorted version of himself, staring back from the bumper with the intensity of a hunter about to pounce. The expression transformed as he realized his role as the hunter was about to end.

The thought of Oswald escaping again burned through him. He opened his mouth in a scream of frustration and rage. The scream cut off as the bus impacted his body and sent him flying, knocking the breath out of him and breaking bones. The pain did not start right away, but he knew it would soon. And he knew the nanos would reduce it before it became unbearable. His worry over the damage to his body occupied him far less than his anger at losing Oswald. *I've survived worse damage than this.* Then he spotted the other bus, hurtling toward him from the opposite direction.

His body rotated while soaring through the night air, giving him alternate glimpses of the bus that had just hit him and the bus now rushing to intersect the arc of his flight. He heard metal squeal and smelled rubber burn as the second bus braked. For an instant, Dean saw the face of the driver pressed close to the glass of his vehicle. The driver stood on the brake, his face a rictus of terror and incredulity as momentum threw him against the windshield. Just before impact, the rotation of Dean's body turned him away, slamming his back squarely into the windshield. He hung there for a second, the force of the collision driving the sharp metal edges of the two windshield wipers deep into the skin of his back on either side of his spine.

The bus lurched to a stop, and inertia tore Dean off the windshield, each of the mangled wipers removing centimeters of flesh before releasing him. Barely conscious now, he curled into a fetal position and rolled. Then the pain started. Everywhere. White-hot hammer heads pounded into every part of his body. At last, a welcome darkness enveloped him.

Dallas, Texas — November 21, 1963

As Dean emerged from a deep sleep filled with turbulent dreams of his childhood as well as his recent past, persistent questions floated to the surface of his thoughts. Why had he been dreaming? He had been twelve years old when he had last dreamt, before his brain had been implanted with one of the first MACHs ever developed. What had happened? He struggled to sift real memories from those of his dreams, then groaned as he recalled his encounter with the buses.

Why had the buses been out so late? And how had he not been aware of them? Dean railed at himself for not being more vigilant. After fifteen years of dependence on the chip, he was finding it hard to fall back on his own, unaugmented senses and memories. Normally, his MACH would have kept him apprised of anything that big and fast moving in his vicinity. But it had let him down again. Not a blip from it, even as he had observed the impending collision unfold.

And still the MACH gave him absolutely no information, not even the "repair mode" message. He had nothing left but his natural-born senses and mental faculties. *Well, plus the nanos—too bad there's not some way I can use them for reconnaissance.*

Dean focused on the information detected by his innate senses. He could feel his body lying on a firm, plastic-coated mattress with the upper section slightly tilted. He smelled rubbing alcohol and other disinfectant odors. He noted an annoying pressure on the back of his left hand, like something affixed there. *Deduction one: I'm in a hospital, hooked up to an IV. Nice work, Sherlock.*

He detected a light scent of perfume mixed with the disinfectant smell, and he heard a soft, musical, female hum. *Deduction two: I'm not alone. Amazing. How do I do it?*

Dean slowly opened his eyes and saw a young woman's smiling face, pretty brown eyes looking at him from behind eye glasses shaped like cat's eyes. She had dark blonde hair, cut short in a bob. She sported a ridiculous-looking old-fashioned nurse's cap sticking straight out of the back of her head. From Dean's angle it looked like white wings emerging from behind each ear, and he smiled in response both to the image and to the woman's smile.

"Well, if it isn't James Dean, back among the living?" the woman exclaimed. "I thought I heard you moaning, and I couldn't believe it. The doctor said you might never come out of that coma. And look at you, conscious and smiling!"

His smile faded as he tried to understand everything she was saying.

James Dean? Coma?

Her own cheerful expression faltered in response, and then she flushed mildly.

"Oh, um, sorry about the 'James Dean' thing. We got to calling you that over the past few weeks. Has anyone ever told you that you look like James Dean? Well, you do, and once we found out your first name is Dean, well it just stuck."

Weeks?

"Wh-what day is it?" Dean croaked.

The woman's smile broadened. "And talking, too! Amazing. I'll go get the doctor. You wait right here." She laughed and then padded quietly out the door. Dean reviewed his brief conversation with the nurse. What was the joke? He finally found it when he looked down at his body. A plaster cast covered each leg, stretching from the upper thigh down to the foot, leaving only his toes exposed. *Okay, I guess I'll wait here.* As Dean continued to scan the room, he spotted a copy of the Dallas Morning News on a small table to his right. He leaned over enough to make out the date printed above the headline: November 21, 1963. He had been unconscious for four weeks. Oswald would kill Kennedy tomorrow. *Deduction three: I'm screwed.*

The nurse returned shortly with water and a resident, who explained to Dean that the casts would be on for a minimum of three more weeks. The doctor also made it clear they would not release him for at least that long, considering the coma he had just emerged from, but Dean could discuss it further with the attending physician when the shift changed at seven-thirty a.m., just eight hours away. Dean counted on the nanos putting his recovery time far ahead of the doctor's projections. *Hopefully, my legs are healed enough already to allow me to walk, because one way or another, I'm leaving tonight.*

As soon as the doctor and nurse left, Dean struggled out of bed and stood rigid-legged on his toes. Using the wall for support, Dean made a complete circuit of the room, looking for anything he could use as a tool. He found his wallet in the first drawer he checked. *Good, but not what I need at the moment.* Then he spied a coat hanger suspended from a peg on the wall next to the door. The hanger was sturdy, with a wooden body and a metal hook so thick he could barely bend it. Perfect.

Dean sat down on a chair and worked the hook between his right leg and its cast. Discovering that the right side of his leg seemed to offer the most slack between the skin and the cast, he shifted the hook over and started levering it up and down, grinding away at the plaster. Soon the point of the hook broke through the cast about three centimeters from the top. With a little more effort, he pulled the hook through the plaster, breaking off a ragged wedge of the cast. Ignoring the pain of the hook digging into the skin under the cast, Dean continued this process the rest of the way down his leg.

As his hands worked on the cast, his mind worked on the problem of stopping Oswald.

So now it's score three for the space-time continuum, zero for me. The closer I get to killing Oswald, the more violently I'm opposed. Any closer than I came this time, and I'll surely be killed. I need to come up with a different approach.

Dean reached the bottom of the cast with the hook, completing the rough channel in the plaster. He dropped the hanger, and pulled on both sides of the jagged cut to widen the channel until the opposite side cracked. He pulled the cast off his leg and bent his knee experimentally a few times. Sore, but not unbearable. He pushed off the chair and gradually put weight on his right foot. The muscles were weak from disuse, and he experienced some throbbing pain, but everything felt whole.

Dean picked up the hanger and repeated the process on his left leg, resuming his ruminations as he dug through the plaster.

The space-time continuum has let me make some modifications. The gunshot obviously caused Oswald to behave differently for the next few days. I'm sure I've made thousands of small changes to history just by being here. I rented a room that would have gone to someone else. I took bus seats and cab rides that would have been used by others. There are pelicans out there with crazy stories to tell their kids. So some changes are allowed. Small changes.

Dean removed the second cast and discovered his left leg in the same condition as the right. He went through some light calisthenics to loosen up his stiff leg muscles. *And get those nanos flowing.* He grabbed his wallet, opened the hospital room door, and peeked out. The clock on the wall showed 12:07 a.m.—the hallway was deserted.

Twelve hours left to stop Oswald. Enough time to make it to the Texas School Book Depository and prevent Oswald from even reaching the sixth floor. But there were a few things Dean needed to do first, like finding some street clothes. More than that, he needed a back-up plan, and that meant making a few changes. He just hoped the changes would be minor enough to slip by space-time's defenses.

Irving, Texas — November 22, 1963

Dressed in a janitor's uniform and carrying a rolled-up dark green towel, Dean emerged from a taxi on West Sixth Street in Irving shortly before 2:00 a.m. He confirmed the arrangement with the driver to be picked up at that same spot in two hours. "Enough time to shower, grab something to eat, and then get back to the hospital to cover my buddy's shift. What a day for my car to break down." He did not expect his errand to take more than an hour, but he wanted to leave himself extra time in case complications arose.

He crossed the street and walked up the front path a nearby house. As soon as the cab disappeared, Dean reversed direction and walked back to the main sidewalk. He headed over to Westbrook, then up to Fifth. As he moved down Fifth, he noted that not a single house on the street had a light on, but he had no trouble finding the Paine house again in the light of the half moon. His goal was not the house itself, but the small one-car garage attached to the west side of the house. Dean paused in front of the garage door, removed a pair of doctor's examination gloves from his pocket, and pulled them on. He reached down and put a hand on the simple twist handle opener in the center of the roll-up door, when a thought occurred to him. *Oswald is sleeping inside this house. I could end this all right now—sneak in, find him, smother him with a pillow, sneak out.*

Acting on this thought, Dean walked past the garage and up to the front door. Holding the towel in his right hand, he reached out with his left and gently gripped the storm door latch. He gave a soft, slow push on the button with his thumb. The button pressed in partway before it stopped and made a loud click. He froze. A dog barked nearby, a few tentative yelps at first, then full-throated baying. A light appeared from inside the Paine house, casting a glow on the east part of the front lawn. Dean backed away from the front door, turned, and walked swiftly back across the driveway, taking cover on the opposite side of the garage. His heart raced.

Okay, okay. Stick to the plan. Small changes only.

After a few minutes passed, the dog quieted; shortly after that, the glow on the lawn disappeared. Dean crouched with his back against the garage wall, facing the house next door, collecting himself, and waiting for his heartbeat to return to normal.

He had no wristwatch, but after waiting for what he gauged to be about an hour, certainly long enough for dogs and people to get back to sleep, Dean returned to the garage door. He twisted the garage door handle and it turned. Stunned, he stared at the handle for a few heartbeats before proceeding. *Finally some good luck—no lock-picking required.*

Taking one full minute to do so, Dean lifted the door four or five centimeters, listening all the while for squeaks or other noises that might disturb the dog or the residents. He placed the rolled up towel on the ground and let the door down gently until it rested on the towel, propped open just a few centimeters. Lying on his back, Dean lifted the door, again slowly and quietly, until it was just high enough to allow him to scoot under. He took great care doing so, testing each centimeter of advancement with hand and foot to make sure he did not bump into anything.

Fifteen minutes later, Dean lay completely inside the garage with the door shut. He sat up, unrolled the towel, and removed a small flashlight. Like the uniform he wore, the flashlight was one of the items he had appropriated from a janitor's closet in the hospital. Dean switched on the flashlight and a pencil-width shaft of light appeared, created by pieces of electrical tape he had affixed to most of the lens. Sweeping the small beam about, Dean viewed the inside of the garage.

It looked as though the garage may never have sheltered an actual car. The small light revealed countless household items, including boxes, tools, and furniture, taking up most of the garage space. He searched for one particular household item, though—an old brown and green blanket wrapped up in a long roll. He found it quickly, and, making a mental note of its position, unrolled it to reveal the rifle that Oswald intended to use to assassinate Kennedy.

When Dean had developed his back-up plan in the hospital, he had considered simply disabling or stealing the rifle after finding it, but had ultimately decided against both of these options. He feared Oswald would have a back-up plan of his own, in the form of a second rifle stashed away somewhere. *No, better to stick with small changes.*

Dean mentally reviewed the back-up plan. It was fairly simple—make subtle modifications to the rifle so that if Dean ended up unable to stop Oswald from firing at Kennedy, at least the shots would miss their mark. These were the smallest kinds of modifications Dean could think of that still had a chance of altering history. He still intended to physically stop Oswald from even making the assassination attempt, but he was now convinced that he needed to first implement this back-up plan; so far, the space-time continuum had been too effective at preventing large changes.

Peeling off some of the tape to expose a larger beam, Dean propped the flashlight to shine on the rifle. Now that he had the actual rifle in front of him, he paused to re-analyze his decisions, wanting to be sure he had considered everything.

Dean pictured the scene as Oswald would see it. At the time of the shots, the limousine carrying Kennedy would be driving almost straight away from Oswald's position in the southeast corner window on the sixth floor. But it would be making a slight right turn; from Oswald's viewpoint, aiming at Kennedy's head, the front of the vehicle would point just to the right, and the rear would point just to the left. Kennedy would be about eighty meters away when Oswald fired the fatal shot. Governor Connally would be in front of Kennedy and just to the right, due to the slight turning of the car. Mrs. Kennedy would be to the left of Kennedy with an unoccupied seat between them.

Dean recalled that most experts believed Oswald had eschewed the scope in favor of the iron sights, so he started with them. He had three options for modifying the iron sights: 1. File down the front sight, causing the shots to go high; 2. Adjust the V-shaped notch of the rear sight to deepen the V to the right, causing the shots to go down and right; 3. Adjust the V-shaped notch of the rear sight to deepen the V to the left, causing the shots to go down and left.

Dean had ruled out the front sight first. To put the shots safely above Kennedy's head would require Dean to file down the sight significantly. That much change would be too noticeable. *My modifications have to be subtle enough to get by Oswald and space-time.* Looking at the tall thin blade of the front sight now before him, he concluded he had been correct to rule out that option.

That decision narrowed his choices to either down and to the right, or down and to the left. Adjusting the shots down and to the right would in all probability put them into Connally's back. And adjusting them further to make them go far enough to the right to miss Connally would probably be too great a modification for Oswald not to notice. Adjusting the shots down and to the left would probably put them into the empty seat between JFK and Mrs. Kennedy, although they could possibly end up hitting her. He found that his earlier reasoning still held, and he quickly came to the same determination. *Possible injury of Mrs. Kennedy versus the almost certain death of Connally—makes the choice easy. Down and left it is.*

Dean removed a small metal file from his collection of pilfered tools and started making careful adjustments to the rear sight. He knew his adjustments were by no means precise, but options and time were both running out. *Besides, this is just a precaution, a fallback in case all else fails. Hopefully, I'll never find out how well I did these adjustments.*

He finished the filing and evaluated his work. It looked like the right amount of adjustment, but the filed areas shone a bit too brightly. Dean had not thought to bring something acidic, but a search of the garage yielded a large jug of white vinegar. He poured some onto a corner of his towel and dabbed it on the bright areas. Letting the shiny metal soak, he moved on to adjusting the scope, a much simpler task. Fairly sure that Oswald would not use the scope, Dean nevertheless made adjustments corresponding to the modifications he had made to the rear iron sight.

He returned his attention to the rear sight. Satisfied with the amount of darkening, Dean wiped the vinegar off with the towel. To ensure he had removed all the vinegar, and to make the modified metal once more match the condition of the rest of the rifle, he rubbed the area with a pinch of oil and dirt. Finished, he wrapped the rifle in its blanket and placed it back in its original position.

He rolled the towel back up with the file inside it, then examined the interior of the garage with the flashlight to make sure everything looked as it had when he had arrived. Convinced he was leaving no evidence behind, Dean reversed his entry procedure. Unsure how long the whole ordeal had taken, he thought perhaps he had exceeded his two hours. He strode off at a fast walk, trying to move quickly but quietly. As he walked, he wedged the towel under his arm, peeled off the gloves, and shoved them into his pocket.

Dean blew out an exhalation of relief as he rounded the corner and saw a cab in the street, brake lights on. He jogged up to the car, opened the rear passenger door, and slid onto the seat. As Dean shut the door, the driver looked back and smiled. "Hey, I was just about to give up on you. All right, ready for another shift at the hospital?"

Dean leaned his head back. The tension and exertion of the past few hours had left his still-healing body sapped of energy. He closed his eyes, thinking of his bed at the hospital. *Actually, this seat is pretty comfortable.*

"Hey? Buddy? The hospital?"

Dean opened his eyes and sighed. "Actually, there's been a change of plans. Take me to Dealey Plaza, please."

"Oh, gonna go see the president, hm? Well, no problem, but you're gonna be there way too early. That parade or whatever they're doing is something like seven hours away. This time of mornin', we'll be there in twenty minutes. Sure you wanna go there now?"

Dean had started to drift away again and had missed most of what the driver had said.

"Yes- well, no. Uh, I... I really need to get some sleep. Can you take me to a hotel near the plaza?"

"Mmm yeah, but—" The driver hesitated, eying Dean's rumpled uniform. "Well, maybe out of your price range. And they all jacked up their rates with this presidential stuff going on. Why not go on back inside and get some sleep? I can come back and pick you up later."

"Ah. Well, it's complicated. I have an appointment before the president arrives that I absolutely cannot miss. I want to get to the area now, so there's no chance of being late. But good point about the money." Dean touched the wallet in his back pocket, recalling how much he had left after paying the cabbie earlier. Not enough to waste on a good hotel. *But there's no way I can stop Oswald if I don't get some sleep first.*

"How about a cheap place? Doesn't have to be really close to the plaza, but close enough for me to walk there." He smiled and added, "I can't afford to keep taking your cab everywhere, you know."

The driver laughed, pulling the car away from the curb and starting down the quiet, dimly-lit street. "Sure thing. I know the perfect place, about a mile from the plaza. Not too much of a dump. I'll have you there in no time. There's an all-night diner not far from there. They have the best steak and eggs breakfast in town…"

The cab's motion lulled Dean to sleep before the driver finished his monologue.

Dallas, Texas — November 22, 1963

Dean sat in a booth in the crowded diner the cabbie had suggested, drinking coffee and waiting for his breakfast of steak and eggs. The large clock above the counter showed it was just after 8:00. He had slept for three hours in the tiny hotel room, and had been pleasantly surprised when the promised wake-up call came on time. Then again, he had paid the clerk five dollars extra for the guaranteed call at 7:30 a.m., which was quite a bonus considering the room cost ten dollars.

He hadn't needed the wake-up call after all, his internal sense of time waking him shortly before the room's alarm clock, which had buzzed shortly before the telephone call. *A back-up to my back-up—I've become quite the believer in them.*

The sleep had been very deep, and it had left him feeling remarkably re-energized. *Maybe the nanos helped, too.* A shower and shave had contributed to Dean's improved outlook, as had his mental review of the successful outing in Irving. Although relieved to have the back-up plan in place, he did not want to put that plan to the test. He intended to intercept Oswald and prevent him from reaching the infamous sniper's nest. To that end, he had made one more change to his appearance. He had discarded the sullied janitor's shirt in favor of a plain work shirt purchased earlier in the morning at a near-by, early-opening thrift store. Dean glanced down at his clean shirt and passable janitor's pants. He nodded, satisfied he would blend in with the crowd of workers entering the Depository later in the morning.

The waitress came over to his table with a carafe of coffee and refilled his cup. She paused with her hand on her hip and looked at him. Dean looked back at her expectantly. She was nice-looking, with medium-length light brown hair and full lips covered with faint red lipstick. Lois, according to her name tag. Lois pursed her lips slightly, then asked, "Have you been here before? You look awful familiar, but I can't remember serving you before."

Dean smiled. "Well, I've been told I look something like James Dean. Maybe that's what you're seeing."

"James D—" Her eyes widened. "Uh, yeah, that must be it." She turned on her heel and took a step toward the kitchen. She swung back again and said, "I'll... I'll go see what's taking your meal so long." She disappeared into the kitchen.

Lois reappeared a few minutes later with his breakfast. She looked ruffled, probably running behind on her tables. She clattered his plate to the table, mumbled an apology, and disappeared again.

Dean dug into his food. He could not remember the last time he had eaten. They must have been feeding him at the hospital while he was unconscious, but he realized his last real meal must have been over a month ago. The cook had prepared the steak perfectly medium rare, and the eggs were over easy, all exactly as he had ordered and delicious.

He bent over his plate and soaked up the last remnants of yolk with his toast, trying to decide what to order next. When he looked up, he saw two pairs of black trousers parked next to his table. Looking up further, he saw they belonged to two Dallas police officers, staring down at him. Dean had noticed them earlier, sitting on the other side of the restaurant and being served by Lois. His stomach clenched, although he could not figure out why they would be interested in him. He hoped the hospital had not reported him missing.

The officer standing closest to Dean was a bit shorter than his partner, with short dark hair under his black hat, and a grim expression on his face. He appeared very fit, and he looked like he intended to beat some sort of confession out of Dean. From where he sat, Dean could not read the menacing man's name tag. The taller, rounder, older officer wore a white cap and had sergeant stripes on his sleeve, and his name tag read "Reynolds". Sergeant Reynolds looked calmer, less angry than his fellow law enforcer. Reynolds did the talking while his nameless partner did the glaring.

"Excuse me, Mr. ... ?" Reynolds paused, waiting for Dean to fill in the blank.

"Sheldon. Dean Sheldon. Would you care to join me, officers?" Dean waved a hand toward the vacant bench across from him.

"Thank you, no, Mr. Sheldon," Reynolds replied, staring at Dean's waving hand. "Actually, we'd like you to place both hands on the table and keep them there while we ask you a few questions."

Uh-oh. That is not the start of a friendly chat.

Dean complied with the request. He noticed stares from diners at nearby tables. He looked up at Reynolds and waited for the questions.

"Do you have some ID?"

Dean nodded.

"May we see it, please?"

Dean nodded at his hands. "Well, it's in my wallet in my back pocket."

Reynolds considered this briefly, then nodded. "Go ahead, Mr. Sheldon. Please remove your wallet and hand me your ID."

Dean pulled out his wallet, removed his counterfeit New York driver license, and handed it to Reynolds. Dean felt confident that the license would stand up to all but the most comprehensive of probing. Rather than give him an alias, Barlow's researchers had easily extracted records on several Dean Sheldons in New York in 1963, picked one whose physical characteristics were similar to Dean's, and created a near-perfect replica of the man's driver license, using Dean's picture.

Reynolds examined the license closely for a minute. "New York," he grunted.

Not sure if that was a statement or a question or a condemnation, Dean simply nodded.

"Mr. Sheldon, can you tell me where you were on the night of October twenty-first?"

The stomach clench repeated, stronger. Dean put a thoughtful look on his face. While he could not precisely recall October twenty-first, he had a very strong, very bad feeling that he knew exactly what this was about.

"I'm sorry, but I don't believe I can. That was over a month ago. I've done so much walking and sight-seeing since I arrived in Dallas, I can't even remember everything I've done, much less which days I've done them."

After the words came out, Dean realized that the last part might have sounded a bit sinister.

"Well, Mr. Sheldon, we have an eyewitness that positively identifies you as the shooter of a handgun near Commerce and Hall on October twenty-first around 10:30 p.m. Does that ring any bells?"

Damn.

"No, sir, I'm sorry, but I'm sure I wasn't anywhere near such an event, or I would remember. Besides, it's pretty dark around 10:30, isn't it? How could someone be positive they saw me?"

"Well, you are a perfect match for the height, weight, hair-color, and hair style given by the witness at the time of the crime report. She saw you very clearly from her second floor apartment window. You were standing directly under a streetlamp at the time of the shooting. Furthermore, you were very memorable to the witness, as you, ah, strongly resemble James Dean."

James Dean? Lois. Dean looked for the waitress, but did not see her.

"Unless you can provide an alibi, we're going to have to detain you for further questioning."

Dean closed his eyes. *Not now. I'm so close.*

He snapped his eyes open when he heard a soft clink nearby, like a small chain being rubbed against metal. Officer Glare reached toward Dean's hands with a pair of handcuffs. Dean tensed.

Sergeant Reynolds backed away a half step, perhaps to make more room for his partner to put on the cuffs, and Dean realized he had no real chance of escape. Reynolds's move, whether conscious or not, had put the sergeant out of Dean's reach, and had also given Reynolds a better vantage point from which to view Dean's movements and respond as needed. Even when in his best condition, it would have been difficult for

Dean to neutralize both men under these circumstances. In his current sleep-deprived, semi-healed state, he doubted he could even take on one of them.

Officer Glare snapped the cuffs onto Dean's wrists. The policeman stepped back a bit, put a surprisingly gentle hand under Dean's arm and assisted him out of the booth.

"You are not under arrest at this time. You are being detained while we investigate the allegations made against you," Reynolds stated.

Dean looked at the clock as the policemen walked him through the now silent restaurant. 8:40. He had less than four hours to extricate himself from the Dallas Police, get to the Depository, and find a way to thwart Oswald.

Dean sat in a holding cell in the Police and Courts Building on Harwood, perhaps in the same cell that Oswald would occupy in just a few hours. *Unless I can get out of here. Unless the back-up plan works. Unless...*

He heard footsteps and looked up, expecting to see Sergeant Reynolds. The sergeant had taken responsibility for investigating the accusations made against Dean, and he had started by taking Dean's statement. Then Reynolds had taken Dean's driver license and disappeared. That had been over two hours ago. The approaching man, however, was not Sergeant Reynolds.

"I'm Lieutenant McCormick," the officer said as he opened the cell door, "I apologize for having detained you so long. Sergeant Reynolds was looking into the allegations against you before he was suddenly, and without my consent, pulled into a special duty detail related to the president's visit."

The lieutenant handed Dean the driver license the sergeant had taken.

"I completed the initial investigation as soon as I found out what had happened, and I'm here to explain the situation to you.

"The witness that identified you is unimpeachable. She is the niece of someone extremely well-connected in the police department. And she described you to a T when she filed the report last month.

"However, we have nothing else. No other witnesses. No physical evidence. You have no priors, either here or in your home state of New York. No outstanding warrants.

"Calls to check out your history and your alibi went nowhere. Nobody's heard of you. I don't know what to make of it, and I'd love to get to the bottom of it, but I don't have the time or the resources.

"So here's the deal. You get your mysterious ass out of Dallas and don't come back. We drop the investigation. Deal?"

Dean glanced at a clock on the wall behind the lieutenant as he reached out and shook the policeman's hand. 11:55. "Deal. One way or another, I'll be out of Dallas by the end of the day."

A patrolman escorted Dean through the building and to the Harwood entrance. Dean trotted down the wide stone stairs, then took off at a sprint as soon as he reached the sidewalk, heading north toward Main. Thousands of people clogged the streets, waiting to catch a glimpse of the Kennedys. Many roads were closed or rerouted, and Dean soon realized a bus or cab would never get him to the building in time to stop Oswald. Since the motorcade would be traveling down Main, he knew Main would be clear once he made his way through the throng of people. Then he could run down the empty street along the front of the crowd. Less than a mile from there to the Depository. He thought he could traverse that in ten minutes, given his current condition. Then reach the sixth floor and get to the southeast corner. *I should be able to make it.*

But when he finally fought his way to Main, he realized this plan would not work. White-capped policemen littered the route, directing traffic and controlling the crowd. What would they do if they saw a man running down Main Street? Odds were good that at least one of them would decide to stop him.

Instead, Dean continued north one block to Elm, then headed west.

Between the normal lunch-time rush and the traffic diverted from Main, Elm contained more cars and pedestrians than usual, but nothing like the mass of humanity packed onto Main. Dean ran down the sidewalk on the south side of Elm, dodging businessmen and bicyclists. He ran when crowds thinned enough to let him do so, jogged when it became too crowded. Because Main was closed, most of the intersections were easier to cross than usual, since not many vehicles drove toward or away from Main on the cross streets.

Dean felt confident about his pace. He knew he would be in trouble if he heard the roar of the crowd from Main to his left, which would indicate the motorcade passing his position. Each time he crossed a street, he glanced left to see if he could read anything from the twenty-deep line of people with their backs to him. Searching for any sign of the motorcade's arrival.

Dean approached the large intersection at Griffin and knew he had passed the half-way point. His legs ached and his breath started rasping in his throat. He had to stop for a red light and wait for a few cars to cross Elm heading north. While he waited, bent over, trying to recover some wind, he glanced over toward Main. The crowd seemed to be behaving the same way it had at the other intersections. *Nothing new is good news.*

As he ran across the wide street, though, Dean thought he detected a distant roar behind him. He suspected the motorcade had just turned right onto Main, in which case he needed to reach Oswald within about ten minutes. Dean tried to pour on a burst of speed, but he had nothing. In fact, the ache in his legs had started feeling more like a fire, and he feared he was actually slowing down.

Dean pictured what was happening at that moment at the Texas School Book Depository. Oswald sitting in his sniper's nest, waiting for the motorcade to appear. Had he noticed the modifications?

The burning in Dean's legs had disappeared at some point, and now they simply felt like iron weights. He had to think, to concentrate to keep his legs moving correctly. He crossed Market, and suddenly he could see his destination ahead and slightly to the right. At the same time, he heard the roar again, this time coming from his left instead of behind him. Less than two hundred meters to go. The sight of his goal and the sound of the crowd combined to push him faster than he had thought possible at this point.

This close to the parade route, the street was closed, so Dean gradually moved into the street, making a direct line for the Depository's front entrance. As he reached Houston, though, he saw that a large crowd blocked the main entrance. Without a pause, he turned slightly and ran up Houston to reach the service entrance. Here, he did have to finally slow down to make a sharp left turn. He entered a deserted dock area, dashed up a set of narrow stairs, and burst through a swinging door into the main part of the first floor.

A few people stood about, and nobody seemed to pay any attention to Dean as he turned right and headed toward the freight elevators and stairs. He made a split-second decision to take the stairs instead of the elevator. He did not have the time to wait for the elevator if it wasn't already on the first floor, and even if it was there and waiting, using it would be an open invitation for space-time to trap him in it.

Dean ran up the first half-flight of stairs, turned left, and ran up the second half-flight. He emerged onto the second floor, in some sort of vestibule, disoriented for a second. Where were the rest of the stairs? He took a few steps, saw the next set of stairs to his left, above the first half-flight he had just used. Dean felt his legs getting rubbery as he started up the stairs to the third floor, so he grabbed the railing on his left and used it to propel himself upward. He continued the dizzying counter-clockwise pattern of up, left, up, left, left, ascending flight after flight.

As Dean pulled himself up the last half-flight of stairs to the sixth floor, the railing came slightly loose from the wall. The sudden shift threw him off balance; he lost his grip and sprawled across the stairs. He regained his footing and scrambled to the top of the stairs. Still off-balance from the frantic, spinning run up the stairs, Dean staggered a few steps as he stepped onto the floor. He regained his balance and saw that stacks of boxes filled the floor, forming rows and aisles. The boxes blocked the opposite corner of the floor from Dean's view, but he knew he would find Oswald there in his shooting nest.

Dean ran along the wall, looking for an aisle that would lead him to Oswald. He partially passed an aisle when he realized that it lead all the way to the southern windows. He attempted to stop and reverse direction, but his right shoe slid on a stray clipboard. His head smacked the floor with a loud crack before he could react. The echo left his ears ringing. As he regained his feet and his head cleared, he realized that crack had been too loud to be just his head hitting the floor. Oswald had fired his first shot.

Dean raced down the aisle toward the windows looking out on Elm Street.

History says Oswald's first shot missed. Even if he discovered and accounted for my adjustments, I still have time to stop him from killing Kennedy.

Dean had almost reached the windows when he heard the second and third shots in quick succession. By the time the echo from the third shot had faded, he had stopped moving. He bowed his head, drained. *The back-up plan. Please, God, space-time, who-ever. The back-up plan.*

Dean snapped his head up, listening as he received an unexpected answer to his prayer. The quiet voice of Oswald penetrated the wall of boxes that separated them, as if Oswald had been talking directly to Dean.

"No, no, no, he's the wrong man. They're going to kill me..."

The wrong man.

Relief cascaded through Dean like a rush of morphine, deadening all the physical and emotional pain. *The back-up plan worked.*

A brief stab of regret followed on the heels of the rush, as he realized that someone else had been injured or killed. *But it was worth it. To save JFK.*

He heard Oswald hurrying down the aisle next to him. Even though JFK had not been killed, someone had still been shot. Which meant the authorities would be here soon. He needed to take the cue from Oswald and flee as well. He reversed his path at a trot. He knew he should be evaluating escape alternatives, but something about Oswald's words bothered him.

Strange, he said the wrong "man"—I think if anyone would have been hit it would have been Mrs. Kennedy. I must have made larger adjustments than I intended. Maybe the shots hit one of the Secret Service men behind the limo.

A few meters from the end of the aisle, Dean saw Oswald rush by, heading toward the opposite corner of the room to the elevators and stairs. Oswald stepped on the same clipboard that had tripped up Dean, and Dean watched the man stagger, the rifle still in one hand. Oswald crashed into a stack of boxes as he worked to regain his balance, and as he did so, Dean saw a folded sheet of paper fall from Oswald's pocket and flutter to the floor. Dean could see that Oswald did not notice him or the piece of paper; maybe he was focused on his failed assassination attempt. *Or on his escape route, like I should be.*

Still, curiosity and the investigator's instinct forced Dean to pause and pick up the paper, which he could now see was a newspaper clipping. *A little souvenir from this mission.*

He could hear Oswald's footsteps echoing faintly as the failed assassin descended the steps. Dean walked quickly toward the steps himself, unfolding the square of newspaper. He stumbled to a stop at the top of the stairs as his brain sputtered, piecing together what his eyes beheld.

The clipping showed a picture of Governor Connally and his wife at a campaign event.

A thick, roughly drawn black X covered Connally's face.
The wrong man...
Oswald had been shooting at Connally.
My modifications put the shots low and to the left.
The wrong man.

"My God," Dean whispered. "I've killed Kennedy!"

Brion Scheidel graduated from North Central College in Naperville, IL, with undergraduate degrees in math and computer science. Amidst working and starting a family, he also completed a master of science degree in computer information science from the University of Michigan, with the never-ending support and encouragement of his wife (and his daughter, who arrived a few years before the degree).

Brion's world is saturated with words. By day, he works in the field of text analytics - making computers figure out what people are talking about. By night, he reads avidly and writes sporadically. His writing includes one-act plays, short stories, song lyrics, poems, writing exercises, and notes for future novels and screenplays. And throughout it all, he talks - in person, by phone, by email, by text, by instant message - with co-workers, friends, and family, and especially with his wife and daughter.

Screaming Mimi

Steven Vallarsa

GUNTHER'S UNIVERSE CONSISTED of a bright, cold, white light shining from high above, and the hardest wooden chair he'd ever sat upon. Hands tied firmly behind the backrest, he'd lost track of how long he'd been sitting there. He looked around the cavernous room once again, hoping to tease out something—anything—about his surroundings. But the blinding light didn't reach the edges of this vast chamber. It faded to darkness along the smooth rock floor without revealing any of the walls. He had given up trying to gauge the room's size from the echo he produced; the preoccupation of his current plight had worn his usually sharp cognition down to uselessness.

A smile twisted on his face. He had memorized the schematic of the Citadel long ago. He knew he sat dead center in the Cavern of Inquiry and that the exit lay over his shoulder beyond the curtain of darkness. There was no information in the schematics about what else might be in the room.

He glanced in the direction of his escape, before turning his head forward at the realization that such a simple gesture may have revealed too much.

He gritted his teeth and played with the rope that cut into his wrists, struggling in mock anguish against its confinement. Gunther wanted his captors to believe he had given up. He forced his mouth into a thin line as he once again failed to wiggle his hands any looser. But he knew he'd free himself eventually. Once he extricated himself enough from his bindings, he could get to the blade concealed in his sleeve. He sneered. How typical of them not to have found it while tying him up. It was only a matter of time before he freed himself, and until then he'd display the panic his captors expected.

He cocked his head and squinted up into the light as he thought of pretending to echo-locate himself once more. A giant screen suddenly flickered into existence before him. He gasped as a lump rose from his stomach. He hadn't expected that. More screens sparked to life, alternating left to right around the first one until seven darkened figures hovered in an arc above him.

The TimeCouncil.

At long last he met his overlords, though not in a manner he'd ever imagined. Of course, he'd never thought he'd get caught either. He turned to face each of the screens in turn, hoping to glean something about the high priests of his craft. Gunther pursed his lips when he found only the silhouettes of the seven greeting him. A light blue glow behind them provided just enough illumination to hint at the features hidden in dark shadows.

"TimeWeaver 341," Councilor One boomed in a voice sounding as ancient as the ages themselves. But a little too loud for ears acclimatized to total silence. Gunther winced and turned his head as if struck. He wordlessly cursed his display of weakness and returned to face Councilor One's darkened image as it continued speaking. "You sit before us for unspeakable crimes, crimes no TimeWeaver should have been able to contemplate. Crimes no TimeWeaver should have been able to commit. Crimes no TimeWeaver has commited for a generation!"

A hissing chorus of condemnation rained down on him. Gunther hunched over as disgrace stabbed at his soul. But only briefly. He clenched his jaw and raised his head, staring dead straight to the first screen as he waited for the scolding to abate, and his trial to begin.

Once silence had returned, the central silhouette spoke again. "Councilor Two will read the charges."

The sound of an old woman clearing her throat pulled Gunther's attention to the second screen. "TimeWeaver 341," the councilor said, "you are hereby charged with the following crimes—"

Gunther shrank. The woman's voice unburied long-forgotten memories of the warmth of his grandmother's smiling face. When TimeWeavers entered the Citadel for training, the memories of their previous existences were supposed to have been completely erased, yet shadowy tendrils of his former life maddeningly clung to the recesses of his mind. Was it this flaw that allowed him to so flagrantly break the rules?

He straightened his back and forced himself not to think of his previous life, the normal existence he had lived before being recruited as a TimeWeaver. He sat still and waited for the councilor to continue, but she remained strangely silent, as if she had to compose herself before reciting her list.

She cleared her throat once more. "Your crimes are as follows," she said quickly, as if trying to rush everything out lest she stumble again. "Unauthorized activity in the TimeSpace. Profiteering in the TimeSpace. Failure to complete the assigned mission. And lastly and most grievously—" Number Two sucked in her breath before spitting out the final accusation in a short gasp, "Dereliction of Duty Leading to Damage of the Space-Time Continuum."

The room fell uncomfortably silent, and Gunther squirmed in his seat as he felt the cold stares of the Councilors boring through him. An unexpected pang of guilt swept over him as that last charge banged around in his head. Out of all he had done—and he had willingly done everything he was accused of—he felt actual remorse over the damage he had caused by deviating so egregiously from his assigned mission. That act went against his very being as a TimeWeaver.

"TimeWeaver 341," Councilor One said, an unexpected note of sadness in his voice. "How do you plead?"

Gunther sucked in a deep breath and steadied himself. "Not guilty." He silently cursed the shallow tone of his voice. He had to remain strong in front of the councilors. Invincible. And so far, he had been nothing but scared and vulnerable.

An audible gasp of shock rang out from the councilors. Apparently, they hadn't foreseen that response. Gunther smiled.

After the murmuring had subsided, the old man continued, now sounding like a disappointed grandfather. "I would so like to believe your innocence, TimeWeaver. I'd do just about anything to alter the doubt you've instilled in me. But the evidence against you is damning. Overwhelmingly so. We have proof—"

"You have nothing," Gunther barked, feeling confidence growing inside of him.

"We have proof of your guilt on all these charges," Councilor One continued. "No TimeWeaver should have been capable of these... these *inexplicable* offenses." The old man slowly shook his head, and Gunther sank in his seat. He was surprised at how sharply the guilt cut him. Years of conditioning told him he'd failed his fellow TimeWeavers.

He immediately shook off the remorse. No, he told himself. It had been worth it. Even knowing all the damage he had inadvertently caused, it had most definitely been worth it. For her.

The old man's stern voice shook Gunther out of his thoughts. "Councilor Three, what have you discerned of his mental stability?"

"From what I can conclude, it's excellent," said the Councilor. Gunther smirked at the surprising compliment. Three's voice sounded younger than the other two. For the first time, Gunther realized that the Council was ranked by age.

"His mental abilities were only rated as average throughout his training, though," Three continued.

Gunther raised his eyebrows. *Average?*

"His early missions were evaluated as average as well," Councilor Three continued in a neutral tone of voice. "Below average in some cases."

Gunther flinched as the councilor's words jabbed him.

"He had even been marked for removal from Weaving duties," the councilor went on. Gunther leaned forward at this new information, waiting for more to be revealed. "But then quite suddenly, unexpectedly, his mission performance improved significantly. His execution became excellent, in fact. And his last mission, before, um, the one in question, was the best Weaving he's ever done, probably *the* best of any TimeWeaver, councilors included." A few of the councilors gasped. "I've delved into the most ancient of records and failed to find any Weaving that was accomplished more quickly and efficiently. If anything, the accused should have been groomed for a councilor's position for when, ah, a vacancy arises."

Gunther looked back to Councilor One, knowing everyone else would do so as well at the pause.

"See? There's no way I could commit these crimes," Gunther said with excitement in his voice at this newfound acclaim of his TimeWeaving skills, even if the TimeCouncil didn't know—and clearly didn't suspect—he had a little help in getting so good so fast.

"You expect us to believe you?" said Councilor Four.

"I'm speechless at what you've done," said Councilor Five. "Completely speechless."

"We have proof in hand of your guilt," said Councilor Six. "By claiming innocence, I can only conclude that you're hiding something from us."

"Preposterous," interjected Four. "He's clearly snapped. Anyone who improved that much so quickly is a danger to us all. We should get right to the sentencing and banish him immediately."

"We really should understand more about this before sentencing him," said Two.

All the councilors started talking over one another, which quickly devolved into a shouting match. Gunther leaned back and shifted in his seat, straining against his bindings as he waited for the argument to end. Almost immediately he stopped and sat erect. Was there now play in the rope? He twisted his wrists with new urgency, trying to gauge their stricture. Yes, the bindings were finally loosening! His heart raced. Just a little more effort, and he could free himself. But if they were sure of his guilt, sentencing would be swift and final.

"Silence," Councilor One roared. Gunther shuddered, and abruptly stopped his fidgeting, eyes wide with fear that he had been spotted working himself free. The room dripped in tense silence.

"TimeWeaver 341," the old man said, "I can't begin to express the disappointment I feel at the crimes you have committed." Gunther opened his mouth to again express his innocence, but something in the cold tendrils of the old man's voice caused him to snap his jaw shut.

"Since before the birth of this universe, TimeWeavers have been mending the stray threads of time that would unravel existence. Yet, even with the knowledge of the harm you could commit—did commit—you not only ignored your mission, you went about changing reality in the most unusual and frightening ways." A murmur rumbled from the councilors. "Your fellow TimeWeavers are working, at this moment, to mitigate the incredible damage you caused. We can't believe the profusion of fresh tears created by your baffling indiscretion. I'm personally amazed that we're still all around to be judging you at all. We haven't seen such wanton damage since I was new to this Council."

The Councilor's voice rose in pitch and intensity. "It may take generations of TimeWeaving to complete the mending, if these tears can be adequately repaired at all!" Councilor One exhaled sharply and shook his head. A pang of guilt once again ripped through Gunther's soul, but he steadied himself against regret. He had done what was necessary. "Everyone on this Council has Weaved," One continued. "We all know the hardships, privation and strain you have endured jumping out of this reality and temporarily into another soul's body to Weave. But never before have we witnessed this kind of bizarre behavior. These events must simply never be repeated. We need to know why you so flagrantly disobeyed your orders and so willfully damaged the time line."

Gunther exhaled, feeling the tension release from his body. Now he knew why he sat in this chair instead of already facing his punishment. They wanted information. The thought of unburdening his soul and dumping the truth on them flickered through his exhausted mind. But he instantly batted that notion away, knowing it would immediately lead to what Councilor Four had suggested. No, he needed to stall them while he worked himself free. Then he could escape.

With Greta.

He caused all the damage, at her insistence, because he loved her. She clearly loved him as well, for she had helped him with his recent missions, making him look so damn good. Yet she inexplicably refused any credit, and insisted that he keep her involvement a secret. In gratitude for her much needed help, he didn't question her baffling request. TimeWeavers anonymously helped each other occasionally, entering a time stream the other was working on to help set up or execute a Weave. But never quite like this. Never to this depth of effect.

Doubt crept into soul like an infection. Why hadn't he so much as flinched when she'd revealed her plan? Payback. Retribution. Vengeance for the horrible man who had raped her. She never told Gunther any details, only that the attack had happened while on a mission. He didn't want details. Gunther wanted to be her sword. Revenge went way beyond the bounds of TimeWeaving. Above and beyond Gunther's sense of duty.

He shook the doubts aside and thought of their success. He had meted out punishment. Most satisfactorily so.

Now, once he freed himself, they would need to flee the mess they had created. If the Council had caught him, they would catch her. It was only a matter of time before she'd be sitting in this chair, facing banishment to some obscure time and place, with no means of ever returning to the Citadel. Or each others' arms. The same fate he was facing now.

He couldn't let that happen. He would rip time apart to prevent it.

His heart sank a little, knowing that if he had convinced her to make their escape after the previous Weaving, none of this would be happening to him right now. They'd be living as free people, hidden away from all this. No more Weaving. No more time mending. No more taxing their bodies to carry out their missions, feeling their life force ebb with every jump. No more not knowing if they'd ever return to the Citadel if their host died during a Weaving.

But she had wanted—had demanded—a deeper revenge. One last Weaving, she had insisted. Just to see how far her attacker had fallen. To confirm the Weaving's success. It was one Weaving too many, and the Council had caught Gunther.

"I don't know what you're talking about," Gunther lied, stalling for time. He only needed a few more minutes, and he'd be free.

"If you will not admit your guilt and tell us why you did this," said Councilor Seven in a high-pitched, whiny voice, "we will have no choice but to, um, extract it instead." The way the youngest councilor emphasized that one word sent a chill down Gunther's spine. The existence of memory extraction had been a whispered rumor between the TimeWeavers. But he had thought it implausible, until now. His chest tightened as a cold, prickly sensation crept over his skin.

"Ah, yes," said One. "If the accused won't cooperate, I do believe we will have to extract his memories and relive his thoughts and experiences ourselves." The Councilor sounded almost gleeful at the prospect.

Before Gunther could again express his innocence, something shoved him down into his chair. It felt like being crushed under an enormous weight. He struggled to move. He couldn't breathe. A tingling radiated from the base of his neck through his skull. He let out a gurgled scream as he felt what seemed like an ice-cold dagger plunge into the back of his head.

"Let's get to the last Weaving first, shall we?" said Councilor One from far away. Then Gunther's world exploded into pain and light.

He stood on the steps outside the YMCA where they rose to the sidewalk, exactly as he'd done all those times before. With the recessed parking lot on one side, this had been such an excellent spot to wait for the car that he decided to commence this latest—and last—Weaving right here. To pass the time he leaned toward one of the building's tinted windows and checked his makeup in the reflection, making sure his lip gloss and mascara hadn't smeared. He had to look perfect for Mark.

Gunther's image smiled back at him at as he thought of the irony: A mark named Mark. It was almost too perfect. Like it had been planned.

He continued to stare at himself, unable to get over how simply adorable he looked all dolled up. With a touch of makeup, slicked-back hair and frilly clothes, he could be a member of an early '80s glam-rock band. Or a beautiful woman. He smiled at himself in vain contemplation. Yes, he initially had doubts about this getup, but now he had to admit that cross-dressing had been the right thing to do for this series of Weavings.

His eyes widened, and his head snapped toward the road. He felt it. Mark. He bounded the three steps up to the street and peeked behind the guardrail protecting the Y's parking lot from the road above. A line of cars sat still on the far side of the broad intersection, waiting for the light to change. One of them belonged to Mark.

Showtime!

He stepped out onto the sidewalk, took a deep breath, stuck out his thumb, and began singing for his ride.

The traffic light changed, and the vehicles made their way toward him. Then past him. He knew the look of those who drove by. He understood that most people were too afraid to pick this *weirdo* up, that he was simply that strange little singing man in the makeup and girly clothes thumbing for a ride. "Screamin' Mimi," they called him. But that was okay. The name added to his mystique. It also took the edge off this dangerous freelance TimeWeaving game he was playing.

Out of this crush of cars, one slowed. As always. A bright smile curled on his pink, glossy lips at the sight: a beat up older model, dating from the '70s. It had once been a bright, metallic gold, but the color had faded to a pasty, taupe mass of dented and rusted steel. He bobbed up and down on the balls of his feet, unable to contain his elation.

Rattling like an old tin can, the car chugged to a stop. Gunther eagerly pulled the passenger door handle, needing all his strength to pry open the big door. The loud creak of grating metal sang in his ears. Delighted by the ruin he'd brought to Mark's life from the last Weaving, he slipped onto the torn vinyl bench seat and yanked the door, which closed with a satisfying clang. He slowly turned his head toward the driver, savoring the sight of the man's shattered existence. Mark was a mess, from his greasy hair to his shabby clothes. But it was the cold sore on the man's lower lip that brought an enormous smile to Gunther's face. That smile wilted at the sight of Mark's dark brown eyes staring at him with an intensity he'd never seen in Mark before. Gunther had to avert his gaze to compose himself.

"You're a little queer, aren't you?" Mark said with a brusqueness in his voice that hadn't been there in past Weavings. The acrid stench of stale cigarette smoke assaulted Gunther's nostrils, and he wrinkled his nose. He glanced back up at Mark, the smile cautiously returning to Gunther's lips, for in this existence Mark had taken up that filthy habit.

"Just happy," Gunther replied, trying to sound cheerful, but unable to keep worry from lapping at the edge of his voice. He wiggled his butt back and forth, feeling the seat's rips and duct-taped repairs through his tight jeans. He calmed his pounding heart by reminding himself that he was witnessing the result of his latest TimeWeaving success.

Mark stared at him for a long, uncomfortable moment. He squinted and a smirk creased his face. Only then did Mark turn to face the road. With a rush of acceleration that sounded like a garbage disposal chewing a metal spoon, the car pulled away from the curb and raced up the hill. Mark's right hand clasped the wheel tightly as his left elbow jutted out the window.

Free of Mark's intense stare, Gunther exhaled and took careful note of his driver. He smiled with satisfaction at what repeated Weavings had done to this horrible man's life.

"What's that song you sing at the bottom of the hill?" Mark asked, not taking his eyes off the road. "Is that Five Bad Boys? It's Five Bad Boys, isn't it?"

The smile wilted from Gunther's face, and a cold tingling radiated from his heart to his extremities. How would Mark know that? How *could* Mark know that? Five Bad Boys was a band from two Weavings ago. It did not exist in this timeline, a casualty of the butterfly effect.

"No wait," Mark said, slamming Gunther's racing thoughts to an abrupt halt. "Backstreet Boys," Mark said with a chilling casualness that caused the hair on Gunther's arms to stand on end. "I meant Backstreet boys."

Gunther exhaled the breath caught in his lungs, then turned toward the road, feeling the prickles of the sweat on his neck turn cold.

No. Nothing unusual here, he tried to tell himself. Just a coincidence. A really eerie one, but a coincidence nonetheless. He really wanted to believe that, but his heart refused to slow, and it continued to slam painfully into his ribs. The throbbing served to emphasize how this exercise at revenge had gone on too long. He was completely frazzled from all the experiences, all these memories. Luckily this would be the last of this set of Weavings. His last Weaving ever. He couldn't imagine Mark dropping into circumstances that would make his life even worse than it had already become.

He reflected on that thought a moment, and a perfectly dreadful notion crossed his mind: could he Weave Mark's life to an even baser existence, even, say, to his suicide?

Such a thought should have been blasphemy to a Weaver. Weavers were supposed to braid new realities to fix stray threads of time that had come undone, not create glaringly obvious new ones. He had already caused enough trouble, even if it was for the greater good. Yet that horrible notion persisted in his mind, daring him to follow through. And if such a malevolent thought had been so easily formulated, perhaps it was simply meant to be. And besides, who could possibly catch him if he did the unthinkable?

"You know..." Gunther began before choking on the words he knew would cross the line. But he plowed forward just the same. "You know, it looks like you have had a rough life. Wouldn't it be great if you could just fix your past mistakes—"

"So, are you a queer or what?" Mark asked, cutting Gunther off.

Mark's interruption caused Gunther's sweet words to burn like acid in his throat. He stared at Mark, realizing he'd already gone too far. Gunther took a moment to compose himself as the stench of those heretical thoughts evaporated, and he formulated a suitable reply to Mark's question. "I'm perfectly straight," he was finally able to say, failing to produce Mimi's usual high-pitched sing-song voice. Instead, the waver in his words betrayed his anxiousness, and he could feel himself shrink in his seat whenever Mark glanced his way.

"Sure you are," Mark said flatly as he hit the brakes and slowed down even though the traffic light ahead was still green. It turned yellow an instant later. Gunther tensed. He had chalked up the "Five Bad Boys" remark as a coincidence. This had become creepy.

Mark moved his left hand onto the steering wheel. "I've always wondered about you," Mark said still staring out the windshield. "Why do you sing like that at the bottom of the hill?"

"Don't you like my singing?" Gunther asked, a nervous warble in his voice.

"No, it's grand. I'm just wondering why."

Gunther felt cold prickles on his skin, and it took a moment to figure out why: there was no emotion in Mark's words. No breath of life. Mark spoke in a dry, monotone voice.

"Why, indeed." Gunther stalled there, as if pondering why he had consistently sung for his ride. "Well, for one thing, it works. You always pick me up—"

Mark's head spun toward Gunther, his gaze once again boring into him with an uncomfortable intensity. "What do you mean *always*?" he snapped. "I've never picked you up before." The crease on Mark's forehead deepened. Gunther's eyes bulged as Mark's grip on the steering wheel tightened, the tendons visibly straining on the backs of his hands. Mouth half open in a hate-filled sneer, eyes squinting suspiciously, Mark glared with a new ferocity. Gunther shrank even smaller into his seat.

Cowering like a beaten dog, Gunther's mouth hung open in disbelief at what had slipped past his lips. That gaffe proved it had been crazy to come back again. It had been crazier still to think he should try yet another Weaving. He needed to save the situation. And quick.

"I mean you picked me up... This time... This one time..." he stammered, feeling sweat trickling down his back. "I don't know where that *always* came from. Silly me." He fidgeted in his seat, wilting even more under Mark's glower. The perspiration covering his body suddenly turned cold. No Weaving had ever affected him so. No simple mistake had ever caused this reaction, and he had made plenty of mistakes during his early Weavings. Raw panic gripped him, and he realized that something had gone terribly wrong. He needed to get out. Get out now. But he couldn't tear his eyes from Mark's hypnotic stare.

"You know, you're pretty stupid to think you could continue

playing this game," Mark said, pure hatred contorting his face. Gunther froze in his seat, unable to protest. "There's something strange about you," Mark continued, his voice stabbing Gunther like an icicle.

"You're different, and I don't like your kind of different."

Gunther had heard enough. His growing apprehension blossomed into terror. Self-preservation filled his mind. He knew he needed to activate his Exit KeyPhrase and jump back to the Citadel. All he had to do was say the right sequence of words, and he'd be out of this mess. He wasn't in the right moment, but he would deal with those consequences later. Gunther opened his mouth, but Mark interrupted him by softening his demeanor and leaning in.

"Don't you want to know how I know?" Mark said in a hoarse whisper.

Mark's words mesmerized him, and the phrase stuck on the tip of his tongue. Yes, he did want to know what Mark knew. How he knew. Whether he actually knew or whether this was the crazed rambling of a guy tortured by the echo of the better life he would have lived. A life not destroyed by expert Weaving. Despite shaking in his seat, Gunther forced his tongue silent, and he patiently waited to find out.

The light turned green, and Mark made a hard left turn, cutting in front of the oncoming traffic. The sound of car horns and screeching tires mixed with a high-pitched scream that Gunther quickly realized was flying out of his own mouth. His body slammed into the passenger door, cutting his scream short and dazing him. The car roared its disapproval as Mark hit the accelerator, which sucked Gunther's body into the battered upholstery. The paved side street became a derelict gravel road that cut through a thick tangle of trees. Mark stomped the accelerator. The car grunted its displeasure and rocketed through the green tunnel. The uneven surface bounced the car around wildly, and projecting tree branches clawed at the car as it shot past. Before Gunther could scream his terror anew, Mark slammed the brakes, and the car skidded to a violent stop.

Gunther grabbed the dash to keep his face from hitting the windshield. He blinked at the beams of afternoon sunshine filtering through the leaves and scintillating across the dust cloud. In that moment, he realized that Mark had tried to knock him out.

Mark jerked the transmission into park and turned toward him, grabbing hold of Gunther's lapel with an iron-fisted left hand. "Listen here you little freak," Mark shouted, spit flying from his raging mouth. "I've had enough of you and what you've done to me. I'm tired of listening to your stupid stories. And looking at that idiotic makeup. Your pretty face is going to pay for everything right here and right now."

Terror gripped Gunther like nothing had ever done before. He was already screaming his Exit KeyPhrase in a high-pitched squeal as Mark cocked his fist to throw a devastating punch his way.

"Happy helps lists Beethoven, Bach, Chopin not only for new Nashville megahits…"

Gunther's world swirled around him. Time itself seemed to draw out past infinity, and he couldn't focus on anything. *Where am I? What am I doing? Who am I?*

There was the sensation of floating weightless, and then he felt a rhythmic tickling sensation pulsing in his head. Before he knew it, that sensation blossomed into irritation and then into a pounding that beat in the rhythm of his heart. The pain became an anchor, steadying him against the rushing world. With each throb he came to realize where he was, what he was doing, and who he was.

And the trouble he was in.

The tattered remains of his recent memories flew past him in a nauseating blur: the Y, Mark, the car, the hill, the gravel road, the fist. As his stomach clenched itself into a tight ball, Greta's beautiful face focused into his consciousness. The whirl stopped, but the reality of his predicament slapped him down. Hard.

Like waking out of a nightmare, he jerked to alertness and realized he sat on the wooden chair in the middle of the Cavern of Inquiry, his hands tied behind his back. His stomach settled, and he pulled his head upright, seeing the screens of the seven councilors flickering above him. He tasted bile in his mouth, and he flopped his head over to spit it out onto the rock floor, hoping to show his contempt to the Seven. Show that they hadn't hurt him. But he only managed to slobber on himself. He used all his strength to look back up to the glowing screens.

"Welcome back, TimeWeaver," Councilor One said in his grandfatherly voice, as if he almost felt sorry for having put Gunther through that horrible experience. "I'm going to skip over the issue of you wearing women's makeup..." A subdued laughter rippled from the other Councilors, "... and dive right into the question of the key you used to return. I'm ever so curious as to what—"

"I think I know what it is," Councilor Seven said. "I believe it's a mnemonic for remembering the first twelve elements on the periodic table."

Silence from the other Councilors told Gunther that they were going through the list of elements to see if that was the case.

"Very good deduction, Councilor Seven," said One after a few moments. "Very good, indeed."

"I must say that's a clever use of words that would only be used in a key," said Councilor Two, laughter in her voice.

"A little something he kept from his pre-TimeWeaver existence?" Three asked.

"If that's the case what else does he remember?" Four questioned.

"Did anyone else find it odd that the victim almost seemed to know what was happening to him?" Six said, jumping his turn.

"Just a coincidence," said Seven. "As we all know, those things do happen ."

"Why were you targeting this one man?" Five asked, speaking louder than the rest.

"Pardon my intrusion," said Six, "but I do believe we should investigate how this Mark seemed to have also known about a singing group that didn't exist in his reality. This is all too bizarre to simply be a coincidence."

"Yes, why this one person?" One said, echoing Five. "We must know what this man did to make you want to exact this kind of revenge upon him. I believe it is the key as to why you went about unraveling time so carelessly."

Gunther realized with a start that during his forced recall and interrogation he had stopped working his hands free. He started his quest for freedom anew, trying to be as inconspicuous as possible even though agony still sparked from every recess of his body.

"I believe I speak for the entire council when I suggest we need to see what happened on his previous Weaving," Seven said with an eagerness that caused the hair on the back of Gunther's neck to stand.

"Quite right," added Five. "We need to understand what he did to cause this Mark to deteriorate into what we just witnessed."

"Yes, what was this man like before the TimeWeaver interfered with his existence?" said Three.

"I think we need to know," said One. And before Gunther could protest, his world once again exploded into pain.

He stood on the steps outside the YMCA, exactly as he'd done many other times. This had always been a good spot to wait for the car to show up, so he had decided to begin this latest Weaving right here. His final Weaving, he thought with satisfaction.

And relief.

This time had to be the last. Gunther couldn't imagine inflicting any more punishment than he already had. Each new Weaving brought a fresh chance at being discovered. And his nerves were frayed enough as it was. With revenge exacted in full, he could finally be done with this exercise.

He leaned toward the window by the Y's front door to check his makeup in the reflection. He stared at himself a while before finally shaking his head. Dolled up in lip gloss and mascara, he looked like a fool. But still, he couldn't tear his eyes off of himself. He sat there gazing at his reflection for a long moment before finally exhaling sharply. He couldn't believe he was going to do this again. He still wasn't entirely sure this would be the best way to handle Mark.

His eyes widened, and his head snapped toward the road. There! He felt it. Mark was coming. He ran up the three steps to the street and peeked behind the guardrail. The familiar line of cars waited on the far side of the intersection. One of them belonged to Mark.

Let's do this!

He stepped out onto the sidewalk, took a deep breath, stuck out his thumb, and began singing for his ride.

The traffic light changed, and the vehicles made their way toward him. And past him. But out of this rush of cars, one did slow, as Gunther knew one would. A smile curled on his pink, glossy lips. No fancy SUV this time, rather a mundane grey sedan.

Gunther was so eager to witness how much further Mark had devolved, that he reached for the handle before the car had even come to a stop. He slipped onto the seat and looked over at the rather ordinary man driving the car.

Success! Gone was the potent presence, the cocky attitude, the powerful aura, the stink of influence. Nothing remained of Mark's previous existence but the shell of a faded dream that only Gunther remembered. Witnessing the excellent results that had flowed from the last Weaving, Gunther couldn't help but smile.

But Gunther knew he couldn't rest on this win. A thrill of exhilaration swept into him. There was one final program to set, and that would be it. He'd be done. So he immediately went to work.

"Thanks for the lift—Say, you're Mark Wright, aren't you?"

Mark bobbed his head at the unexpected recognition. He stared at Gunther, eyes wide in disbelief. Gunther could almost see the gears working in his head, as Mark tried to figure out how this crazy little man could possibly know him. The honking behind them broke Mark's stare, and he turned his attention to the road, gently pressing the accelerator.

"Yes. Yes, that's me." His voice sounded both worried and curious. "How… ? How do you know my name?"

Gunther breathed in deep, and laid the groundwork for the next phase of this Weaving. "Oh, I voted for you for mayor last year." Gunther contorted his face and looked away to make it seem as if that sentence had accidentally slipped past his lips and that he immediately regretted saying it. His acting had improved steadily, and he was confident he had nailed it this time.

Mark kept taking short, worried glances Gunther's way as he drove over the hill and into the valley beyond. Gunther furrowed his brow, suddenly concerned that Mark would think him insane and demand he leave the car at the first stop light. But Mark only asked the question lingering in the air. "I didn't run for office. What do you mean voted for me? I'm definitely no politician." Mark's nervous laugh betrayed his insecurity. Gunther turned to smile back at Mark, relieved he hadn't lost him. He patiently waited for what he knew would come out of Mark's mouth next.

"Besides, why would you have voted for me? If I had run for office, I mean."

Gunther spoke coyly, steadying himself as he tried hard to keep the smile from working its way past his ears. "Actually, I only voted for you because of your hot wife." Again, he cringed in mocking disbelief of what he had just said, hoping he wasn't overacting. He waited for Mark's next line. Seconds passed like minutes, and Gunther wondered if he pushed too hard. Thoughts of failure and having to restart this Weaving to get the required reaction from Mark flooded Gunther's mind, and he drooped in his seat.

"Okay, now I know you definitely have me confused with someone else."

Gunther used all his might to keep his grin from lighting up his face at the laughter in Mark's voice. Every one of Mark's responses had been perfect. This Weaving would be a breeze. No worries.

"Julie, hot?" Mark then asked himself out loud.

"Julie? Who's Julie?" Gunther asked. "No, your wife's Annette. You know, the tall blond with the cute dimples? She's your wife, isn't she?" Gunther leaned back and waited for this information to bang around inside Mark's skull.

"Annette?" The name slipped out of Mark's open mouth like a ghost as he stared through the windshield, his complexion turning pale.

"I... I haven't thought of Annette in... in years... We went out for a little while in high school before..."

Gunther jumped at the opening and turned to face Mark. "Before you dumped her to go out with that Erika, right?" Gunther said, entirely too much glee in his voice. But he didn't care about keeping up appearances. Mark had been hooked. He could reel him in and finish this Weaving clean and easy. And the quicker he accomplished this, the quicker he could get home.

Gunther used Mark's stunned silence to lean in closer, as he continued his work in a hoarse whisper, like he was telling a deep, dark secret. Mark instinctively leaned sideways to listen.

"And Erika ended up dumping you," Gunther continued with glee. "You tried to get back with Annette, but she had moved on, hadn't she? And, well, long story short, now you're with *Julie*," he finished with a slow yawn.

Gunther tilted back, barely able to contain his excitement at how well things were going. "Why on earth would you dump that goddess Annette?" he asked, calmly waiting for the reply. Gunther bit his tongue to prevent himself from laughing. The Weaving on Mark back in high school had been very effective. Oh, how easy it had been to convince him to break up with Annette, leading him to this very moment, the cusp where Gunther could easily turn Mark's life in a new direction.

"I don't know," Mark stammered as he cowered and took furtive glances toward his inquisitor before hitting the brakes hard to stop for a red light.

Gunther held his thoughts there, waiting until the car had completely stopped, and Mark turned his head. "Wouldn't it be great to be able to just go back and change that. That one. Little. Thing?" Gunther saw Mark's eyes widen with hope. "Fix your mistakes? Live the life you should have?" Mark sat transfixed for a moment, before gently bobbing his head.

Gunther leaned in, and Mark mirrored him. "It's too bad you can't just do that." Gunther whispered, laughter in his voice.

Jaw clenched and breathing hard, Mark stared at him. "Get out!" he finally said.

Gunther smiled. He opened the door just as the cars behind began honking.

Gunther crashed back to the present with such force that his eyes bulged, and breath refused to flow into his lungs. Terror clung to his body like ice-cold sweat. Surprise gripped him when he realized exactly where he sat and what was happening.

The room went strangely silent, and a calmness filled his soul. *There*, he thought to himself. *That wasn't so bad.*

A great heave convulsed his body, and vomit spewed out of his mouth, splattering onto his lap and overflowing onto the floor below with a sickening plop.

His head pounded in time with his heart, each throb slamming harder than the last against his skull. When the final remaining wisp of energy evaporated, his eyes shut, and his head flopped down as if he was a rag doll.

As the drumming in his ears slowly subsided, he heard the Councilors arguing amongst themselves. They shouted about why they had left the memory extraction so soon. About why no one had detected Gunther's perverse use of Weaving to adjust people's past to warp their future. About why they weren't banishing him this instant.

Then Seven's shrill voice cut through the argument. "I'm curious as to what the accused did on the previous Weaving. Let us try one more extraction."

No! Gunther wanted to scream. *No more memory extraction.* He started shaking with the thoughts of what that would do to him. *I'll tell you want you want to know!* Tears flowed unchecked from his eyes with the realization that he had truly been broken. He would have screeched out his confession to the Council if it would save him from more torture. If only he could raise his head and work his mouth. *I'll tell you everything. I'll even tell you about Greta. Just no—more—pain—.*

"Look at him. The accused can't take any more of this," said Six.

"It could kill him," added Five.

"That's a chance we'll have to take," continued Seven. "We need answers to prevent this from ever happening again. Then we can banish him."

Why? Gunther wanted to ask, but too weak to speak. Why *are you savaging me like this?* He knew that voice. That tone. If only he weren't in such a state, Gunther could concentrate and figure who this Seven was and how he knew him.

The councilors argued over each other until One's steady voice cut their quarrel short.

"I'm afraid I have to agree with Seven. I feel we're missing a critical piece of information that may be revealed if we witness what happened one Weaving past."

Exhausted from the ordeal, Gunther slipped into unconsciousness as the ice-cold knife once again plunged into his skull.

He cowered on the steps outside the Y, waiting to feel Mark's presence, but wishing that he wouldn't show up. Yet he remained here fidgeting in his tight, frilly clothes, feeling like a fool with the makeup he had somehow been convinced to wear. He refused to look at his reflection in the window, knowing an idiot would be staring back at him. Still, he somehow believed that this was the correct way to go.

His eyes widened, and his head snapped toward the road. There! He felt it. Mark was coming. His heart thundered in his chest as he crept his way up the stairs. Once he crested the final step onto the sidewalk above, he peeked nervously behind the guardrail. He swallowed hard at the line of vehicles waiting on the far side of the intersection. One of them was Mark's.

Do it like she told you!

He stepped out onto the sidewalk, took a deep breath to calm his racing nerves, stuck out his thumb, and began singing for his ride.

The traffic light changed, and the vehicles made their way

toward him. Then past him. He flinched with each amused gaze shot his way. They laughed at him. Mocked him. He shrank. But didn't run. Somehow he had been convinced that this getup would work brilliantly, even though a powerful desire to retreat beat in his heart.

He was about to lose his nerve when an SUV slowed down. Mark. Gunther stood blinking at the stopped vehicle before reaching out a numb arm and fumbling with the door. Breathing hard, he pulled himself up into the seat without looking at his victim.

"Hey there, Screamin' Mimi!" Mark laughed. "Need a lift?"

Gunther made the briefest eye contact. Mark was obviously amused at the cowering cross-dresser in his passenger seat. Gunther's gaze quickly fell to the floor while he tried with all his might to overcome his embarrassment and make his move.

He exhaled and turned back toward Mark, steadied himself, and faked a look of utter surprise at his driver. "Hey, you're Congressman Mark Wright, aren't you?" Gunther realized he was mumbling and turned his wide eyes back to the floor. More than anything he wanted to leave, but needed to see this through.

"Congressman?" Mark laughed again. "I wish. No, I'm your mayor. *Mayor* Mark Wright."

Gunther felt as if he had been thrown against a brick wall.

Then, nothing.

Am I dead? Is this what death is like? It's very peaceful. I like being dead.

The earlier suffering was gone, replaced by serenity. Like floating in warm water. This moment felt right. He felt the gentlest of pulsations tickling throughout what would have been his body if he were alive. He inwardly smiled at being freed from his torment.

His bliss quickly faded when the tingling sensation turned from pleasurable to irritating, and the tickle became an uncomfortable warmth. Soon, the warmth amplified itself into a stinging itch blanketing his body, an itch he couldn't scratch to relieve. That itch twisted itself into a searing pain, as if his body was being immersed in boiling water. Then, a new pain superseded everything else, and his head began to pound in rhythm with his heart.

His heart! Through the agony, he came to the awful realization that his heart did beat and that he was indeed alive. *Kill me now!* he silently screamed through his shattered thoughts. But the throbbing slowly lessened in intensity, and with the pain subsiding, increasing awareness of his predicament rose up in its place. The cavern. The chair. The TimeCouncil. Memory extraction. Greta.

He sat, limp, waiting for the blows against his skull to finally diminish enough for his senses to return. Stars left his vision. He tasted blood. The sound of the councilors arguing over him replaced the roar that had been banging around in his ears. A dull numbness blanketed his body. Only his sense of smell failed him, which wasn't surprising considering that he struggled to let any air flow past the mucus that filled his nostrils.

He waited for the inevitable vomiting, but nothing happened. *There*, he thought to himself. *That wasn't so bad. I survived.* Just then a violent heave surged through his body, and he once again retched. Wave after wave of increasing agony contorted his stomach as it emptied itself until nothing was left, and continued on into dry heaves of ever increasing torment. It was as if his insides were violently forcing themselves out.

Each reluctant breath felt like fire down his lungs. A frigid sweat coated him. He whimpered as he sagged forward, the bindings at his back the only thing keeping him from falling into the mess he had made on the floor below.

The bindings! He had once again forgotten about his restraints. The exertion of his torment had sapped the last bit of energy he possessed. Though he had the will to free himself, he no longer had the ability. He drooped, resigning himself to his fate with the knowledge that he had gambled greatly, and lost. Tears filled his eyes as he realized he would never see his beloved Greta, but he at least had the satisfaction of knowing he had ruined Mark's life on her behalf.

The councilors' voices blended like mush in his aching ears. But Gunther could tell they were once again arguing. Out of the cloud of voices, he grasped hold of the discussion, steadying himself.

"No! It can't be her," said Two.

"I told you she'd be back," said Three bluntly.

"What are you talking about?" asked Four.

"Something that we thought we had taken care of before your time on the Council," said One. "Something, unfortunately, we will have to deal with again right after we resolve the issue of this TimeWeaver."

The grating voice of Councilor Seven cut through the din. "I really must insist on one more memory extraction."

Gunther was beyond reacting, but a storm of indignation immediately rained down on Seven from the other councilors.

"He's already suffered enough."

"Can't you see any more will kill him?"

"Any more is madness."

"In his condition he's no longer of any use to us."

Those words blessed Gunther with a tinge of relief and hope. He opened his eyes just in time to hear Councilor One call for everyone to meet him in his chambers to discuss sentencing and the return of "that meddlesome woman."

One by one, the screens flickered out.

It was now or never. The opportunity renewed his strength. He felt his energy return and went about freeing his hands, but the glow of one final screen remained. He forced his head up to see who was still gazing at him, which of the councilors was keeping him from finishing his bid for freedom.

"I'm still here, Gunther." The piercing voice of Councilor Seven rang like a nightmare through Gunther's ears.

"You poor, sad, pathetic little man," Seven continued as Gunther strained to keep his head facing the Councilor's silhouette. "You think your bonds are loosening?" The laughter in Seven's voice put a fresh chill through Gunther's soul.

Gunther felt his bonds tighten. "Oops!" Seven laughed. "Sorry to have to led you to believe you could escape. I heard you're rather good at slipping out of knots."

Gunther meekly wiggled his wrists, finding them as tightly bound as when he first awoke in the chamber.

"You were waiting for just this moment," Seven continued. "And yes, I know about the blade in your sleeve. I'm the one who tied you up. I gave you some *special* rope of my own design, just to tease you." Seven laughed.

Seven leaned forward, his features almost breaking out of the shadows. "She told me you know the way out of the Chamber of Inquiry. Why waste that bit of information when we could use it to break you?"

In the pause, Gunther's mind caught something. A resemblance. Seven was familiar. It wasn't the voice, but the way he delivered his words. He struggled to make the connection. He needed to hear Seven speak further.

"The secrets to the Citadel are just too valuable for anyone else to know. Especially those unquestioning servants of the Council." Seven leaned back. "You're too good of a man, and therefore a danger to my plans, Gunther. And you're not going to stand in my way. I've already made it the Council, and this is just the beginning."

Gunther's thoughts blocked out the whine in the voice and concentrated on the rise and fall of the words. Suddenly, recognition blossomed.

"Mark!"

"I see you remember me now."

The sound of a closing door indicated someone else in the room behind Seven. His silhouette turned. "Come here, my darling Frieda. Come see the conclusion of your devious plan."

A new shadow entered the screen and leaned down before it came to a rest beside the councilor. "So there he is." The woman's matter-of-fact voice sounded eerily familiar.

She then leaned forward and a wave of long hair fell over her shoulder, which displayed familiar contours to her face. She turned to catch the light.

Gunther's blood froze. *No! It can't be!*

He called her Frieda, but it was Greta. She looked at him with a deviant smile and cocked her head ever so slightly. "So pathetic," she said, her words hitting Gunther's soul like a sledgehammer. She turned toward Seven, and Gunther couldn't look away from being witness to a long, passionate kiss, the kind of kiss she used to give him. He remembered those soft lips against his.

The spell was quickly broken, and Gunther bobbed his head and shook uncontrollably. He had to warn Seven. The Council. Everyone! All the events of the recent past now made sense. Greta's help. Her insistence at punishing this one man...

"That was me you were Weaving against," Seven said, as if on cue. He paused for effect as what little color in Gunther's face drained away to white. "Did that tiny brain of yours ever suspect that I would be Weaving in that man's body?"

Not until this moment.

"How convenient that we can only Weave through the bodies of those mentally unstable," he continued. "And who's more unstable than a politician?" He laughed.

"You were never able to figure any of this out, even with the help of your accomplice, that mysterious woman—" Seven paused. Only for a second, but hesitation was there.

"Oh, did One bring up that woman?" Greta interrupted, her voice smooth and confident. "She's nothing but a tired old legend, I assure you. But she does sound like someone I'd be friends with." She laughed as she leaned in and gave Seven another open mouth kiss. While he was preoccupied, she looked over his shoulder at Gunther, giving him a wink.

Tears flowed uncontrollably down Gunther's cheek.

She pulled away and looked at Seven. "Darling, you don't want to be late to the sentencing. You know, you should suggest that he be banished into that strange little man's body. Wouldn't that be a superb conclusion to what we've done to him?"

The councilor beamed a smile. "Brilliant!"

"Now go," she continued. "I'll have a little surprise waiting for you before you get back."

Those words! That was exactly what Greta had told him before his last mission. Before he was betrayed. Before he ended up tied to a chair.

Gunther heard a door close behind Greta—Frieda—this unknown woman. She leaned forward, revealing her beauty out of the shadows to him once again.

"I'm so sorry about all this, Gunther." She almost sounded sincere, but Gunther was going to believe it, regardless. He couldn't resist loving this woman, even after all she'd done to him. "But playing the two of you against each other has been the most fun I've had in eons."

"Greta, whoever you are, you lied to me," Gunther mumbled.

She laughed, then leaned forward until her face filled the screen, but instead of the sweet angel he remembered her features appeared darker, more sinister. "I've had many names, Gunther. I'm one of the original TimeWeavers," she said. "We were still new to Weaving, and in our experimentation, I ended up unstuck in time. They took it upon themselves to try to stop me. Kill me. Considering all I had done for them, that hurt." Her face was so twisted she appeared insane. And apparently she was. "So ever since, I've been having fun at everyone else's expense."

She leaned back, returning to shadows. "You're a sweet guy, Gunther, and I'm so sorry about what's going to happen to you, but I have to retreat to obscurity for a little while. Don't worry," she laughed. "I'll be back to cause some more mischief long after you're gone." The screen blinked out, and Gunther returned to darkness, not feeling anything but a broken heart.

"Hey buddy, do you want a lift or what?"

The voice slapped him back to the reality that he was standing there on the sidewalk with this thumb out. He absentmindedly opened the rusted car door and climbed in, settling himself onto duck-taped seat. He tried to think of where he was and what he was doing, but this mind was a jumbled mess of memories. Or were they dreams? He didn't even know why he was standing there thumbing for a ride. Why he was now sitting in this stranger's vehicle. Why he was staring blankly straight ahead. The cold shock of not even knowing who he was struck him with enough force to loosen the memory of the chair, the councilors, the banishment...

His mouth opened and his started his key. "Happy helps lists—"

"Save your breath," the man said. "Your key won't work anymore. Neither does mine."

Gunther's head spun to the driver and for the first time saw that it was Mark. The Mark from the first extracted Weaving, after Gunther had destroyed his once grand life.

"Seven!"

"Call me Wilhelm. I've been waiting for you to show up," he said. "She told me. At the end. We were both played for fools by that girl."

Gunther's mouth hung open, and Wilhelm continued to answer the questions Gunther was too shocked to ask.

"That bitch betrayed me just like she betrayed you. As soon as you were banished here they arrested me, tied me up to that chair, extracted my memories to find out more about what was going on." Gunther saw Wilhelm flinch at the recollection of horrible memories. He could relate to that. "But like you, I didn't betray her," Wilhelm said. "Even though I had my doubts, I still didn't betray her." He shook his head.

Gunther stared at Wilhelm, still processing what had happened.

"But we have to get back. We have to tell the Council everything we know about that woman. To stop her from ever doing this again."

"How? They canceled our keys."

"I know how the Council plans to start cleaning up your Weaves. They have someone Weaving in town right now to start a patch. Something to do with a motorcycle thief. We'll find the Weaver and get a message back to the Council. Easy."

A high-pitched honk from behind made Wilhelm nod toward the open door, which Gunther dutifully yanked shut. Wilhelm turned forward to start up the hill, but before he could hit the accelerator, the roar of a high-performance motorcycle echoed beside them. A woman in a tight, red, leather suit stopped her bike beside them, flipped up her visor, and winked at them with laughing eyes.

"Greta!"

"Frieda!"

She flipped down her visor with her middle finger, then pulled a handful of throttle, wheeling straight up the hill with the shrill of the bike's powerful engine.

They both stared in silence at the woman until she disappeared over the hill in a thunder of horsepower.

Wilhelm turned to Gunther as they slowly pulled away from the curb. "I think our job just got a lot harder."

When Steven Vallarsa isn't writing he's riding his motorcycle. Or dreaming of all the exotic locals he'd be riding his motorcycle if reality didn't so rudely get in the way. In real life he's a 46 year old machinist who lives in Holland, Michigan with his wife and two children, all just as crazy about motorcycling as he is.

Silent Night

Tim Rohr

NOW

A LL MEN HAVE A MONSTER within them. Some cages are just stronger than others.

Darnell's boot smashes through the old factory door like a runaway bull. The door shatters, the effect of long exposure to salt air. Shards of rotten wood spiral through the darkness. Knocked from its hinges, the door falls inward in three pieces. The handle assembly and padlock, still attached to the frame, clatter in the otherwise quiet night.

"How far?" he asks.

I check the readout on my phone. "Two hundred meters. Up the stairs."

He holds his crucifix out away from him so he can look at it. Sometimes he kisses it. Not today. Today he stuffs it in his shirt.

"Come on," he says. "We got this one." He takes off at a dead dash into the black of the factory's interior, the light from his comm gear bouncing like an LED will-o-the-wisp, and all I can do is try to keep up.

I've seen him like this before. Focused. Intense. He's always had a melancholy streak. Hated me telling him he was brooding. But this is different. Ever since the shift calling herself Silent Night brought down the Harrison Building, killing herself and two hundred thirteen souls,

Darnell has been darker. More withdrawn. Hell, if I were the only one to walk away from the Harrison that day, alive and unhurt, I might let the monster show a bit, too. Especially if, like Darnell, I had lost my wife and two kids in the destruction.

Forgive me if I understand him just a little.

It's not that the shifts deserve to die any more than they already do for ripping apart the fabric of existence, threatening reality itself. It's not that we kill them any more dead. Ever since Silent Night, for Darnell it's been fuck the shifts. Fuck space-time. For him, it's personal.

I race through the factory, catching Darnell on the stairs to the second-floor office. That's where the department scans show the shift we seek has gone to ground.

"You know what I hate about shifts, Mick?" Darnell asks like we've spent the last ten minutes talking over coffee instead of racing across town. "It's not the things the shifts do. Chronos jump through time. Spacers teleport. Kinetics move shit with their minds. I get it." His voice is flat and even. These things hardly register on the piss-Darnell-off scale. "It's not even the way they use space-time as their own little scratching post."

We reach the office door and position ourselves one on each side, ready to breach. I've got my Sig Sauer in one hand, phone in the other. He holds his weapon with two hands.

"Then what?" I whisper. "What do you hate about them?"

"What'd this one do?" he asks.

"What?"

"The shift. What did he do?"

Confused by the sudden change, it takes me a minute to check my phone again. Shifts have only one talent with space-time. The scanner can detect them all, but we're most concerned with the Chronos and the Spacers. They're the ones doing the real damage. I read the information off the phone. "Chrono." That's strange. "He's got to be the third one today—"

"Chronos are the worst," Darnell says, shaking his head. "Hate them the most."

Silent Night was a Chrono.

I decide to let it go. Tread lightly. Like I said, Darnell has a dark streak. Sometimes he's just like that. I may never know what Darnell hates about shifts. And that may be just fine.

"Ready," I say, stuffing my phone into a pocket of my vest. "Three, two—"

Darnell turns the knob and shoulders his way through the door. Cursing, I follow.

The office is a single room lit by a pair of fluorescent lights that cast everything in green. A third light, this one orange, flickers on and off. In one corner, part of the ceiling has melted, and it drips into a puddle on the floor. I can see the night sky, outside. The desk that sits the center of the room has been altered, as well. It changes halfway across. One half is normal. Boring. Standard middle-management suffocation. Pens and papers, desk calendar, and the odd request, denied, for time-off. The other half sags like licorice left in the sun.

A gray-haired man, the only other person in the room, stands beside a steel file cabinet. We keep our weapons trained and stay away from the desk.

"I see I'm the one," the man says like he's been expecting us. It's tough to tell. Always is with shifts. "Introductions may be in order—"

"You know what I hate about shifts, Mick?" Darnell asks, catching my eye. "The flatness. The goddamn lack of affect."

A gunshot. Not my weapon.

Blood on the wall.

The gray-haired man falls to the floor.

"Like they don't feel a thing." Darnell holsters his weapon and walks past me, out the door. "Come on. Let's go."

NOW

Personally, I don't have anything against the shifts. They do what they do, and we hunt them down for it. Like Darnell says, there isn't a prison or cell built that's going to hold them. That's why we're authorized, as officers of the Temporal Preservation Agency, to use lethal force. Find a Chrono or a Spacer right after he's jumped, before he can recharge for another jump, and make introductions with a bullet. Simple. Reality, preserved for another day. Or until the next shift.

The TPA app on my phone beeps out a notification. Another detection. Darnell and I aren't even back to our vehicle. That makes four today, at least—our one and three more fielded by other agents. Why are so many coming to this point in time?

"Where?" Darnell asks. He must have heard, too.

I pull the phone out and read the message. "Not far. Five minutes, maybe."

He checks his watch. With its silver-nickel finish and large, round face, the timepiece doesn't fit with the rest of our tactical gear, but he insists on wearing it, just the same. "Then let's go. Is any other team closer?"

"Five minutes? I doubt it."

"Put the word out, anyway. We're on it. It's ours."

Darnell slides in behind the wheel and barely waits for me to scramble into the passenger side before throwing it into drive and squealing out into the street. I relay the address from the detection, then key in a message to the other teams and push 'send'.

"Why here?" I ask, the strangeness of the situation hitting me again. "Why now? Why so many?"

"Why so many questions?" Darnell says. "Why try to understand them? They tear reality apart, and you think you're going to figure them out?"

"It's just odd. You don't think it's odd?"

"Not anymore," he says. We come to an intersection, and he flips on the vehicle's flashers before powering through a red light. "You're trying to find rules, Mickey. I know. I used to do it, too. We've torn down the old laws of the universe, and you're trying to figure out whatever has been raised up in their place. But there's nothing."

"There are always rules."

"Did you see that desk, Mickey?" he asks. "What about the roof? In a universe where bricks can turn into water, do you think you're going to make sense of anything? They don't make a protractor for the way this world bends."

"Fine," I say. Not that I'm conceding the point. I just don't want to have the same old argument about transmogrification—the changes that happen when the shifts break space-time. Most scientists take the transmog phenomena as a sign that reality is failing, charting the escalation of changes and their increasing oddity as proof. Darnell and I have very different views on the inevitability of the universe ending, and I'm not going to convince him while we charge off to stop our second shift of the day. "But there has to be an explanation why so many Chronos are jumping to this point in time."

"You listening, Mick? There's no explaining it."

"No explaining the universe, D? Fine. But the shifts are human, and they make their decisions for very human reasons."

"Shifts aren't human, Mick," Darnell says, his voice cutting through the car like a ten car train. "I don't know what they are, but they're not human." He looks out his window. "Demons, maybe."

He says the last part quietly, like I wasn't supposed to hear. It's alright. Darnell and I reached an understanding a long time ago about our different beliefs. Long before Silent Night, back when we were just a couple of Chicago beat cops, he asked me to come to church with him and his family, some sort of charismatic, revivalist service. In return, I asked him to come to a meditation seminar down on the beach.

We never discussed religion again.

Maybe I should have, after his family.

I shake my head. "All I'm saying is they're here for a reason," I say. "They're *now* for a reason, and I want to know why."

"Yeah," Darnell says, "Maybe this one will tell us if they're in town for a convention, or something."

If you don't shoot him, first, I think. But only think.

"Turn here," I say as we near the target.

Darnell pulls into an alley and kills the engine. He leans forward to peer out the windshield at the buildings around us. "Which one?"

"End of the alley. Looks like a—" Oh, shit. I zoom in on the phone's map to be sure. "A church." Of course. I see no way this can go wrong.

"Maybe we ought to wait for—"

But Darnell is already out of the vehicle. I start to wonder just when I got this feeling in my stomach, like my insides want to float out of my mouth. Worry is a slow bleed. I'm full-out hemorrhaging.

I exit the vehicle and follow Darnell. The night is cold, and a pair of dumpsters layer on the smells of garbage. Orange peels, coffee grounds, and leftover pizza, all of it rotting and all of it mingling with the smell of salt from the lake.

Yeah, Chicago and salt. The big girl, Lake Michigan, went all briny. You can thank a Spacer for that one. Shadowstalker. I hate it when they get names, when they're around long enough that the name sticks, but that's what this guy called himself. Old Shadowstalker played the odds one too many times and wound up with a bad jump. Him on the bottom of the lake, needing to rest and recharge before he could jump again, and the lake transmogged to salt water. They found his body a week later. And that wasn't the only thing they pulled from the lake. The beaches smelled of dead fish for a year after that.

We come up on the back corner of the church, and Darnell pauses beside the sort of thick, heavy, wood door that hasn't been made for a century or more. The thing is varnished and well cared for, a stark difference to the rest of the alley around it. No chance we'll be able to force our way through it like we did at the factory.

I check the phone one more time. "We're close."

Darnell reaches out to touch the door. He speaks without pausing his inspection. "Did I ever tell you I thought Carmen was having an affair?"

I nearly drop the phone in the process of stuffing it into its pocket. It's not that Darnell thinks his wife was having an affair. He mentioned that to me while she was still alive. It's that he hasn't spoken of Carmen since her death. Not once.

"Yeah," I say. "You had me talk to her. Wanted me to see if I picked up on anything. Which I didn't, remember?" Find anything out, that is. I did talk to her. Just conversation, nothing to get her radar up. Carmen read not guilty in every possible way. She was happy with Darnell. With their family. I already told all of this to Darnell. "Why are you bringing this up now?"

Darnell's shoulders sag, and his hand slows. "Because I'm more sure of it than ever."

Meaning he ignored everything I told him I'd learned. Meaning he's been thinking this over, chewing on it, the two years since her death. What has that got to be like? To have something like that worrying at your conceptions of the world, teasing you that what you thought you knew, you didn't know. What you thought you loved, you didn't love. The worst part, with Carmen dead, there's no figuring it out. There's no resolution, no closure. If it's been bothering him this long, it's no wonder why he's been so withdrawn.

"Darnell, you gotta let it go."

He holds his hand up, palm to me, like he's asking for silence. But then I see he's showing me something. I look closer. A fine dust coats his glove where he's rubbed it against the door. A matching swipe mars what had been a smooth finish on the wood door. He smiles, but there's no mirth, there. It's the sort of smile more at home in a dungeon. A headsman's smile.

"Transmog," he says. He brushes the dust off his glove, then draws his weapon and stands directly in front of the door. "You ready?"

Before I can respond, he kicks the door square in the middle like a schoolyard bully out for a stomping. The door explodes in a cloud of pale dust and darker grit. I bury my face in my elbow so I can breathe without inhaling the cloud as it swirls around me. Darnell just stands there as the dust washes over him. My cough turns him, and I have to fight to keep from recoiling. In the light spilling from the now open doorway, I see him. He's covered in the dust. It coats his face, hiding his skin's normal rich, umber tones beneath a ghostly patina. His eyes and teeth, yellow by comparison, seem borrowed from the dead. And not just because of the color.

"Let's go."

I follow him through the cloud though everything in me is screaming that something is wrong. My guts have frozen over, knotting up my middle with a tension I can't seem to shake. I have the feeling that if I don't get Darnell away from here, we're going to do something we'll regret.

Well, I'll regret it. Darnell may be too far gone.

"Darnell—"

"I saw him, Mick."

"Who? The shift?" A new worry jolts through me that maybe we're too late.

"The guy," he says. "With Carmen."

"Oh." We still have time. I hurry forward to catch Darnell by his shoulder and whisper, "Something's wrong. We need to wait."

"A couple of times," he says in his same, flat tone. "Never his face, though. Isn't that strange?" He shrugs out of my grasp and strides up to a door marked *Conference Room A*.

"Darnell!" I whisper, though it comes out as more of a hiss. I can't help it. It feels like my insides, all my frozen insides, have been tossed on a hot griddle, and I'm crackling away with the certainty that we need to get out of here. Now.

"I asked her about it. About him. You know what she said?" He does an imitation of her voice that comes off creepy and hyperbolic. "'I ain't been with nobody but you all day, baby.'"

"Darnell!" I grab a fistful of his tac-gear as he reaches for the doorknob. "You need to stop. We need to wait. You're not thinking clearly."

He stares at me, so unnerving with his fever-yellow eyes in that pale dust whiting his face, and it's all I can do to meet his gaze. But, after a moment, I feel the tension in him break. His posture sags. His eyelids droop. He nods. I tap my fist on his chest twice and turn to lead the way out.

Three steps. I put my gun away.

Three steps. The door latch clicks, behind me.

I whirl in time to see Darnell step through the doorway, his weapon at the ready.

"Damn it, Darnell!" I know I'm too late. Whatever madness, whatever danger was lighting signal pyres before, whatever that little voice in my head was whispering about that I thought maybe—just maybe—we could avoid, it's in there. Conference Room A. And, now, Darnell's in there with it.

I draw my weapon and cover the intervening distance in two steps, if my feet touch the floor at all. I'm tweaking on so much adrenaline I wouldn't be surprised if I flew. I feel like some kind of cornered animal with no option but attack. My heart pounds in my chest. The blood roars in my ears. I push my way through the door, afraid of what I'll find.

The room is empty save for Darnell, me, and a little girl, maybe nine years old. The room's chairs, office-style metal frames and cheap cushions, are embedded in the rooms walls. They stick out at all angles, some sunken more than halfway, though the walls show no damage. It's like the room was built around them.

I swing around to clear the room, but there's no one else. Just the girl. "Where's the shift?"

Darnell holds his weapon steady on the girl. He's locked in. Fixed. For her part, the girl meets Darnell's gaze without flinching. Without worry. In fact, she cocks her head to the side as if to get a better look at him. Red curls fall in front of her shoulder. She holds a threadbare, stuffed pig in one hand.

"Where's the shift?" I ask again.

"It's her." His voice is dark and vacant. I haven't heard him like this since I found him wandering the streets four blocks from the rubble of the Harrison building.

"What are you talking about?" I ask. "It's just a girl. Maybe our scan is off."

"The scan isn't off."

"Then the shift got away."

"No, Mick. She didn't."

"Darnell, she's just a kid," I say. I want to go closer to him, but don't. I don't want to startle him. I just need his finger off the trigger. I give the girl a reassuring smile, but she's fixed on Darnell's face. "A kid. Shifts don't show until puberty, at least."

"Still looking for rules, Mickey?"

"Darnell, don't." I point my gun at him. I don't remember raising it.

"She's a shift, Mick," he says. "A Chrono."

"No, she's not."

"A Chrono took Carmen from me. The kids."

"That was two years ago, D."

"Yeah," he says. "Two years ago. Today."

Today? Did I lose track of the day? Of that particular anniversary? Oh, this situation gets better and better.

"Darnell, don't," I say. "We'll figure this out."

"It's okay, Mick," he says. "I know what I have to do."

"She's just a goddamn kid!"

"No, Mick. She's not. They're not human."

He sets his weight ever so slightly. I can see the tension in his hand, squeezing down on the trigger.

Sounds wink away, like all the air in the room has been sucked out.

A gunshot.

My weapon.

Blood on the wall.

Darnell falls to the floor.

I don't know how long I stand there, before something tugs at my shirt. I look down. It's the girl.

"Come on," she says in a clear, pixie voice, slipping her hand in mine. "Let's go."

THEN

Carmen swirls the straw in her cola, sending ice cubes tinkling around the glass. She glances at the bags on the table.

"What's with the take-out, Mickey?" she asks.

I clear my throat. I've never been a good liar, at least around the people I'm close to. Why did Darnell ask me to talk to her? And why did I agree?

"Darnell's idea," I say, trying to sound natural. Which means, because I'm trying, I'm probably coming off just this side of a ventriloquist's dummy, wooden and over-acting. "He had to work late, and he said you'd wanted him to pick dinner up on his way home. So he asked me."

She sets her drink down on the counter and looks in the first bag. "He's always thinking of us."

Just then, the twins, Molly and Jake, go tearing past the dining table on their way to the living room. It looks like Carmen was in the middle of putting up the family's nativity scene when I interrupted her. The manger lays on its side, and the three wise men stand nearby as if in consultation over the disaster.

Carmen holds a finger up, and calls to the kids without taking her nose from the bag she's inspecting.

"Rugrats! Say hello to Uncle Mickey."

And just like that, two bundles of curly-headed, squealing, five year old energy accost me. Jake hugs my leg and Molly jumps into my arms. Carmen calls me their uncle, but there's no way anyone would mistake me for a blood relation. The twins favor Carmen's Puerto Rican heritage more than Darnell's African-American, but that's still a long way from the pasty Irishman in their apartment.

I give Molly a squeeze and ruffle Jake's hair. "Alright, you two. Off you go. Let me talk to your mama."

"Can we play with the wise men?" Jake asks.

Molly hops in place. "And wind up the manger and make it play carols? Please, mommy?"

"Carefully," Carmen says. Smiles splitting their faces, the twins dash away and leave Carmen and I alone with the take-out. After a moment we hear *Away in a Manger* floating in from the living room. Carmen turns my way. "What's up, Mickey?"

I take a deep breath. "Are you okay, Carmen?"

"What do you mean?"

"Just the way you said that, about Darnell thinking about you. It just sounded, I don't know..." It sounded nothing of the sort, but this is what Darnell wanted.

Just be yourself, he said.

My cop self. All I have to do is get the suspect talking. God, Darnell is going to get an earful when I see him.

I push all of that to the background and finish, "I just want to make sure you're okay."

She smiles. "I'm great, Mick."

"Because I know our hours haven't been very regular since we left Metro and signed on with the TPA. And until they get control of the Chicago Experiment, that's not going to change."

"The Eye? They haven't figured that out yet?"

The Eye is what most people call the government experiment that first tore space-time open. What makes shifting possible and agents like Darnell and me necessary. It's supposed to be at the center of the experiment, in the TPA complex here in Chicago, but I've never seen it. Frankly, I don't really care to. That thing scares me.

The carol coming from the living room changes to *Oh, Holy Night*.

I shrug. "Still can't get near it, last I knew. Too much radiation."

A frown slides over her face, but finds no purchase. A smile replaces it. "They'll figure it out."

"It's just, it can make for a lot of late nights." I nod at the take-out. My pretense. "Missed dinners."

The Chinese *was* Darnell's idea, just not exactly the way I led her to believe.

"Darnell loves his work," she says. "You know that."

"Yeah."

"But he loves his family more." She gets a distant look in her eye, like she's remembering something, and a smile spreads on her face. "Darnell and me, we're good. I still love him crazy."

The carol changes again. The twins hum along with *Oh, Christmas Tree*.

"Of course, I didn't mean—"

"And the hours aren't so bad," she goes on, digging out cartons of rice from the nearest bag. "Darnell and I have actually been spending more time together since he took that job. He's really putting in an effort. Almost like he's making up for lost time." She smiles again. "I can't remember when we've spent so much time together."

I feel like a gobshite. She's in love, and any half-blind fool can see it. Darnell owes me, and I may never collect. That's how I feel. I may never collect because I don't want to be owed over this. I don't even want to remember this. I need a shower. It's time for me to go.

I get up. Make my excuses. Carmen wants me to stay for dinner, but I convince her I have somewhere else I need to be.

I leave the kitchen. The apartment. The floor. I leave the Harrison building behind, never knowing this will be my last time.

A month from now, it will be a pile of rubble.

NOW

In the alley, it hits me. I killed my partner. Darnell. I drop the girl's hand and lean against the wall. Darnell was right, the universe doesn't make any sense. Not anymore. I turn my face to the bricks, but not because of the tears I feel in my eyes. I swipe my tac helmet off and press my forehead into the roughness of the wall. The pain. That's what I want. The pain is a distraction. The pain is a reminder. And it's not enough. Not for what I deserve.

"We shouldn't stop here," she says. "Bad people."

I turn so I can see her. She's so out of place in this dirty, stinking alley. Out of place in this city that makes no sense. Her shiny black shoes, green dress, and white stockings are so crisp and new you might think she's on her way to grandma's Christmas dinner. Her freckled face is clean and her blue eyes, big and open. Not yet weighed down by the reality of a universe that's changing beneath us.

And she's a shift. I knew it as soon as she spoke to me. You can't miss the flatness of a shift, the unnatural, knowing calm. And even though hers isn't the complete detachment I've seen in some, on this girl it's enough to make her some sort of bizarro Shirley Temple. I swear I'll scream if she starts dancing.

"What's your name?" I ask.

"Olivia," she says. Then she holds up her stuffed pig. "This is Oscar. Oscar the Wild. He's a wild pig."

I sniff and scrub my eyes. I squat, leaning back against the wall, so that I'm level with her. There's a part of me that just wants to sit down. Have a moment. I just killed my partner. If there's anything else that needs doing today we'll have to get someone else. A stand in. I killed my partner. My day is full. I'm done.

But that won't help me, and it won't help Olivia. Darnell's response to her won't be unique. Any TPA agent she runs into will shoot first and see little girl later. If at all. So I bundle up all that emotion, all the rage and the guilt and the frustration and the sadness, and I push it into a little box in my brain. It doesn't want to fit. It's like one of those stress balls that spread and squirt when you squeeze them, but I force it in and jam the lid down. It's going to hurt when I open that box again, but I promise myself I will open it. I promise Darnell.

"Where are you from, Olivia?" I ask.

"What a silly question," she says, with only a hint of her feeling that it's a silly question entering her voice. "I'm from here. What you really want to know is when I am from."

"You're a shift." Not that I needed the confirmation, but when she nods I can feel the emotions rattle the box, trying to get out. I killed my partner over a Chrono. Whose side am I on?

"You're on your own, now," she says like she could hear my thoughts. "But don't worry, you've got me. And Oscar."

"Thanks."

"But Oscar doesn't like you."

I don't know why it hurts that Olivia's stuffed animal doesn't like me. But it does. "Oh."

"He just has to get used to you," she says. "You're different."

I'm a TPA agent who killed his partner over a shift. Different? I'm a goddamn paradox.

"You should put that away," she goes on with a glance at the pistol still in my hand. "We should go. Bad people are coming."

I stare at the weapon that killed my partner. I don't want to put it away; I want to throw it in one of those dumpsters and run as fast as I can the other direction. I can't do that, though, and still protect Olivia. If I walk away from her now, I killed Darnell for nothing. There's no way I let that happen. I slip the pistol into its holster.

You're right, little girl. Bad people are coming. Bad people are everywhere. Just look inside of me. My cage is torn apart. Have you seen my monster?

"No, he is not a monster," she says to her pig. "He's just confused."

"Help me understand," I say. I close my eyes and lean my head back against the alley wall. "Why did you come to this point in time? Why did so many of you come to today? What's so special about now?"

I wait. No response. When I open my eyes, she's gone. Oscar the Wild sits across from me in the alley, leaning against the opposite wall. Staring at me with mismatched button eyes, head cocked like a perturbed judge. I look both directions down the alley, searching for Olivia, but see no sign of her.

But I do see them.

Four Kinetics round the far corner of the alley, hugging the walls and moving in short bursts. Four more come around the church side. With their skinny jeans, tight jackets and matching Andy Warhol hair, they resemble spiders emerging from their den. As much as Chronos and Spacers have a flatness to them, telekinetic shifts have a high-strung twitchiness to the way they move. A dead giveaway if you know what to look for.

The bandoliers of threaded, half-inch machine bolts helps with identification, too. Kinetics like to have something close at hand that they can push like rudimentary projectiles. Every member of this gang wears one.

I stand up, drawing my weapon as I do. I fish out my badge. Hold it so they can see. Use my big-boy voice. "Federal agent. Stay where you are!" Of course, asking a Kinetic to stand still is a little like asking a jackhammer for silence. These don't even hesitate.

The one I take for a leader is close enough I can see his face in the light spilling from the church. Despite the night's darkness, he wears small, circular shades, mirrored gold and glossy. He swings his head back and forth as if looking for something. Probably more agents. Or my partner.

"Wrong alley, Federal Agent." He holds his hand in front of his chest, palm up, and two bolts slide from their leather sleeves in his bandolier. They hover over his palm, spinning slowly. "Wrong night."

I dive to the side as the bolts shoot through the air. They slam into the wall behind me with metallic pings and sprays of mortar. I need cover. Kinetics aren't like other shifts. They don't need to recharge between each use of their ability. They will eventually fatigue, but with eight of them in this gang, it's not like I'm going to wait them out.

I roll to my stomach so I can push the rest of the way to my feet, but there, under my nose, are shiny black shoes. White stockings. I look up to see the girl. Shirley Temple in a fury.

"You might want to run," she says to the gang leader.

He laughs at her. "A Spacer, just off her jump, talkin' like that? To us?"

Spacer? No, she's a Chrono. She admitted it. Shifts only have one talent.

"That's what you want to spend your jump on," the leader goes on, "asking us to play nice? How long's it gonna be before you can jump again, little girl?" He holds his hands up before him, and four bolts slide out of his bandolier. "An hour? Two?"

"You'd be surprised."

This is crazy. If I don't do something, this girl is going to get herself killed. I raise my weapon, but I can see in the leader's face I'm going to be too late.

"I like surprises," he says. A bolt shoots out at the girl.

"No!" I scream, but the girl vanishes. The bolt sails harmlessly through the space where she'd been.

"Surprise," she says from behind the leader.

Eyebrows climbing his forehead, the leader spins. It probably saves him, because the three gang members left in that end of the alley launch bolts of their own at Olivia's back. She disappears again, leaving the leader standing before the speeding attacks. One rifles past his face close enough to move his hair. Another leaves a red streak along his side where it grazes his ribs.

Things are happening too quickly for me to process. The girl is a Chrono, but she's teleporting like a Spacer. Except, Spacers and Chronos require time to recharge before they can jump a second time, and Olivia's hopping around the alley like a firefly on a black night. Behind a dumpster. Beside one of the Kinetics. At the far end of the alley. I'm not the only one amazed by her. Two of the Kinetics turn and run, leaving their friends behind.

The transmogs start piling up as her teleportations break reality over and over in this confined space. Small things, first. The light spilling from the open doorway of the church changes from a whitish yellow to a deep red. The hard plastic and steel wheels of one of the dumpsters pop like balloons bursting, and the dumpster crashes to the cement with an enormous clang. Then, bigger changes. The corner of the building opposite the church turns to sand, falling into a pile like the world's biggest hourglass. One of the Kinetics disappears through the cement, the stone beneath him sounding like rotten wood as it breaks. For the space of three or four seconds, every shot the leader of the gang takes changes from a steel bolt to some sort of yellow bird that flies off into the night. But those aren't the worst.

A small, black orb forms in the air between me and the back door of the church. It floats about waist high and gives off a pale light. Silvery threads slide across its surface like a shifting skin. The orb grows to the size of a basketball, bulging out in all directions. Reality bends around the edges. The door frame, straight and square just a moment ago, curves around the orb like the reflection in a funhouse mirror. This isn't good. I've only heard about these things. The black bulge is a voidspace, a hernia of anti-space into our reality. Unchecked, the voidspace will explode, tearing a hole in space-time and wreaking devastation over who knows how much of the city.

I need to stop the girl. Stop her and somehow get away. When I look for her, though, I see what she's doing. She teleports herself between two of the remaining Kinetics and stands there just long enough for them to notice. By the time the Kinetics launch their bolts at her, she's already gone, leaving them to push their projectiles at each other. One bolt embeds itself in the forehead of the far Kinetic up to the hex head. The man's eyes roll up and he crumples. The other Kinetic bellows in pain and holds his arm where a bolt passed through it. He stumbles out of the alley.

The three Kinetics left standing get smart about their fight. Not very smart, else they'd be running already. But they get smart enough to put themselves in the center of the alley, backs together, facing out. Now, wherever the girl appears one of the Kinetics spots her immediately and looses a bolt in her direction. No more crossfires for them. They've got her on the run. She needs help.

I raise my weapon. They must have forgotten about me, just lying here, because none of them even looks my way. I put two bullets in the chest of the nearest Kinetic. He staggers back and falls partway through the dumpster, slipping through the box like it's a hologram rather than steel. Another transmog effect. The man's feet still poke through to the outside.

I swing my gun over at the gang leader and squeeze off two more rounds, but he's faster. He's spotted me. His hand is up, between us, and I watch my bullets stop short. They hover near his hand.

"Wrong alley, Federal Agent," he says. Then the bullets are rocketing back toward me. There's nowhere for me to go. I close my eyes, waiting for the impact, waiting for the end.

It never comes.

"You should have run," Olivia says, very close. I open my eyes to find her standing in front of me, in the path of the attack.

I scramble to my feet, ready to scoop her up and make a run for it. With only two of the Kinetics left, maybe we can make it to the far end of the alley. Before I can touch her, though, I see the bullets. They're hovering in front of Olivia's face.

The leader's chin stretches his mouth down, wider and wider. "What the hell? That's not—"

His voice cuts off as the bullets tear through his mirrored shades. Shards of glossy lens fall to the alley floor.

The last Kinetic screams and runs away.

I know how he feels. I look at Olivia again. Chrono. Spacer. And, now, Kinetic. What the hell is going on? The gang leader was right. I finish his sentence.

"That's not possible."

I'm sitting down. I don't remember lowering myself. Pain in my backside tells me it probably wasn't the gentlest of landings. I have the presence of mind to check the voidspace. Shrinking, thank goodness.

Olivia turns to me and smiles. Her eyes are heavy-lidded, blinking slowly. Her head rocks forward and back, side to side, like she's not sure just where center is. Her breathing is slow and deep. She looks ready to collapse. After the display she put on, I can understand.

"Who—" I clear my throat. "Who are you?"

"What a silly question," she says, sleep beginning to slur her words. She reaches out her hand without turning, and Oscar flies to her. "I'm Olivia. What you really want to ask is who you are." She sits in my lap, holding the pig tight. I'm too surprised to stop her.

"Who I am?"

She nestles her head against my chest and closes her eyes. "Mm-hmm."

"Who am I?"

"Silly," she says with a sigh. "You're my daddy."

THEN

There's a strip of trendy, bohemian shops across from the Harrison, and a coffee shop on the corner where I sometimes meet Darnell before we head to the station. I come through the side door. The owner, Taj, knows us—Darnell and I used to patrol this part of the city—and makes sure we're taken care of. My coffee is waiting on the counter when I arrive. Black with a little sugar, the sort of coffee I learned early on I could replicate under the worst of conditions. Like stakeouts. Parade duty. Or the precinct pot-o-surprise.

That Taj has my coffee ready means Darnell is already here. I lay my two bucks down and take my joe. Taj waves at me from the kitchen and motions to the front, where the cafe has a few tables of outdoor seating. I nod my thanks and head in that direction.

Outside, Darnell sits at the table nearest the street. His coffee and a bagel sit on the table before him, untouched for all that I can tell. He stares off, down the street, but he doesn't look lost in thought. He's watching something. I glance that way myself, but whatever it is I can't spot it. I see people walking down the sidewalk, a couple of cars crawling along the road, the Harrison building, but nothing that should have so captured his attention.

I sit down in his line of vision. "What's up?"

"Nothing," he says. "Just looking."

"At what?"

He shakes his head. Sits up straighter in his chair. "Nothing." He glances at my coffee. "Your normal swill?"

I take a sip and make an exaggerated sigh. "Only the finest swill from Taj."

"I'll never understand you," Darnell says, sipping from his own foam cup. "Taj makes the best chai latte in the whole city."

"The whole city, now, is it?"

"The whole city, and you order boot polish."

"With sugar."

"Sometimes I think you'd prefer it if Taj kept yesterday's pot around, just for you."

"Ooh," I say. "I'll have to suggest that to him."

Darnell shakes his head, chuckling. "Crazy Irishman. You probably would."

He takes a bite of his bagel. I catch his glance over my shoulder.

"Darnell?"

"What?"

"Darnell." That draws his eyes to mine.

He shrugs. "I'm just looking." He's almost as bad a liar as I am, at least when he's around me.

"You're watching."

He picks his bagel up and tears a hunk off, but he doesn't put it in his mouth. Instead he stares at it. It takes him several seconds to speak.

"How did it go, last night?" he asks.

Last night. Take-out.

I don't know what I expected him to say, but it wasn't that. I could lay out my impressions of Carmen, what my intuition told me and what I observed about her mannerisms. Truth is, I still feel more than a bit slimy, working Carmen like a suspect, so I keep it simple. "She loves you."

He smiles, hesitant and fragile, like a boy learning the girl he's interested in has a crush on him, too. "She wanted me to thank you for stopping by."

I make a disgusted sound. He holds his hand up, the piece of bagel still pinched between his thumb and finger.

"I know you didn't want to do it," he says. "And I won't ask you again. Just, thanks."

"Can we drop it? She loves you crazy—her words—and that's that. I just want to enjoy my swill and sugar."

He lets the silence be, but only for a few moments.

"She asked me if *I* was happy," he says like he's thinking back. "Me."

"And what'd you say?"

"That I love her crazy."

"See?" I pluck the still uneaten bite of bagel from his grip. "All better. Now, can we drop it?"

"Yeah," he says. "Sure."

I can't even count to five before I catch him glancing over my shoulder again.

"What the hell, D?"

"Look," he says, nodding at whatever it is he sees.

I turn. A black sedan has pulled over, across from the Harrison, pointed down the street away from us. Carmen gets out of the passenger side but leans back in to hear something the driver says to her. Whatever it is, it makes her laugh as she closes the door.

I'm a cop. Well, used to be a cop. In some ways, I guess, I still am. And I know Darnell. I know what he's making of this.

"It's nothing, D," I say. "She just got a ride."

Carmen walks around the front of the car, like she's on her way to the Harrison's front doors. The driver has his hand out the window. Dark skin. A silver watch with a big, round face. Carmen takes his hand, gives it a squeeze and the driver the sort of smile I've seen her give Darnell a thousand times.

"They're friends," I say, wishing I didn't sound like I was making excuses.

When Carmen reaches the sidewalk in front of the Harrison she turns. The driver waves to her. Carmen blows him a kiss as he drives off.

"Innocent." The word almost fails in my throat. I turn back around, shaking my head. "I'm telling you D, she loves you—"

"I know," he says. "She's a good woman."

"You married up, that's for sure." I can see it still bothers him, though, so I say, "Why don't you just ask her?"

"Ask her if she's seeing someone else?" he asks. "Just how do I do that? How, without saying that I saw her because I was sitting here, spying on her? How do I ask if she's having an affair without coming across like that's exactly what I think is happening?"

"Is that what you think is happening?"

"No," he says, his eyes turning to the side.

Color me unconvinced. "Darnell?"

He sighs. "It just eats at you, Mickey."

"Well, when you get to thinking about it, just remind yourself that you're an idiot, and let it go."

"Yeah."

"A lucky, lucky idiot."

That makes him smile. "I get it. I get it."

"Good," I say, and sip my coffee. "Cause I can remind you, if you need it. As often as you like."

"Crazy Irishman."

When we leave the cafe, Darnell tells me he wants to show me something. He takes me by another of the shops in the strip, a little boutique with jewelry, scarves, and handbags in the display. We stand at the window, me, waiting for Darnell to explain, and Darnell, just standing. Staring. At what, I can't tell.

"Do you see it, Mickey?"

"No, D," I say, trying not to let my impatience show. "Want to give me a clue, here?"

There are necklaces and rings. Watches and bracelets. Scarves that are knotted and scarves that hang loose.

"The watch."

I spot it, then. A metallic watch sits in its open box on a shelf, tucked in with others. But I've seen this watch before. Silvery-nickel finish. Large face. The guy in the sedan had this exact watch.

"Darnell—"

"You think she likes it?" he asks. "You think that's the sort of thing she likes?"

Is that why she's with him, he means.

"What happened to the lucky idiot?"

"I'm buying it," he says, brushing past me to go inside.

I stand, somewhat in shock, and watch from the sidewalk as he talks to the shop owner. Darnell points to the display at the window and hands over a credit card. The owner calls to someone in the back, and a young girl with dark hair comes over to collect the watch. She delivers it to the register. It takes only a minute or two before Darnell emerges from the shop with the watch on his wrist. He holds his arm at different angles as if examining the look.

Words failing me, I shake my head.

"I can't lose her, Mickey," he says as if that should explain. "I can't."

"Well, you haven't," I say. "Not yet. But, you keep on like this, and—"

"I don't know what I'd do. I'd go crazy." He looks me in the eye, and I see something there that scares me. I don't recognize it. Not yet. But I will come to. It's the first hint of the monster within him, loosed. "If someone wants to take her from me, I'll kill him."

"Kill him?" I ask. "Are you listening to yourself? You need to get a grip, D. What if the world takes her from you? People die all the time. What if the universe just decides it's her time?"

He crumples his receipt and tosses it to the side. "Then I'll burn it down."

His words should bother me. Instead, staring at the receipt, all I can think is I hope he's happy with the watch, because there are no returns. Not now. No going back.

NOW

Olivia wakes up after a couple of hours. Through the open back door of Darnell's car, I see her stirring. I drove us far away from where she fought the Kinetics. I'm still not sure what she did or what she is, but that level of shift activity had to be lighting up the TPA screens back at headquarters. Before long, we would have teams of agents swarming over us. Questioning us over the Kinetics. Finding Darnell. Killing the girl.

My daughter. I'm not sure whether to believe that one, so for the past hour or so I've been sitting outside the car, leaning against a building, and staring through the open door at her as she sleeps. The Agency doesn't really have a protocol for handling messages from the future. I think they figured the conversation would never get that far. But I haven't been just sitting here while she slept; I've been working on my own method for testing her story. A question. A question I only just decided on, with an answer both absurd and non sequitur:

What did yesterday's clouds remind me of?
The blanket is the color four.

It's not perfect. I'm only an amateur temporal mechanic—tinkering with the spark plugs, changing the oil; anything heavier I outsource to the big brains back at the agency, the ones who get paid to figure out a way to contain the Eye and put an end to this mess. I do keep up with the papers they publish, though, the research and theories they write about in the popular science magazines, so even I can see the loopholes in my test. A good Chrono could beat it, find some way to come up with the answer. Best if I come to terms with that, and not put all my faith in it as a verification of the girl's story.

You're my daddy.

I shake my head, trying to dislodge those words. At least the test is more than I had an hour ago.

She sits up with her feet hanging off the seat, out the door, and rubs her eyes. Without looking, she floats the stuffed pig up from the floorboards. Picks him out of the air. He stares at me over her arm. She yawns and gets out of the car, closing the door behind her with the same telekinetic ability that picked up the pig.

"You shouldn't do that," I say.

"Do what?"

"That," I say, pointing at the door. "Even small pushes can be detected by the agency. After the alley, they're bound to be on the lookout for anything unusual."

"No," she says. "They won't. They're too busy. You said that was the point."

"The point of what?"

"Of so many of us jumping to this point in time."

That perks my ears up. I scoot back so I can sit up straighter. "Why?"

She yawns again and sits down, cross-legged, on the sidewalk so that she's facing me. "The blanket," she says before her yawn is completely spent, "is the color four."

I stare at her, only realizing my mouth hangs open after several moments have passed. "How..."

"You told me. In the future."

"I did?"

She nods. "Oscar heard it, too. We both thought it was silly."

We're quiet for a long moment. I study her, but, as with the more powerful shifts, her flatness masks her signals. I can see a resemblance in her features. Her red hair and greenish-blue eyes. The nose that curls funny, just there. The slant of her cheekbones. But resemblances can be faked. Search long enough, and you'll find a dozen girls who might look like my extended relations. Still, there's a part of me that has already accepted her. I think it's the part of me that realizes I killed my partner for this girl. It sits in my mind on a box full of pain and whispers, *Would it be so bad? It might explain a whole lot. You know.* Then it points to the box.

"You could have gone back for the answer," I say. "Waited for me to ask the question, waited for me to provide you the answer, then looped back to when we first met."

"A loop?"

"Yeah, a loop."

"There are no loops."

"What are you talking about?"

"That's what you told me," she says. "There are no loops."

"No loops?" I say. "If a shift goes back in time and tells himself to have eggs for breakfast instead of a bagel, he's changed the past."

"Mm-hmm."

"And, and if he changes it in a way that could only change because he was there, then he's created a loop, right?" I rub my face. "What am I doing? I'm arguing with an eight year old."

"Eight and three quarters," she says, lifting her chin a little higher. "And there are no loops."

I sigh, knowing she won't understand. "There would have to be a world, a timeline, where the Chrono would have had his normal breakfast, without the future-him intervening." I use my fingers to illustrate the point. Two index fingers, one for each shift, alternating their place. "Once the future-him changes things, there would be a loop. The original has to go back and do the same thing, or the loop breaks."

She stares at me with a blank expression.

"It means—"

"There are no loops," she says. "No timelines. No infinite futures. There is only one timeline. One now. One future."

"But the Chrono who goes back in time—"

"Was always there."

"That's..." I search for the words. "That's impossible."

She shrugs. "I think that's why it breaks things. Like, the universe."

"No, that can't be right."

"You gave me a message to deliver to you," she says. "Made me memorize it. You said it would help you understand."

"I gave you a message?"

"It goes like this." She closes her eyes like she's remembering. "What happens if a Chrono goes back in time to kill himself? If your answer makes a paradox," she pronounces each syllable deliberately, like it's a word she's had to practice, "then you're wrong. There are no paradoxes." She smiles and opens her eyes.

I take a second look at her face. "How old did you say you are?"

"Eight and three quarters," she says. "What does 'paradox' mean?"

"It's something that..." I look for a way to explain the idea to a child. "It's something that can't be."

"Yeah," she says. "That's what you said before. I thought this-you might say something different. Doesn't matter though, right? If they can't be, they can't be."

Well, when you look at it that way. "So how should I think about things?"

She shrugs. "I don't know."

I feel my eyebrows pinch together and my head cock. "What do you mean, you 'don't know'?"

"I don't know."

"What kind of a message is that? Aren't you supposed to teach me something? Help me understand?"

"You said the message would do that," she says. She leans forward and squints her eyes at me. "Did it?"

"No," I say. *No paradoxes.* What sort of a theory about time could involve no paradoxes? Try as I might, I can't come up with a model that would work that way. Future-me must have been wrong, because Olivia's message isn't opening any doors in my mind. I throw my hands to the side. "I give up. How do you think about time?"

"I don't know."

"You don't know?" This is great. I get a message from the future, but the messenger can't explain it to me. I take a deep breath. "You said one future. One now." I think that through. Shake my head. "That would mean the future's already written. We couldn't change it. I can't accept that."

She sighs. "No, Daddy—"

I raise a finger. "Don't call me that."

She goes quiet. Just stares at me. Her hands squeeze Oscar, one after the other. I can see, even through her calm-sea demeanor, how much those words hurt her.

Would it be so bad?

"O-okay," I say. "I'm sorry. You can call me that. For now."

She smiles. A flicker that passes over her face before disappearing. A bird, flying, falling, halfway across the sky. "Not... ," she pauses as if searching for a word. "Not an *only*-future." She leans on the word "only" like it's important. "One moment, one future, but every moment a new future."

"New," I say. "How does that help?"

"It doesn't," she says. "Not on its own, anyway."

"I think this is the worst message from the future, ever," I say. "And when you think about it, that's saying something."

"I don't know how to explain," she says. "I just do what I do."

"Try," I say. "I just shot my partner over you. Help me make sense of that."

"Okay," she says, getting a look of concentration on her face. She bites her lower lip. "Okay. You know things in the future can cause stuff to happen in the past, right?"

"You mean cause and effect working in reverse?" I remember something like this in an article one of the brains at the TPA published. It's new stuff, cutting edge theory that borrows from quantum physics. I struggle to remember what he called it. "Atemporaneous causality?"

She gives me a quizzical look, trying to repeat the phrase. "A-tempo... Are those even words?"

"I think so. And, no, I didn't know that."

"Whatever you call it, it's true. The now is more than just what happened in the past. It's the future, too." She floats Oscar up between us. "Grab him."

I do as she says and take hold of one of Oscar's arms. She takes the other in one of her hands and gives him a tug.

"Hey," I say. "I thought you wanted me to grab him."

"I did," she says, smiling. "He's like our now. You're the past, and I'm the future." She gives him another tug, this time to the side. I hold on.

"So we share him?"

"More like fight, I think."

"And I'm supposed to think about this and the other idea, too? Every moment a new future? I don't get it." I think my head might split open. I say so.

"We both pull on Oscar," she says. "The future and the past. You want him to play the way you want to play, because if he doesn't, in the next moment—" she jerks Oscar to the side, out of my grasp "—there might be a new future." She looks at Oscar, held outstretched in her hand. "You have to imagine that there's another you, here," she says. "Holding him. It helps to imagine that."

"But how does that help with paradoxes?"

She only shrugs and smiles in answer, leaving me to talk it out.

"The Chrono who goes back in time to kill himself," I say, thinking things through, "comes from a future. Comes from *the* future. And in the next moment, there may be a new future." A little piece of what she's saying slips into place for me. "But he's already there." I feel my eyes open wide with realization. "The Chrono who goes back to kill himself, does."

She smiles and claps like I've performed a trick. "He plays the way he wants to play. And we get a new future." She looks around us. "And the universe breaks open a little more."

I'm quiet for a time, thinking this through. Olivia lets me. In fact, I get the impression she's got nothing more to tell me, and that this is all supposed to make some sort of sense, now. Apparently, I know what I need to know. Unable to fully let go of the idea of paradoxes, though, I can't help the frustration that leaks into my voice. "You still have a paradox."

"No paradoxes," she says.

"The Chrono still has to go back in time to kill himself, but he can't because he's dead."

"No, he doesn't have to go back anymore."

"Because we got a new future? What, he's splintered off?"

She nods. "Time is a pretzel stick."

"A pretzel stick?"

"We break off little pieces of it." Oscar begins to rise out of her lap. "Move them around." He floats across the space between us and settles beside me. Looking at me. "Glue them into new spots."

I get it. Not completely, it's going to take some time to really think the idea through, but I can at least see the edges of it. "It doesn't matter that the Chrono didn't live to travel back in time to kill himself. Once he jumps, a Chrono splinters away from that future, and we get a different one."

"See?" she says to Oscar. "I told you he would get it."

Two blocks away, a police cruiser tears through the intersection, lights spinning and sirens wailing. I tense, but it's gone as soon as I notice it. It's a good reminder. We're not out of the woods, yet.

"Why are you here, Olivia?" I ask. "Why are so many of you here?"

Her smile disappears. "Because something is going to happen to the Eye tonight. We don't know what, and we don't know how. Oh, and we don't know who."

"But you know when."

"Eleven thirty two. Are you surprised?"

"Somehow, no."

"Whatever it is that happens," she says, "changes the Eye, starting what you call a 'chain-reaction of disintegration.'" She cups her hand and holds it near her cheek, whispering like she's sharing a secret. "It means things start falling apart, and there's no stopping it."

"Things?"

"At eleven thirty two tonight, someone is going to cause the end."

"Of time?"

"Of everything."

NOW

The clock in the car says it's ten past eleven by the time we enter the TPA complex on the outskirts of the city. I thought about stealing another car, but there isn't time. Besides, this way I can keep tabs on the the other TPA agents with the built-in scanner. Things have slowed down. There's an almost eerie silence, now, but I keep the speakers on just in case we might pick up any more chatter. Surprisingly, the team that was sent to the church after we left reported nothing unusual besides the dead gang of Kinetics. I thank my good luck and ignore the TPA's calls. Better if I don't try explaining things just yet.

I park and Olivia starts to get out, but I put my hand on her arm.

"Wait," I say, then can't bring myself to continue.

"Go ahead," she says.

"Did I..." I clear my throat. "You said I coached you on what to say. So, did I..."

"No, Daddy, you didn't die." I breathe a sigh of relief. She goes on, "But you were dying."

I don't know if there's a name for the gymnastic maneuver my insides try, or for the emotions I feel. "Dying? Of what?"

Her voice gets very quiet. "You told me not to tell you."

"Oh."

"But you didn't say anything about Oscar the Wild," she says, holding up her pig. "Would you like him to tell you?"

"N-no, that's alright."

She looks out the window at the TPA building, at the various windows lit up in the darkness. "It's why you didn't jump with the rest of us."

"Me? Jump?"

"You're the best shift anyone has ever seen, and with all three powers." She smiles. "But you say I'm the best *you've* ever seen. You think I'll be better than you, someday."

I open my mouth, but too many questions clog my brain, and I say nothing. I swallow. "All three powers? Like you?"

She nods.

"When did that happen?"

"You changed the Eye," she says. "In the future. Tweaked it, you said. Nobody understands it like you do. Anyway, what you did made lots of things possible."

"Like multi-talent shifts?"

"And how to use the talents over and over, without having to wait. You even say there's a fourth talent waiting for us, but you haven't figured it out, yet."

"I changed it? The Eye?" I ask. "In the future? Then why can you do it here and now? I haven't changed it yet." But I realize the answer before she even responds. "Atemporaneous causality. I did it in the future, but the effect reaches back for everyone."

"You got Oscar to play the way you wanted."

"So anyone can use all three powers, now?"

"Only if they realize the others are there," she says. "And how to use them."

I grip the steering wheel like it's my life preserver in this chaos. Multi-talent shifts. That goes against everything I've been told about space-time. Everything I believe. "What happens with so many people using so many powers? Doesn't that weaken reality even more? Olivia, you saw what happened in the alley."

"I think you were scared," she says, her eyes going distant. "You never said so, but I could see it."

"Things must have been pretty bad."

She nods.

"I'm sorry, Olivia."

She shrugs. "That's why we came back. We had to try."

A new thought occurs to me. "What about your mom?"

"What about her?"

"Who was she—is she?" I ask. "What was she like?"

"You told me not to talk about her, either."

I look out the windshield again. "Oh."

She stares out her window. Her breath fogs the glass. "She's beautiful," she says, her voice a whisper. "A doctor, taking care of you, at first, anyway. With a smile like... like... I don't know. Like summer. Warm. And the prettiest, red, curly hair you've ever seen."

"The prettiest?"

"That's what you say."

We sit in silence for a long time. When I speak, it's not the question I intended to ask. "What am I dying from?"

She bites her lip. "You're not, yet." Olivia points at the clock on the dash. Eleven eighteen. "We're running out of time. Let's go." And she steps out of the car.

I have to hurry to catch up to her before she reaches the front door. I don't know how I'm going to explain her to security, but I know I'll never manage that if it looks like I don't have her under my control. When we reach the first turnstile checkpoint, I realize security won't be a problem.

The guard on duty slumps over one of the turnstiles. Blood drips from his face.

"Close your eyes, Olivia," I say, hurrying to check on the guard.

"Why?"

"You shouldn't see this." I check the man's pulse. Find none.

"I've seen worse, Daddy," she says, looking past the guard, further into the complex. "A lot worse."

I slow at her words. What must her life have been like before she came here? I can only imagine, but there is something tragic in hearing her say it. Even more in how little it bothers her.

"Are we too late?" I ask.

"Not yet," she says, pointing to the digital clock on the wall. Eleven twenty. "Come on."

We set out at a run. There's no one to stop us. Everyone we see is dead. Some lay crumpled against the wall. Some are embedded in it.

"Olivia," I say, half out of breath, "wouldn't it be faster to teleport?"

"Not this close to the Eye," she says. "Too dangerous."

It doesn't look like the person we're out to stop is too concerned with that. Transmogs are everywhere. We pass a wall that looks like crystal melted into slag. Another that is made up of rubble and debris, each individual piece floating in the air. A room that has water spraying into the hallway from all around the door. A checkpoint at the beginning of the restricted area of the complex is reversed, with the metal detectors and turnstiles on the ceiling, and the ceiling tiles as the floor.

My head is a like a shaken snow-globe spinning with everything Olivia has revealed, but mostly with the notion that I'm a shift, too. That's insane. What am I doing here, following this girl who claims to be my daughter? Am I just looking for justification, playing out a bad hand of cards to see the end of the game? She says we're saving the universe. You might say that's the every day job of a TPA agent. I worry that her story is maybe just close enough to the agency's mission to give myself the excuse to stay with her, to not ask the harder questions. But at this point we're beyond that. Something or someone is attacking the agency. Someone is trying to get to the Eye.

Still, I find myself reaching out with my mind, wondering what it would feel like to work with space or time.

Which is probably why the floor, cracking, doesn't register immediately. I slow. Olivia runs ahead. It cracks again, this time under her. Suddenly, I put it together.

"Olivia, wait!"

It's too late. The floor gives way beneath her, breaking apart like frozen, hundred year old glass. She's falling into a black pit so deep I can't see the bottom. She screams. I scream. And I find it. The fabric of reality. Space-time. Whatever you call it, I have it, but only by a fingernail. And I have her.

I catch her. I don't really understand how, but I have a hold of her. Kinetic. I set her on the far side of the pit just as I feel this thing I have slip out of my grasp. I slump against the wall, breathing in great heaves.

"Wow," I manage.

"Wow," she says. "Good job, Daddy."

"Thanks. But maybe teleporting is worth the risk. I don't think I could do that again."

She glances up the hallway behind her, then turns back to me. "Okay."

She disappears, only to reappear at my side. Then she takes my hand, and just like that we're standing outside huge, yellow, metal doors. One moment there, the next, here. But, in the middle, I could have sworn I sensed something. It felt like I swiped my hand over a smooth table and felt a joint between two sections. Or more. Multiple sections, all sharing that one edge.

One of the yellow doors hangs, slightly ajar. Signs mark this area restricted, for authorized personnel only. Those authorized personnel make a neat pile in the corner, beside a pallet of red barrels.

I reach for the handle to swing the massive door open, but Olivia throws her arms around me in a hug so tight I think my insides might crack.

"What's that for?" I ask.

"It's just good to have you back, Daddy," she says. "Oscar says he likes you again, too."

"Well, thank you, Oscar," I manage, unsure what else to say. "Smart pig."

Together, we open the door and step into an enormous control room. There are stations and consoles, computer screens and microphones. Like a NASA mission control room went on a shopping spree. The far wall is composed entirely of some sort of thick glass with a single door at the far end, and looks out into another huge, dimly lit room. The door is marked, "CAUTION," and has a black skull superimposed over an orange radioactive symbol.

I've never been to this part of the complex. My security clearance would have had me stopped three or four checkpoints ago. Even so, I'm guessing the Eye itself is through the glass, out there in the darkness, somewhere. I don't really have time to think about it, though, because a man stands at the main console in the center of the room. A man I recognize. I think I might faint.

THEN

Tires squealing, I skid to a stop at the police line around the Harrison. Around what's left of the Harrison. Dust still plumes from the pile of rubble, testament to how recent the collapse, and how violent. My stomach is a porcelain balloon. I try Darnell's phone again. Still nothing.

One of the cops manning the yellow-tape barricade comes over to tap on my window. He's new since I left the force. I don't recognize him. I don't bother rolling the window down; I get out.

"You can't park there," he says. "We need you to move your vehicle back—"

I flash my TPA badge. He stops talking.

"Were there any survivors?"

"Not that I'm aware of, sir. But it's still too early to tell."

I draw my weapon and step under the rope. Check the TPA app on my phone. The readings are all over the place, with residuals and transmog ghosts clouding any chance of accuracy. Whatever happened here was massive. I wish I had Darnell with me. We've never encountered anything like this before. But it was still early when this happened. We weren't on shift. I was on the way to meet him for coffee when the notification came across my phone.

The police line is a block and a half from the Harrison, so it takes me some time to cover the distance. With each step, the devastation magnifies. Rebar twists up out of concrete forms like compound fractures. Broken glass and shattered brick spreads over the street for hundreds of yards. Pieces of the building lay stacked like a pile of second-hand blocks.

I thought I was ready. I thought I had checked the despair clawing away at my middle. I was wrong.

Directly in front of the Harrison, I fall to my knees, sobbing.

I find Darnell an hour later, a couple blocks from the destruction. He's wandering the streets, covered in a white, dusty powder. When I call to him, he slowly turns, like a creature out of one of those Saturday matinee monster features. His eyes, yellow against the white and bloodshot besides, find me and lock in. Lose their glaze. I've seen nature programs on television with hunting lions that were less focused. But tears have carved paths through the dust on his cheeks, sending those images out of my head. That's my partner, alive. I run to him.

"They're gone, Mickey," he says, flat like he's in shock. "They're all gone."

"What happened, Darnell?" I ask.

"Carmen. The kids. All gone."

"Darnell—"

"Gone!" He throws his head back and screams until his lungs empty and his voice rattles in his throat. Then he punches the wall beside him. His hand sinks into a thick, gelatinous imitation of stone. A transmog, this far away from the Harrison.

"Darnell, let's get you cleaned up."

"I killed her, Mickey," he says.

I feel like someone has driven an icicle down my spine. I take Darnell's shoulders and turn him to face me. "What do you mean? Who did you kill, Darnell?"

"Silent Night," he says with a horrified sort of recognition passing over his face. "I saw."

"Saw what? Saw who?" I give him a little shake. "Darnell, who did you see?"

"I saw her," he says. "I've seen her so many times."

"Who, Darnell?"

"Oh, my God!" he says. He screams again and tries to break out of my grip. I hold on, and his wail breaks into sobs, and he leans on me. "I was there. I saw. The tree. Presents. And I heard… oh, my God! Silent Night! I killed her, Mickey. I killed her!"

"Silent Night?" I ask. "A shift? Is that what you're saying?" I hate it when they get names.

"Carmen. The kids. They were there. It's Christmas, Mickey. Christmas! The decorations. The tree. They're dead!"

"Tell me what happened, Darnell."

"We had a deal." I can't keep up with the emotions passing over his face. Horror. Anger. Fear. "Me and God. And I failed. It wasn't enough."

"It's not your fault, D."

"So much time jumping."

"Silent Night was a Chrono?" I ask. "And she's dead now?"

"She's dead, Mickey. Dead!" He wails again.

He's in shock. I'm not going to get anything more, for now. I put my arm around him.

"Come on," I say, leading him back to the police line and the paramedics I know will be there. "Let's get you cleaned up."

Once I've left Darnell with one of the medics, I coordinate with the other TPA agents showing up to secure and process the scene. It's some time before I can find that medic again, and even longer before I connect with Darnell. Seems he wandered away from the ambulance shortly after I left.

In the end, he finds me.

"Mickey," he calls from another ambulance. He waves me over. He looks better. Someone must have cleaned him up. There isn't a trace of the dust that had coated him. His eyes are closer to the Darnell I know, too. Not so haunted.

"Darnell," I say. "What happened?"

"I was hoping you could tell me," he says. "I don't remember."

"Don't remember?"

"I woke up in the back of this ambulance. The paramedics say they pulled me out of a building."

"You don't remember?" I ask, still not understanding. Maybe not believing.

"Mickey," he says, alarm entering his voice. "Tell me. What happened?"

"You don't remember Silent Night? A shift? A Chrono?"

He looks to the side. Shakes his head. "No. I remember the building shaking. The wall cracking." His eyes suddenly go wide. "Mickey, that was my apartment. Mickey, that was my apartment!"

"Darnell—"

"Where's Carmen?" he asks. "The kids?"

"I—Darnell..." I don't know how to say it.

I don't have to. I can see the understanding spread, burning through his expression like a torch set to paper. He screams. I can't move. I can't move while my partner screams and the medics rush over to restrain him. Can't move while they sedate him. While they close up the doors and drive him away. I can't move because I want to scream, too.

I file the paperwork later. List the cause of the collapse as an unknown shift calling herself Silent Night. Then I set out to see if there's enough scotch in all of Chicago to make me forget I ever heard of her.

There isn't.

NOW

I know it's him the moment I see him. I think I knew it before, maybe even before I hit the bottom of that bottle of scotch. Darnell. He stands near the center of the control room at a console, typing commands into the system.

He barely glances up at our entrance. White powder from the church door still coats his face, though now tears have trenched darker canyons over his cheeks. He looks remarkably well for someone I just shot a few hours ago.

"Mickey," he says. His voice is hoarse with old tears and cracking under new ones. "Don't try to stop me."

Relief shudders through me, chased hard by a cold terror. Darnell is alive. Darnell is here.

"Darnell, I shot you."

"No, you didn't," he says, and waves his hand in my direction. Something floats toward me. I pluck it out of the air when it gets close enough. A bullet.

"But, the blood."

"Smoke and mirrors," he says. "It was my blood, but not from the bullet. I teleported it. Pushed it. I created just the picture you'd expect to see after shooting your partner."

"You're a shift." The words burn coming out of my throat.

"Yeah, well, you're all kinds of cozy with them these days, aren't you?" He glances at Olivia. "Don't worry, I'll take care of them all."

I reach out to pull Olivia behind me, but she's slid to the side, out of my reach. "Since when?"

Darnell slows what he's doing. "Two years ago. When the Harrison came down. I-I jumped. Shifted."

"That's how you survived."

"Yeah, me," he says. "Me. I survived. Just. Me!" He throws his head back and screams. Around the room, computer screens explode and sparks fly through the air. The stations on either side of Darnell crumple. "Molly and Jake were five feet from me. Carmen... What would it have taken to bring them with me? But I didn't think about that, did I?" He pushes a button and I hear the hum of machinery from in where the Eye is. "I just saved myself."

"You didn't even know what you were doing," I say. "You can't blame yourself for that."

He laughs, though I hear no amusement in it. "You have no idea how much I blame myself. No idea the things I blame myself for."

Then I hear Darnell's voice from the side, where Olivia is. "Don't try it, little girl."

I look that way. Another Darnell stands beside Olivia, looming over her. A duplicate. He must have jumped back to this point from somewhere in the future. Olivia looks up at him, not at all surprised.

"Olivia," I say, "don't do anything. Let's just talk."

"I thought I was special," the new Darnell says, studying Olivia's face. "I thought I was unique. Of all the shifts, the one who didn't need to be put down. I'm surprised you haven't put it together yet, Mickey. Teleporting, pushing."

"And jumping through time," I say.

Darnell hisses like I slapped him. "Who else could use all three talents? I was chosen. Chosen by God to do His work. We had a deal. I would do His work, and in return I could see Carmen again." His voice catches, and he looks at Olivia with so much hate I think he's about to strike her. A moment only, it breaks, and his expression turns vacant. His eyes, hollow. "Now I see I was just another devil. I guess even God needs a devil now and then."

"What happened?" the old Darnell asks.

The new Darnell turns that way. A broken table leg floats into the air not far from the original Darnell, the broken end sharp and splintered. "She tried to attack me with that. Pushed it."

"Chrono and Kinetic," the old Darnell says.

"Better figure on Spacer, too," the new one says.

"Just as I suspected, then."

"We aren't unique." They share a look. An understanding seems to pass between them.

"I was never chosen."

"Not special."

"No different from any of them."

"All that time."

"All those jumps."

"So much destruction."

"For nothing."

"Nothing."

"Oh, my God! Carmen!"

"We're monsters," the new one says. "All of us. Monsters without cages." They share a moment in silence.

The old Darnell sniffs. "That's why we came. It ends tonight."

"Watch her," the new Darnell says, walking in the direction of the console where the old Darnell stands, "when you go back."

Go back?

The table leg falls out of the air, but before it hits the ground, it stabilizes and points at the old Darnell. It shoots through the air like a javelin aimed for his heart. At the last moment, the old Darnell disappears and the table leg sails through empty space. The new Darnell—the only Darnell, now—steps behind the console without missing a beat, taking over whatever it was Darnell was trying to do.

"Don't try that again, little girl," he says. "That's the only warning you're going to get."

In the far chamber, huge, robotic arms swing a glowing platform out of the deeper shadows and into view. The platform is round and flat, with blue lights dotting the outer ring and a larger orange light in the center. On top, hovering over the orange light, is a black sphere the size of a small car. Silver threads slide across the surface like veins. The Eye.

My breath catches in my chest. "That's a voidspace. A stabilized voidspace!"

"No, Mickey," Darnell says. "That's hell. It's what I deserve. I killed my family."

"No, you didn't. That was Silent Night."

He leans over onto the computer screen, covering his face with his hands. His body shakes. "Silent Night. I heard... heard that. The music. Playing through the wall." He goes back to typing, moving even more frantically.

"Slow down, Darnell," I say. "You don't have to do this."

"Yeah, I do. God has one more job. One more job for His devil." He looks at the Eye. "That's where all the shifts come from, and where I'm going to send them. I'm going home, Mickey."

I share a look with Olivia. What am I supposed to do? I sent her back here for a reason. My daughter. But why me? What can I do? She smiles like she understands. No, she smiles like I understand. My stomach falls to my knees.

"I love you, Daddy," she says.

"Olivia? Olivia!"

She disappears. Steps from the shadows behind Darnell. A handful of glass shards floats beside her. And I think, just for a moment, that she's going to succeed. That Darnell is too distracted.

Then, gun in hand, another new Darnell appears behind Olivia.

"I warned you."

"Darnell, don't!" I say.

"I'm sorry, Mickey," he says. "I warned her."

"But not me." Another Olivia appears beside him.

I feel like I'm in a car crash, or about to be in one. Like I'm skidding on ice toward oncoming traffic, seeing the impact to come. And knowing, no matter my foresight, that when it comes I will still be surprised by the sheer ferocity of it. Darnell and Olivia stand perfectly still, locked in their standoff. I don't know if any of us are breathing. Water drips over in a corner where a desk slowly melts.

A small, cardboard banker's box on the desk beside me rattles. Then, again. I don't want to take my eyes from Darnell and Olivia, but I do. Transmogs can be dangerous. Deadly, even. I reach for the box, but before I touch it the lid pops off and a swarm of hummingbirds flies out, blues and greens and yellows and the sound of a bee's nest, kicked over. I stumble back and cover my face as they dart around me. A gun fires, over where Darnell and Olivia were standing.

"Olivia!" I scream.

The birds clear, and I can see again. I want to run to Olivia. I want to dive for cover. Scream for help. But I don't do any of those things. I'm too astounded by Darnell and Olivia. They're moving through the room like hummingbirds, themselves, fighting in ways I've never seen. Debris flies around the room like we've stepped into a poltergeist rave. I count six Darnells and at least four Olivias. While I watch, one of them will disappear from one place only to appear in another, dodging some projectile. Or they disappear and don't reappear, and I figure they've gone to another point in the fight. I can't keep track of it all.

Transmogs begin tearing the room apart. A thick goo drips down a wall, covering monitors and control systems before hardening into an amber-like lacquer. A terminal erupts into a green and purple fire that sparkles and cracks around the tongues of flame. Worse, I see a ripple pass through one of the great panes of thick glass separating us from the Eye. The glass steadies and I'm thankful we dodged a bullet. It's still intact, still shielding this room from the Eye's radiation. Then one of the hummingbirds flies over and hovers at the glass as if looking for a way through. I can't count to two before it falls to the floor, dead.

"Oh, shit," I say. I look for something I can do. My daughter came back through time to me—to *me*—for a reason. Because of something I needed to do. I draw my weapon.

There. Through all the chaos of the fight—Darnell and Olivia appearing and disappearing, new copies of them popping up in unexpected places and vanishing just as quickly, the transmogs, and the debris flying around like improvised artillery—through all of that, I see one Darnell standing still, working at the same console where he's been since the whole thing started. I take careful aim. I may have only one chance at this.

To my left, Olivia screams. One of the Olivias. My daughter. I've already passed the point of accepting her as my own, and no matter that there are six or seven of her now in the room, her scream connects with something deep and primal in me. I swing my gun over. She's taken some sort of metal shard in her side. She lays on the floor, propped against the wall, bleeding. A Darnell stands nearby, raising his weapon.

I shoot, and that Darnell falls. I swing my weapon back to the original Darnell, at the console, but before I can fire again, a boot kicks the gun from my hands. I hear a voice at my side.

"Stay out of this, Mickey," Darnell says. "You're not one of us. I don't want to have to kill you. This is just something I have to do."

I look in that direction, but the Darnell who spoke has already vanished.

I'm crouching behind a station, watching the fight, watching my daughter fight, when Darnell's words hit me.

You're not one of us. A shift.

But I am.

You're the best anyone has ever seen, Olivia said.

I reach inside for that place where I found space-time, before. My hand slides past, like I'm feeling newly polished steel. I don't have enough practice, but I can't fail. Not at this. I block out the screams, coming more quickly, now. Some are Darnell's. Most are Olivia's. I tell myself if I don't do this, she dies anyway. We all die. It doesn't make it hurt less.

I hunt for the edge I remember. Nothing. I try again. And again. Still nothing.

Why me? What can I do? Even if I get a hold of one of the talents, I can't use it the way Darnell and Olivia can.

Nobody knows the Eye like you do, I hear Olivia's voice again. *You even say there's a fourth talent out there, waiting for us.*

That's when I remember the feel of the edge. Not a single edge, but multiple together. My perspective shifts, inside, like a twist, and I find it again. Space-time. All the talents, available to me. There, Kinetic pushes. There, Chrono jumps. There, Spacer teleports. Three talents.

No. I go back and test the edge again. Not three. Four. There's a fourth edge. The fourth talent. And I realize, in that moment, that this is why I sent my daughter back. I did more, in the future, than just discover the possibility of a fourth talent. I discovered the talent, itself, and I knew I could do it again. With no idea what to expect, I seize the edge and tug.

Time lays itself out before me.

I can see the past and the present, even a little of the future. I see the whole, sad story that brought Darnell to this point. How he thought Carmen was having an affair. Cheating on him. How he watched her, and how it destroyed him. He never saw the guy's face, he said, but that isn't a problem for me. The fourth talent is clairvoyance, and I see into the car that drops her off. I see who bought her flowers, who spoke to her on the phone, and who she met at a hotel. I see Darnell.

He fixated on her after her death. Became obsessed with seeing her. I see him crying in quiet moments, dealing with the guilt of having not saved her or the kids and wrestling with the knowledge that he, too, was a shift. Then he started traveling back in time to be with her. Over and over he jumped, two years of jumps, spending all the time he could with the wife he thought he'd killed, becoming the very affair he suspected

Carmen of having in the first place.

What I see next is so horrible I release the talent, but not soon enough. I see more of Darnell's story, right up to a few hours ago, right up to this very room. I'm leaning on the side of the station when I come back to myself, my head sagged and my breath coming in short bursts. I cover my mouth, but it doesn't help. I vomit.

"Oh, Darnell," I whisper.

The room is quiet. I hazard a peek over the station that's giving me cover to see a scene like frozen chaos. Pieces of desks and computers float in the air. Steam billows out of a vent in slow motion. Parts of the room have melted and sag. Other parts are blackened, and still others, rendered translucent. In the next room, the Eye has grown huge. It's nearly as large as the containment platform it sits upon. The blue lights surrounding the platform change to red, and a siren begins sounding a warning. I count eight Olivias dead on the floor, and at least a dozen Darnells. There are two Darnells standing, one at the same console where he's been, and one across the room. Only one Olivia moves, the one slumped against the wall, bleeding, with a shard of metal in her side. The Darnell who's not at the console holds a gun in his hand. He starts in Olivia's direction.

I know what I have to do. As much as I don't want to do it, I seize space-time and tug at the clairvoyance talent. I stand.

The Darnell with a gun stops and points the weapon in my direction.

"Wait," Darnell says from the console. "Just watch him."

"Darnell," I say. "D, don't do this."

"I already did," he says.

A woman's voice comes over the speakers with a recorded message. "Magnetic containment systems offline. Containment failure in two minutes. Non-essential personnel should seek immediate shelter."

"You don't have to do this," I say. "Stop it. Put the containment field back."

"You don't know what I have to do, Mickey. The things I have to be punished for."

"Yeah, I do." I circle slowly through the room, hands open and held out to show I'm no threat. I steal one last look at Olivia. She doesn't look good. So pale. Eyes closed, her chest, barely moving. I turn to face Darnell at the console. I don't like putting the other Darnell behind me, but I try not to let that show. "You blame yourself."

Darnell closes his eyes. He's trembling and shakes his head. "You have no idea."

"You wish you could have saved Molly. Jake." He flinches with each name and throws a baleful stare my direction, but I grit my teeth and finish, "Carmen." His anger breaks, and he sobs into his hands.

"I killed her, Mickey," he says. I don't correct him. Not anymore. I saw the truth of things with the clairvoyance. I let him talk himself through it. "I-I went back to see her. That first time. Just to see her. Maybe... maybe just to say goodbye, you know? It was so sudden, I never had the chance to say goodbye. But then I saw her. She was laughing. You know I was always a sucker for her smile."

"Yeah, D. I know."

"I didn't mean... didn't mean to..." His sobs break through again, and he has to collect himself before he continues. "I went back, Mickey. I went back so often. For two years." He smiles through his tears, and for a moment, I see the Darnell I knew from before. He shrugs. "I just couldn't be without her. How could I be without her?"

I have to bite my cheek and suck my lips to keep from crying, myself. "It was too much. Too many jumps to the same place."

"I was being so careful," he says, like he's pleading. "Never to the same spot twice. I jumped to places all around the Harrison."

"You wanted to spread out the effect."

He nods. "Just in case. See, I was special, Mickey. All three talents. I was different." He glances in Olivia's direction, over my shoulder. "I *thought* I was different. I made a deal with God. If He let me travel back to see Carmen, if He let me use my abilities without tearing the universe apart, I would get rid of as many shifts as I could. Do His work. Be His sword, on earth."

"It doesn't work that way, D."

"I did my part! He failed, Mickey. Not me. God." He's screaming. "He can go to hell, for all I care, now."

"Darnell—"

"I hate them, Mickey."

"'Them,' Darnell?" I ask. "Shifts? You're one of 'them.'"

The woman's voice returns. "One minute to containment failure."

Darnell nods. "That's right Mickey. I am. You're not. Don't try to stop me."

"You're going to have to shoot me, Darnell," I say, walking slowly but steadily for the console where he stands. I put my hand in my pocket and close my fist around the bullet I thought had killed Darnell. "If you want to stop me, you're going to have to shoot me."

"Well, I suppose it's only fair, right?" He looks behind me, in the direction of the other Darnell, and nods. "You shot me, so..."

Behind me, the other Darnell raises his weapon, pointing it at the back of my head. I don't have to see it; I've got a hold of space-time. I'm seeing the whole room. I'm seeing everything.

"I'm sorry, D."

"Yeah, me, too," he says. "Goodbye, Mickey."

The Darnell behind me fires his weapon. I see it a moment before it happens. I watch the bullet spin through the air, drilling itself forward. I see it penetrate my skull. I see the path it's on, the path it would travel were I not here.

Darnell, at my back.

Darnell, in front of me.

I teleport, appearing back by Olivia, behind the Darnell who fired. At the same time, I pull my hand from my pocket, open my fist, and give the bullet a push. At the console, Darnell stares at the spot I vacated, shock peeling his eyes wide. Then the two bullets strike home. My bullet takes the Darnell who fired; his bullet takes the other Darnell. They both fall over, dead.

"Thirty seconds to containment failure."

Thirty seconds. I start for the large windows. Maybe I can get a better look at the Eye.

"Don't, Daddy," Olivia calls, her voice weak.

I stop and turn back to her. Dark rings shadow her eyes, and the blood has made a pool beneath her. "We've only got seconds, Olivia."

"Don't. That's how. That's..." She shudders a breath in. "You.

Dying. That's how. Too close."

I snap my head back to the windows. A dozen birds lie dead at the base of the wall, looking like blobs of bright paint. I back up out of instinct.

"What do I do?"

"Console."

I sprint to where Darnell was working. Try not to notice him, but that doesn't work. He's there. My partner. Dead. The blood, so brilliant against the white dust on his face. His eyes, open but unseeing. Remembering the church, earlier, I check his pulse to be sure. He's really dead this time. Somehow, it doesn't bother me as much as it did before.

"Ten seconds to containment failure."

"I'm here!" I call to Olivia.

"Two. One. One. Blue," she says, sounding like she's fading into unconsciousness. "Two. One. One..."

"Olivia?" No response. I punch the numbers as quickly as I can, hoping she was only repeating herself, not passing out midway through a longer code. After the numbers, the screen changes.

Are you sure you wish to abort? I press the blue 'Yes' button.

"Magnetic containment restored," the woman's voice says.

I close my eyes and sigh. Then I catch my breath.

"Olivia!" I rush over and kneel beside her. I can hardly find a pulse, so I ease her down, laying her head in my lap. "Olivia, no. No! You can't leave now."

Her eyes flutter open, and she smiles. "Daddy."

I try to speak, but all I can say is, "That's me."

"It will be... good... to have you... back. Not dying."

Closing my eyes sends tears rolling down my cheeks. "I-I can't wait." A flash of horror seizes me. "But how can I send you back? In the future. How can I send you back here, to die? I won't do it. I won't!"

"Silly," she says. "You don't have to. Not anymore."

Relief surges through me, and I can't hold back a hitching sob. "No loops."

"Keep Oscar for me," she says.

I look around for where she dropped him. He's face down, not far away. I float him over to me and catch him in the air. "I've got him."

"Careful," she says. "He's... he's a wild pig."

"I will."

She closes her eyes.

Breathes one last time.

And then my daughter dies in my arms.

I sit there. I don't know how long. I'm too exhausted to care. Too drained. I sit until I hear voices and the sound of people running this way. Someone lifts Olivia out of my grasp. Though my head weighs a hundred pounds and my eyelids feel carved from stone, I look up.

"Sir, are you okay?" a woman asks. She's a paramedic. With a smile like... like summer. And the prettiest, red, curly hair I've ever seen. "Sir, are you okay?"

I smile. "No," I say. "I'm not. But I think I will be. In time."

Tim Rohr graduated from Hope College, where he studied English Literature and Creative Writing. He lives in West Michigan with his wife and children, near the shores of what locals call, with something of an aboriginal sensibility, "the big lake." You can catch up with him at www.timrohr.com.

Acknowledgments

This anthology would not have come together without the help and support of a great number of people. Primarily, we'd like to thank our families for putting up with us and for dealing with the amount of time a project like this requires. A special thanks also goes to Digital Dreaming for handling our various artwork emergencies, no matter how short the notice, and to Emily Taylor for lending an extra pair of eyes to the proof process. Finally, we need to extend our sincere gratitude to all those who read our previous anthologies, and especially to those who offered encouragement that we should continue. We cannot say how much your support means to us.

Cover art "Origins"
by Digital Dreaming

MifiWriters

MICHIGAN SPECULATIVE FICTION

x/0

MIFIWRITERS.ORG